Berkley Sensation Titles by Michelle Beattie

WHAT A PIRATE DESIRES
ROMANCING THE PIRATE

Romancing the Pirate

MICHELLE BEATTIE

BERKLEY SENSATION, NEW YORK

THE BERKLEY PUBLISHING GROUP
Published by the Penguin Group
Penguin Group (USA) Inc.
375 Hudson Street, New York, New York 10014, USA
Penguin Group (Canada), 90 Eglinton Avenue East, Suite 700, Toronto, Ontario M4P 2Y3, Canada
(a division of Pearson Penguin Canada Inc.)
Penguin Books Ltd., 80 Strand, London WC2R 0RL, England
Penguin Group Ireland, 25 St. Stephen's Green, Dublin 2, Ireland (a division of Penguin Books Ltd.)
Penguin Group (Australia), 250 Camberwell Road, Camberwell, Victoria 3124, Australia
(a division of Pearson Australia Group Pty. Ltd.)
Penguin Books India Pvt. Ltd., 11 Community Centre, Panchsheel Park, New Delhi—110 017, India
Penguin Group (NZ), 67 Apollo Drive, Rosedale, North Shore 0632, New Zealand
(a division of Pearson New Zealand Ltd.)
Penguin Books (South Africa) (Pty.) Ltd., 24 Sturdee Avenue, Rosebank, Johannesburg 2196,
South Africa

Penguin Books Ltd., Registered Offices: 80 Strand, London WC2R 0RL, England

This is a work of fiction. Names, characters, places, and incidents either are the product of the author's imagination or are used fictitiously, and any resemblance to actual persons, living or dead, business establishments, events, or locales is entirely coincidental. The publisher does not have any control over and does not assume any responsibility for author or third-party websites or their content.

ROMANCING THE PIRATE

A Berkley Sensation Book / published by arrangement with the author

PRINTING HISTORY
Berkley Sensation mass-market edition / September 2009

Copyright © 2009 by Michelle Beattie.
Cover art by Judy York.
Cover design by George Long.
Cover hand lettering by Ron Zinn.
Interior text design by Kristin del Rosario.

ISBN: 978-0-425-23085-5

BERKLEY® SENSATION
Berkley Sensation Books are published by The Berkley Publishing Group,
a division of Penguin Group (USA) Inc.,
375 Hudson Street, New York, New York 10014.
BERKLEY® SENSATION and the "B" design are trademarks of Penguin Group (USA) Inc.

PRINTED IN THE UNITED STATES OF AMERICA

10 9 8 7 6 5 4 3 2 1

For Bryan, who has given me everything that matters in the world: two beautiful daughters, a lovely new home, and a partner I can count on. It hasn't all been easy, but it's sure been worth it. Thank you for all your hard work, which has enabled me to be a stay-at-home mom and to pursue my dreams of being an author. You're my rock, and I love you very much.

One

Port Royal
1657

Alicia Davidson felt the contempt through the small crowd that had amassed around the freshly turned earth surrounding her father's grave. It was like the blade of a cold dagger being slid across the back of her neck. Though the sun was blazing down upon the shifting crowd, Alicia shivered. Wiping her damp cheeks, she pulled her attention from the dirt that was being dropped by shovelfuls onto the sturdy wooden box below her feet, and examined the crowd. Who was it that was aiming such hostility toward her?

She saw the faces of many friends as well as customers of her father's, who'd been one of two blacksmiths on the island. Some of those faces had tears pooled in their eyes; others simply watched solemnly as the clergyman recited a last prayer before slipping away. Alicia's eyes shifted to the right, where a few people huddled in a small circle. It was when they broke apart and moved away that her gaze connected with the stranger left standing alone at the edge of the congregation. His eyes narrowed and the full impact of his disdain hit her.

His dark brown hair was long and loose, framing a face that seemed carved from stone. There wasn't a drop of sympathy in his eyes, nor a hint of compassion in his expression. She had no idea who he was, and given the flat line of his mouth and the waves of bitterness that continued to pour from him, she had no inclination to find out.

Forcing her attention back to the only matter of importance, Alicia knelt and bowed her head, hoping everyone would take her gesture as the sign it was. She desperately wanted to say her last good-bye alone. Women walked away, skirts swishing in the grass. A few hands squeezed her shoulder as a sign of encouragement. Their sympathy was both a comfort and a harsh reminder that her dear father, who had been loved and respected, had gone to join her mother. Tears that should have been spent by now filled her eyes. A deep sense of loss squeezed her heart.

A shadow fell on the ground next to her a moment before she heard her aunt's voice.

"Alicia, dear, come back to the house, have something to eat."

"I'm going to stay a little longer."

Her aunt Margaret was nearly sixty years old and had always made very clear her disapproval of the man her sister had chosen. Even now, Alicia noticed her aunt's gray eyes were as dry as the earth that lay at their feet.

Aunt Margaret tsked. "Child, he is gone. Best to move on."

Because she was used to the woman's coldness, she didn't react to it. "I need a moment," Alicia repeated.

"Fine. But do not be long. It is dreadfully hot and there

is no point in wilting out here. Besides, it is only proper you make an appearance; I have a houseful of people who wish to offer their condolences." Margaret fanned herself as though to reinforce her point. "In the meantime, I will have your things sent to my home."

Alicia pushed herself to her feet, moved slightly so the sun wasn't beating directly in her eyes. "I thought I made it clear where I belong."

"Really, child. You cannot stay alone in that little hovel. It is not proper."

"It's my home, Aunt Margaret. I'll not be leaving it."

The other woman took a full breath, expanding an already impressive bosom. Her tiny hands clutched the curve of her parasol. "I will not have any niece of mine living alone, without proper guidance. You will come with me, be given a maid, and I will find someone to teach you etiquette and decorum. You will not work in that filthy blacksmith shop, and if it takes us three weeks, we will scrub those hands until they are no longer stained black. When we are finished, you will no longer be the object of disdain and pity that you have been since Jacob allowed you to work that shop. And," she added, with a pinched mouth, "you will have the finest of dresses." She said the latter with a pointed look at the simple gown Alicia wore.

"This isn't the place, Aunt Margaret. We can discuss this later."

Her aunt feigned remorse well. "Of course, child. We can talk later." As she stepped away, Alicia heard her aunt mutter, "He has some nerve, coming here."

Alicia ignored the comment. Her aunt was always annoyed or complaining about someone. In the past it had been her father. She waited until her aunt was well past the line of headstones and then unbuttoned the collar of her dress. The breeze coming off the ocean carried the tang of salt with it. Alicia took in a cleansing breath now that she could breathe without feeling as though she were being choked by her collar.

The respite from the cloying heat felt amazing and she sighed. She took her time saying good-bye, allowing the tears to come as well as the memories. She talked to her father as though he were there, and by the time she stood, wiping the dirt from her skirts, the pain around her heart had eased.

It wasn't until she straightened and took a step to leave that she noticed the stranger was still there.

His expression hadn't softened and she found herself casting a furtive glance around, but they were well and truly alone. What did he want? She wasn't helpless the way her aunt thought she was, but she was certainly no match for him in strength.

Alicia's mouth dried like cotton when he began to walk toward her. Despite her galloping heart, she didn't move. He was at her father's funeral. Surely Jacob Davidson must have known this stranger. His gaze never left hers, and when he stopped opposite the grave from her, she was able to see his eyes were dark brown and were framed by black lashes and a cut of black brows.

He said nothing, but his eyes finally shifted to the grave between them. With nothing more than a creak of his knee-high boots when he crouched down, he grabbed a handful of dirt and let it sift through his fingers over the casket. Then, with a last scathing glance at her, he stood and left as silently as he'd come.

Two

You can't mean to run this shop by yourself, Alicia. It's madness!"

"Thank you for the encouragement, Charles. I always know I can count on you," Alicia responded. Judging the embers in the forge, she picked up the billows. They whooshed as she pumped air into the fire; the red of the coals brightened. Only midmorning, her shirt clung to her back and the tendrils of hair that had escaped her braid stuck to her cheeks. Breathing was becoming more difficult, and Alicia knew by the end of the day her lungs would hurt from the effort.

She wouldn't have it any other way.

"You know I didn't mean it the way it came out. It's not that you're not capable. The problem, my dear girl, is that you're too capable."

Alicia replaced the billows on the hook her father had fashioned onto the edge of the long worktable.

"I've never known efficiency to be a negative trait."

"It wouldn't be if you were a seamstress."

"You know that's never going to happen."

"You're eighteen. You shouldn't have to worry about keeping a business afloat."

"My mother taught me about numbers and ledgers. I know how to manage them."

"You think the Navy will continue to buy swords from you now that your father is gone? It was one thing to have you work with your father—they managed to turn a blind eye to that out of respect for Jacob. It'll be another to them when you're the sole proprietor."

Alicia set her teeth. "I'm trying to be patient because I like and respect you, but I'm getting tired of your constant discouragement. It's all you've been telling me for a week now."

"And I'll keep telling you until it starts to sink into that thick head of yours. You're choosing an impossible road. It'll do nothing but make you miserable."

Alicia sat on the table. Despite the messy nature of her work, the surface was clean and clutter free. Tools were always replaced after being used. Her gaze met Charles's.

The father of three rambunctious boys and a sweet yet shy daughter, Charles had worked at the shop nearly as long as Alicia could remember, which, owing to the fall that had left her scarred and wiped her memory clean, was about six years ago. He'd been loyal, hardworking, and like her aunt, firm in the belief that a blacksmith shop was no place for her. Unlike her aunt, however, he acknowledged her skill.

"I've never cared what people thought of me." There was a spark of a lie in there, but she wouldn't give Charles more ammunition. If he knew she sometimes wished she were included in the social activities of people her age, wished people wouldn't look the other way when they passed her on the street, he'd jump on the fact. Then he'd team up with her aunt and she'd never hear the end of it.

"As for work, all the Navy will care about is that their swords are better than those of their enemies. This shop can give them that, *I* can give them that." And she had for the past two years. She took great pains with the craftsmanship of her swords, and it always filled her with such pride when she saw an officer walk by with one of her blades at his side.

Charles rubbed his coarse whiskers. "I don't believe your father ever told them it was you who forged those swords, which is my point. They won't be happy about it."

"They had better get used to it, or they can go elsewhere."

He frowned. "Thinking like that will sink this business. The Navy is our biggest purchaser. We lose them, we may as well close the doors."

It was Alicia's turn to sigh. "What else would you have me do?"

He ladled a cup of water from a cask near the door and swallowed it in a large gulp. His eyes wouldn't quite reach hers. "Anything else. You should go with your aunt. You'd have an easier life with her."

"I'm not interested in easy, Charles. I need to be true to myself. I'd be miserable if I went with her. Besides, putting on a fancy dress and primping with my hair doesn't change who I am on the inside. Can you honestly see me spending my days having tea and talking of all the eligible bachelors?"

He shook his head. "At least it's more ladylike. And living with her, you'd have a chance at getting married."

"Even with this?" Alicia asked, tracing the scar that slashed from her right earlobe to mid-cheek.

"Since when has that bothered you?"

She shrugged. "It doesn't." Which was the truth. Most often she was too busy working to even think about it.

"Besides, it's not the scar, Alicia, it's the smell of ash and smoke that is more of a deterrent."

Alicia grinned. "That isn't normal?"

"Blimey, you're a handful. I give up," he said, throwing up his hands. "I've said my piece, I don't imagine you'll listen to me any more than you do your aunt."

"I appreciate your concern, but no. I've made up my mind to work my father's shop."

"Your mother wouldn't have wanted this," he said.

The jab hit its mark, bruised her heart. "Perhaps not. But she never stopped me from coming here with him. She knew how I loved to work alongside him. Charles, Jacob taught me this."

"Because he lost his sons," he reminded her gently.

Alicia inhaled sharply. "If you're saying he'd never have had me in here if Daniel and Eric were here, then you're wrong. He *breathed* this shop, and he was proud to have me here. There's nothing he'd have loved more than having all his children work with him. He always had time to explain and teach. Your son Jack is proof as he's spent many hours in here at my father's side."

Charles lowered his gaze, being properly reminded of the man he'd worked with for years.

"And the fact remains, Charles, that Daniel and Eric *are* gone. This shop is not only my father's legacy, it's all I have left of him and, in a roundabout way, all I have left of the brothers I don't remember.

"From the first time I saw my father shape steel, saw

him create something beautiful from nothing, I knew that was what I wanted to do. Did my mother like it? No. But she understood it. You won't change my mind, Charles. No one can. It would be easier to rip out my heart while I was still breathing."

He locked eyes with her for a long while. Long enough for the half-burned logs to roll and spark in the forge. Long enough for Alicia to feel the sweat run in a sticky trail down her temple. Then he nodded and went back to work. They said nothing more, though their words hung in the air as surely as the smell of heated steel.

For the past seven days her aunt and a few other well-meaning acquaintances of her father's had stopped by to offer the same advice. Well, the others had offered. Her aunt had actually ordered Alicia to come live with her. She, like Charles, had discovered that they weren't the only stubborn ones. The little house and the blacksmith shop were all Alicia had left, and she wouldn't leave either behind to satisfy someone else's belief of what was proper.

The town was mostly quiet as she made her way home later that evening. A few children raced by her, leaving the youthful smell of sweat and energy in their wake. The lamps hadn't been lit yet and long shadows crossed the street. Through windows she saw the glow of light and the flutter of family life. Her feet stopped, and Alicia found herself jealously watching. What she wouldn't give to have that again.

"Move along," a harsh voice commanded from behind her.

Alicia spun around. "Pardon me?"

"I told you to move along. These are well-kept houses and the people here make an honest living. Go back where you belong."

It wasn't until the man grimaced at her clothes and face that she remembered she was still filthy. Her hands, despite scrubbing, bore the traces of her work and no doubt her face was as grimy as her clothes.

He didn't move, so Alicia did. Though she held her head high—she wouldn't apologize for being who she was—she left nonetheless. She turned down one street, then another, until her little house came into view. It was dark and empty. The truth she'd been working hard to avoid suddenly pelted her. Nobody was waiting for her, or would, if that stranger, Charles, and her aunt were any indication, ever again. She was a blacksmith now. And as much as she wanted this life, she knew it would come with a price.

A swelling emptiness engulfed her and she sought refuge in the room her parents had shared. She hadn't been in it since her father's death when she'd come to pick his burial clothes. Now, looking about the tiny room, she felt an overwhelming need to be close to them, to the people who'd loved her as she was, without trying to turn her into what they thought she should be.

At the foot of the bed lay a simple trunk. She'd never seen it opened and had never wondered what was inside. But now, desperate to feel a connection to them, Alicia lit a candlestick, placed it on the floor, and knelt before the trunk.

The lid opened easily and with it came the smell of both her father and mother, a hint of smoke mixed with lavender. Sniffling loudly, she began to sort through the contents. There were several trinkets, worn blankets, and a few of her mother's dresses wrapped in paper. Alicia unwrapped one and pulled out a yellow gown, very plain in design but beautiful in its simplicity. She remembered it had been Anna Davidson's favorite before she'd died last spring. Standing, Alicia held it upright to see if it would fit her.

Perhaps she could wear it to church, prove to people she could be pretty if she chose.

A small wrapped package fell from within it and plopped onto the wooden floor.

Curious, Alicia set the dress on the bed and picked up the bundle. Turning it over, she saw her name, in her father's hand, across the front. Frowning, she sat on the bed and pulled open the string that held the package closed.

Inside were two letters. Her name was on the first; the second, bearing her father's seal, had the name "Blake Merritt" neatly written in the middle. Who was Blake Merritt? she wondered. But she set it aside and carefully opened her letter.

My dearest daughter,

Hearing her father's voice as she read the words, Alicia had to fight the tears that pricked her eyes.

> *If you are reading this, then it means I've gone to be with your mother. Before I explain anything, please know you were one of our greatest joys. We could not have loved you more.*
>
> *However, you weren't always ours. When you were twelve or so, we found you and your natural mother washed up on the beach. You were both hurt. Your mother was very distraught and you, my dear girl, weren't conscious. Before your mother died, she begged us to keep you safe. She was afraid the pirates who had attacked your ship would learn of your escape and come for you. Your name, and the name "Samantha," were the last words she spoke.*
>
> *You were hurt and bleeding, and we took you*

immediately inside our home. You had a large cut across your cheek, which we tended to as best we could, but as you know, it left a deep scar. We fretted over you for days, and when finally you awoke, you remembered nothing, not even your name.

Looking back, I can see it was selfish not to tell you the truth, but your memory never returned and we had promised your mother to keep you safe. We decided it best to let you believe you'd fallen as a child, and the scar and memory loss were a result of that accident. We wanted to spare you the pain of knowing your family had perished at the hands of pirates.

There's a plantation on the other side of the island and the owner, Oliver Grant, had taken in three strangers about the same time we'd found you. It was when they all escaped a year later, stealing his ship in the process, that I suspected the truth. There was a young woman among them named Samantha. I can only assume it was the same Samantha your mother had spoken of.

I'm terribly sorry, Alicia, and I hope you can forgive us for our selfishness. You see, we'd already lost Eric and Daniel, and by the time word got round of the other survivors, you were as much ours as you could ever be.

Should you want to seek out Samantha, then take the other letter to Blake Merritt. He's a good man, and you can trust him. He doesn't come to Port Royal, but you should be able to find him, or get word of him, in Tortuga.

You've often asked me why there's a white cross at the top of the rise behind the house and who it belonged to. It was cowardly to lie, but that is where your mother rests.

I pray you can forgive us for our deceit.

Lovingly,
Your father.

Alicia stared at the parchment, numb and shocked. For years she'd had bits of pictures or sounds flash through her head. She'd never made sense of them, couldn't as they were so fleeting and jumbled. Was it her memories that had been trying to resurface? She'd assumed it was dreams.

She jumped to her feet, the letter clutched in her hand. Her head spun. Samantha. The name resonated but she couldn't say it was because she remembered her; it simply sounded familiar. Was it possible she had a cousin? Could she even have a sister?

And her mother's grave was behind the house? Her *mother's*? Which meant she wasn't Alicia Davidson. Her knees gave a violent shake. Who was she? She tried desperately to remember anything of what her father spoke of, but she couldn't remember a sister, cousin, or a mother who wasn't the one she'd buried five months ago.

She placed an icy hand to her forehead, her breath shaking. What kind of person couldn't remember her own mother? *I'm not who I've always thought I was.* And the certainty of that cut deeply. She dropped to the bed. Why hadn't they told her before, when they could have been there to hold her, to explain? When they could have gone with her to look. When she didn't have quite so much responsibility.

She had a shop to run now. She couldn't, wouldn't, walk

away from it. She'd meant what she'd said to Charles—the shop was her world. It was where she'd played, where she'd worked, where she'd stood next to her father and listened with patience and an equal part of awe as he'd shown her about blade smithing.

She didn't imagine it would be a simple matter to locate Samantha; there must be hundreds of women with that name scattered around the Caribbean. How did one even begin a search such as that? It wasn't as though she had a well of money she could dip into. The shop made a living but didn't allow for much else. Besides, she'd never— that she remembered, she thought bitterly—been to sea. She knew nothing of ships and sailing. In fact, she'd never really liked sailing. Was it because she'd hated being at sea or because, deep down, she knew what it had cost her?

Her heart began to hammer, bringing with it a fierce desire to know everything she'd lost. She'd found a piece of that now; how could she not look for the rest? Her tumbling thoughts shifted to the shop and what she'd do with it, followed closely by her aunt and what she'd have to say about all of this.

Margaret wouldn't approve of Alicia running about the Caribbean by herself, but her aunt wasn't her concern. Regarding the shop—her heart missed a beat—she could talk to Charles; she'd make him understand. And it would only be temporary.

Alicia sighed. She had to know. She had to find out about her history. Not knowing would be far worse. With a slight tremble in her hand, Alicia grabbed the other letter.

Blake Merritt.

"Well, Mr. Merritt, I hope you're easy to find."

Three

Alicia awoke the next morning, after precious little sleep, with a very clear plan in her head. It was ridiculous to go out looking for Samantha until she had as much information as possible. And the only person who could provide it was Oliver Grant. Because it was Sunday and the shop was closed, Alicia had the day to herself and she packed a small lunch into her satchel, threw in a dagger for good measure, and not wanting to alert Charles of her intentions just yet, proceeded to walk to the home of her father's attorney.

It wasn't far, but the road offered no relief from the blazing sun and soon her gown was sticking to her back. Her cheeks were hot and no doubt she'd have a sunburn to show for her efforts. Another thing for her aunt to criticize, Alicia thought, kicking aside a stone, which rolled across the dirt into the thick underbrush that lined the route. Although uncertainty trotted through her head about the idea of seeking out Samantha, there was one thing she knew for certain. A reprieve from her aunt was more than in order.

Finally arriving at the tidy home of the attorney, Alicia knocked on the heavy door. He answered promptly and, despite the surprise on his face, invited her in. She gratefully stepped into the coolness of his home.

"I thought our appointment to read the will was tomorrow."

She held up a hand. "Yes, Mr. Fritz, it is. Or it was. I was hoping we could postpone it, for a little while," she added.

He frowned. "Whatever for? Your father's made some provisions, and it's best if we sort them all out as quickly as possible. There are issues about the blacksmith shop that you need to know."

Her hand flew to her throat. "I haven't lost it, have I? I assumed it was mine and—"

"Dear girl, it is yours. But there's also someone else that—"

Alicia expelled her breath in a rush. Well, if it had to do with Charles, he wouldn't mind if they waited a few more weeks.

"Thank goodness. You scared me for a moment. Well, then, I think it can wait. What I'm actually here for is to ask if you know where the plantation of Oliver Grant is."

Mr. Fritz's forehead creased in puzzlement. "Yes, but it's rather far. Why do you need to go there?"

"It's something my father suggested. I can't explain it any further than that at the moment."

"You're alone?" he asked.

"Yes."

He shook his head. "Dear girl, you can't go there all by yourself. It isn't right. Does your aunt know you're here?"

"No. And I'd prefer it remain that way."

A hint of a smile pulled at his lips. "Well, can't say that I blame you." He paused, studied Alicia. "You say your father wanted you to go see Oliver Grant?"

"Yes," she lied without question. If she was to find Samantha, and in turn, her past, then she'd do what it took to get it.

He nodded. "Wait here. I'll get someone who can take you."

It was a stately home, tall and commanding with a carved front door. An assortment of baskets overflowing with vibrant blossoms spread along its porch. The grounds were impressive with their carpet of emerald-colored grass that not a single weed dared to mar. The silence was equally awe-inspiring. Other than the slight breeze ruffling the palm fronds, or the occasional cry of a bird, the stillness was a presence in itself.

Surely it was inhabited to be so well kept, and yet from where Alicia stood at the base of the porch steps, not a single soul was to be seen.

She threw a glance to the end of the road, where she'd asked the driver to wait. The horse stood patiently, swishing its tail lazily; its driver must have been waiting inside the carriage, where it was cooler. Looking once more at the door, Alicia exhaled a breath, placed her hand onto her knotted stomach, then climbed the three steps.

Alicia's knock was answered by a large black woman with a frown that creased her wide forehead.

"Yes?"

"Hello. I—well, that is . . ." Alicia shook her head. She'd never anticipated it would be easy to explain what she was looking for, but neither had she expected that the words would lodge in her throat. But if Samantha had indeed been there and had stolen a ship to escape, Alicia wasn't sure of the reception she herself would receive by asking about her.

"I'm sorry," she said, forcing a smile and wiping her damp hands onto her skirt. The maid's face remained stoic. "I was hoping I might speak to Oliver Grant."

Her large brown eyes didn't so much as blink. "Ya can't. He's dead."

The bottom of Alicia's stomach fell in disappointment. "Oh, I'm so sorry. I didn't know."

The woman shrugged, almost as though she didn't care.

"Would it be possible to speak with Mrs. Grant?" Alicia asked, hoping her trip hadn't been for naught.

"The missus don't take callers no more."

Alicia sighed. This wasn't going the way she'd hoped. But who was left that she could talk to, that could tell her about Samantha? She wrung her hands together, not sure who to ask for next. This had been her only hope of possibly finding a link to her past, to her family.

"What did ya need?"

"I was hoping that I could speak to someone who could tell me about a woman that worked here. Her name was Samantha and I understand she escaped—"

"What do ya want with her?" she asked.

Taken aback by the rudeness, Alicia paused. "It's a long story. But I think she's part of my family, or at least that she may be." She shrugged. "I just wanted to know about her."

In a sudden transformation that captivated Alicia's attention, the woman's eyes filled with warmth and her smile reached out and wrapped around Alicia as surely as her strong arms.

"Child, come with me. I'll fix ya a cool drink, and we'll

have ourselves a nice long talk outside in the garden." She yanked Alicia by the hand, giving her no choice but to follow. She drew her into the marble foyer and down a corridor to the large and speckless kitchen at the back of the house.

Before she knew it, Alicia was sitting in the middle of the garden, a glass of sweet tea in her hand and the smell of flowers surrounding her. Fanny, as she'd introduced herself while she'd made the tea, sat across from her, eyes dancing with delight.

"Tell me how ya know Samantha," she said.

Because her manner had warmed considerably, Alicia told Fanny everything that she knew, ending with her decision to come there today in hopes of learning a little more. When she was done, Fanny had tears running down her dark cheeks.

"What's wrong?" Alicia asked quickly. Surely not any more bad news.

Fanny blew her nose into a handkerchief she drew from her apron pocket. "She'll be so happy yer alive."

Alicia's stomach flipped and she leaned forward in her chair. Behind the bodice of her gown, her heart was beating a frantic drum.

"She remembered me?"

"Of course she did, child. She's ya sister, ain't she?"

"I have a sister?" An impression flashed through her head. It didn't stay long enough to grasp it all, but she was able to make out a few things. "She has light brown hair?"

Fanny nodded and soon they both had tears falling freely.

"Yes, child. And she's lovely." Fanny sniffled. "She spoke of ya often. She loves ya very much. Ate a hole in her soul, thinkin' ya'd died and she was helpless to prevent it."

"But it was pirates. What could she have done?"

Fanny slapped her thick thigh. "That's what I's told her every chance I got. Didn't matter none. She felt she should have."

Alicia accepted the handkerchief Fanny pulled out of another pocket while trying to calm her emotions. Though the tears continued, she managed to steady her racing heart.

"Will you tell me everything?"

Fanny nodded, and before long, her happy tears ebbed.

"He found 'em on the beach, promised 'em work and shelta." She grunted. "It's not what they got, that's for sure."

"There were more with her?"

"Two men from ya father's ship. Joe and Willy." Her chin lifted. "Good men, both of 'em. They escaped togetha."

Alicia searched her memory, but nothing shifted. "The five of us were the only ones that made it off the ship?"

"Far as she knew, there was only three. She said she never saw ya that night, it ate at her somethin' terrible."

Alicia shook her head, it was all so unbelievable. She had a vague recollection of being cold, and very afraid, but nothing past that. She listened as Fanny told her, in more detail, about the pirate attack and that it was Joe who'd thrown Samantha overboard in order to save her. They were found by Oliver Grant and taken back to the plantation.

"It was a great day," Fanny said, smiling, "when they escaped. Gave us all somethin' to smile 'bout, knowin' they was free on his own ship."

"You didn't like him?"

Fanny's eyes narrowed. "He was evil. The devil hisself couldn't have been any more vicious. We's all glad he's dead."

"And you never heard from Samantha again?"

"No. But wherever she is, child, can't be any worse than livin' here was."

"Thank you, Fanny, for telling me. I'm glad she had a friend while she was here."

"Samantha had many friends here, child. Everyone who knew her liked her."

"Did anyone ever call her Sam?" The words came out as fast as the thought occurred to Alicia and she was taken aback by the sureness that she'd called her Sam.

Fanny smiled, leaned back in her chair. "Joe called her Sam. I always thought it suited her."

Alicia's heart shook. She had a sister. Sam. She pressed her trembling fingers to her lips.

"I have some stories, if ya have the time to hear 'em."

"Please," Alicia replied.

Upstairs, directly above the garden, Lewis Grant sat in his father's study—a study he hadn't been allowed in when his father was alive—and started to pay attention to the conversation drifting through the open window.

It grated on already raw nerves that as Oliver's only son he'd been denied the title of overseer. Though he was considered the heir, it was in name only. Lewis had gained nothing from the death of his father nearly a year ago other than a larger allowance. The respect, the damn acknowledgment that he was worthy and capable, had died in Barbados with the man who'd never looked at him with anything but disappointment.

It had never mattered to Oliver that his son had a head for figures or a deep desire to learn the operations of the plantation. All Oliver had seen was a son that hadn't grown into the physical image his father had wanted. It wasn't Lewis's fault that his height had never surpassed his mother's. Or that his bone structure was slight and far more suited to a woman than a man.

But since Oliver himself had rarely dirtied his own hands with the disciplinary areas of the plantation workers, Lewis had never understood why his size was an issue to his father. Couldn't Nathaniel continue to discipline the workers the way he always had? And couldn't Lewis then do the rest? Unfortunately Oliver had refused to listen to logic.

The rebuff, however, had only stopped Lewis for so long. On days like today, when Nathaniel—the bequeathed overseer—was busy in the fields, Lewis came to the office, studied the ledgers, and devoured everything he could find about his late father and the business he'd been denied. At twenty, he was more than capable of running the plantation. But the will had been ironclad.

Still, these visits had offered more than a knowledge of the plantation. It was on one such visit, the night he'd learned of his father's death, that he'd found the journals about Samantha. Every day since Oliver had found her on the beach had been precisely recorded. Her beauty, her spirit, her refusal of Oliver's advances that had led to his father raping her. The fury he'd felt when he'd tried a second time, only to have her attack him, help his slaves escape, and take his ship had all but leapt off the pages. He'd dedicated nearly two journals to the quest to find her and his ship, only to fail in the end. The ship and Samantha were still missing.

His father's failure gave Lewis extreme pleasure. Oliver had never acknowledged his own son's worth. He'd trusted hired men to act as his advisors and step into his shoes when he'd set off to search for Samantha, and he'd named those same men in the will.

But Oliver had been wrong about his son. Lewis was smart and worthy. And he'd just heard something that would finally allow him the chance to prove it. He'd just heard that fat Fanny say something that had sharpened his attention.

Sam.

Samantha had escaped five years ago. Not long after, word began to spread. There was a new force in the Caribbean waters, a pirate so cunning nobody knew what he looked like. Sam Steele. Nobody had mentioned Sam in nearly a year, and Lewis couldn't help but wonder if it was possible that Samantha and Sam were the same person. After all, she had managed to attack his father, free a dozen or more slaves, and steal his ship all in one night. Surely if she could manage that, it was conceivable she could be a pirate. And, he thought, Sam Steele was known to use a sloop as his flagship. The fact that the ship she'd stolen from his father was also a sloop seemed too tidy to Lewis.

This was his chance. His opportunity to get the ship back, to show everyone that Lewis had accomplished the one thing Oliver had failed to do.

But his aspirations didn't end there. Surely the treasure and riches she had accumulated were extensive. A little jaunt through the Caribbean was worth the blackmail he could profit from if Samantha was indeed Steele. He'd not only come back with his father's ship, but return with the respect he deserved.

And judging from what that worthless Fanny was discussing, all he had to do was follow this Alicia girl.

Charles dropped the sword he was working on. It clanged to the floor.

"Are you mad?" he demanded.

"I can do this," Alicia tried again. In retrospect, she should have eased him into the subject, rather than simply asking him to run the shop while she went to search for someone she herself hadn't known about until the night before last.

"No," he stated, picking up the steel. "No, you can't. You are far too young and naive for this kind of undertaking."

"I'm not a child, Charles. I can take care of myself."

His eyes bulged in his head. "Here maybe, where you know people and it's familiar, but out there?" He gestured to the window, his arm waving madly. "I'll worry myself sick about you." He wiped the sweat from his brow. "Your father must be rolling in his grave as we speak."

Alicia sighed. "He's the one who told me, remember?"

"I'm sure he hadn't figured on you going it alone. How are you getting to Tortuga anyhow?"

"I bartered passage," she said. He raised an eyebrow and she added, "I'll need money to do this and I don't have very much to spare. You can't afford to come with me and I can't afford a chaperone."

"I'm sure your aunt would pay for one."

Alicia laughed. "If she knew about this, she'd lock me up in her house, never to be free again."

"Not a bad idea," Charles mumbled, running his hand over the blade.

"I'll be fine. Pounding on steel day in and day out has given me strength. Besides, I haven't worked years in this shop without learning how to use each and every weapon."

He sighed heavily. "And you'll be taking along at least five of each?"

She smiled affectionately. "I promise to get word to you as soon as I can."

Charles leaned heavily against the workbench. "Tortuga of all places is not where a young woman ought to be, especially by herself."

"It won't be for long. Only until I find Mr. Merritt."

He rubbed his stubbled jaw. "It strikes me as odd that your father would send you to someone I've never heard of."

Alicia shrugged, examined the rows of knives, and took two that were small enough to hide. She slipped them into the waist of her trousers. She chose a small pistol that would be easily concealed and ignored Charles's tortured moan as she did.

"Well, it must be someone he trusts, or he wouldn't have." She picked a sword, held it out, swished it back and forth, and added it to her arsenal.

"Here," Charles said, taking a larger pistol from a shelf. "You better take this as well."

Four

The rum wasn't working, and it wasn't from a lack of effort on Blake Merritt's part. He hollered for another and knew he was in dire straits when the wench who brought it to him didn't stir a reaction from him no matter how much bosom escaped her bodice. Normally he would have taken her up on her wink and seductive laugh. He'd have followed her upstairs and buried his problems with meaningless sex. But nothing was normal and hadn't been for almost a week. Not since he'd gotten word.

He swallowed half the contents of his mug in one long gulp.

"Blake, lad," thundered a voice over the curses and carousing that had the walls of Doubloons trembling. "Where ya been? 'Aven't seen ya in months."

Blake raised his head, his gaze scaling the giant's body until he reached the man's face. "Well, then, Captain, I take it you haven't been around much, because I've been here for days."

Captain took a seat, saving Blake's neck. His large hand covered a good portion of the table when he leaned forward.

"No, can't say I 'ave. I've been a little . . . preoccupied." He grinned.

Knowing just what he meant didn't help Blake feel any better. He himself hadn't been able to summon up a desire to do more than drink lately.

"So," Captain said, smacking the table and making it quiver, "what's bringin' ya by, then? It's not like ya to stay fer long."

Blake shrugged, not in the mood to discuss his problems.

Captain's booming voice made Blake wince. "'Tis a wench. 'Tis always about one, ain't it? Which one wanted ya to marry her this time?"

Despite his mood, Blake chuckled. Captain was right. Every time he came to Tortuga, he seemed to find himself at the receiving end of a marriage proposal.

"Not this time. Although I must say, as much as I hate those proposals, I'd greatly prefer one right about now."

Captain's eyes danced and he leaned back in his chair, which groaned under the effort. "Well, let's see if we can change yer luck."

Shaking his head, Blake went back to drinking. Captain, though, was determined in his quest. He was scouring the room, listing off reasons each of the women he spotted wouldn't work. "No, she's trouble, likely to cut yer throat during the throes of passion if yer not careful. That one is too old, that one too young. Her ya said no to at least twice already." He turned back to Blake, his gray eyes laughing. "Now I see why yer alone."

Blake raised his mug in salute and took another long gulp. He nearly choked on it when Captain slapped him hard on the back.

"By God, lad. There's one fer ya! And if ya don't want her, I'll have her fer meself!" he said excitedly.

Blake shouldn't have looked. He should have listened to the warning bell that chimed in his head a moment before he raised it to see who Captain had spotted. Instead his eyes made contact with the woman—girl—in question and he groaned, wishing yet again that the damn rum had taken him to oblivion.

Alicia Davidson. She stumbled when she recognized him, but after catching herself, turned from Blake and continued on to the barman. Perfect, Blake thought. Not only was the rum ineffective, but one of the reasons he'd needed the alcohol to begin with was now across the room from him.

"Land sakes, lad, how do ya do it? The woman barely steps into the door and already she targets ya?" Captain shook his head in disbelief. "Whatever spell it is ya have on the wenches, lad, could ya teach it to me?"

"Right now it isn't a spell, Captain, it's a curse. And you can have her, I'm not interested."

His friend licked his meaty lips. "Yer loss. Wish me luck," Captain said, grinding his chair back against the scarred wooden floor as he stood.

Blake grimaced. Luck. He didn't remember what that was anymore. Leaning back in his own chair, he watched Captain stomp over to Alicia and grinned despite himself when she took a step back. Captain was heads taller than anyone else, and with his large girth and booming voice, most people tended to be afraid of him at first, until they got to know him and realized he was more jellyfish than shark.

Despite the fact that her presence tightened the muscles across his shoulders, Blake found himself watching her and Captain. What could they be talking about? he wondered. Surely she had no business in Tortuga. Shouldn't she be home mourning her precious father?

Suddenly Captain's face lit up brighter than the candles clustered on the tables. He turned to Blake, his grin from ear to ear. Blake's stomach clenched. What was going on? Then, before he had any more time to ponder that, Captain took Alicia by the arm and led her straight to their table. Was he stark raving mad?

"Blake, lad," he bellowed, swinging an arm around Alicia's shoulders, the weight of which had her stumbling. Captain yanked her back. "Ya did it again. 'Tis you she's looking for."

"Fantastic," Blake muttered. "My luck keeps getting better."

She didn't look any happier than he did, which was some comfort.

"*You're* Blake Merritt?" she asked.

"Last time I checked."

Alicia exhaled heavily. "Well, this is unexpected."

"As is your presence here." He looked over her brown trousers and white shirt. "Mourning periods must be getting shorter and shorter."

Her mouth pinched and he saw her hands curl and uncurl at her sides. "I *am* in mourning, but it's not practical to travel in a heavy skirt. And I'm here because I require your help."

Blake crossed his arms over his chest. "I wasn't aware that I'd given you the impression of someone who cared."

"Blimey, Blake," Captain whispered, or tried to. With Captain, even his whispers echoed.

"You haven't," she answered. "And had I known it was you he'd sent me to, I may have reconsidered."

Blake gestured to the door. "It's never too late."

"And give you the satisfaction? I think not."

"Well, let's say I am not in the giving mood. Whatever it was you needed from me, you'll have to find elsewhere."

"What is it ya need?" Captain asked.

Blake was glad when she turned her face away from him. It gave him an opportunity to study her. She was dressed as a man; she'd tied her hair back in a braid that fell in a thick rope to the middle of her back. At the grave site he'd concentrated mostly on his loathing of her and the bitterness he felt toward Jacob. He hadn't paid attention to the details. Now, by glow of candlelight, he saw her hair was the color of honey fresh from the comb. The fact that he noticed it did nothing to improve an already sour mood.

"I'm looking for someone. Her name is Samantha. She was last seen five years ago leaving Port Royal on a stolen sloop."

"Well, now that we have so much to go on, let's not waste any more time. I mean, five years. Why, she's practically around the corner," Blake taunted.

Alicia's cheeks turned bright red. Blake called out for another rum. The girl was insane if she thought he'd sail aimlessly, to help *her* no less. "Over my dead body," he grumbled.

"Samantha . . ." Captain said with some thought. "Are ya family?"

Alicia nodded. "She's my sister. But I don't know where she is."

"Good luck," Blake answered. When his rum was brought

to him, he smiled his warmest smile and flirted with the wench. It gave him supreme satisfaction to see Alicia frown.

"And she's in a sloop, ya say?"

"No," Blake corrected, wiping his mouth. "She was five years ago."

Alicia glared at Blake, her blue eyes sparking. He smiled in return.

"That's what I was told," she said, once again talking to Captain.

"Hmm . . ." Captain said, rubbing his protruding belly. "I don't know 'ow much value this is to ya, but me knows a Samantha."

"Oh, good. I'll go ready the ship," Blake muttered.

"She's about yer height, a little older. Her hair is darker than yers, but I know her and Luke own a sloop." He shrugged. "Might be the same girl."

"You expect me to sail off to . . ."

Captain finally turned from Alicia to Blake. "St. Kitts."

Blake choked. "You want me to sail to St. Kitts on the *chance* that this is the same woman?" He looked from Captain to Alicia, not sure who was crazier. "I won't waste my bloody time, nor that of my crew."

"How far is St. Kitts?" Alicia asked.

"At least a six days' sail, longer if ya get bad weather."

Alicia paled and her hand fluttered at her stomach. She swallowed hard. "That long?"

Blake gulped his rum, glad when his head swayed a little. Maybe it was finally starting to take effect.

"Doesn't matter how long it takes as I won't be taking you."

Her hand dropped back to her side. "We've never met. Why is it that you hate me so?"

Though the rum was starting to work, it wasn't enough

to shut out her words. And it certainly wasn't enough to tell her the reason for his hatred.

"I've heard of you, let's leave it at that. And I won't sail you anywhere. Therefore, it appears you've wasted your time."

"I don't relish the idea of sailing with pirates either, Mr. Merritt, but I was sent to you."

Blake's teeth gnashed at the term. Perhaps to others there was little difference between privateers and pirates, but to Blake the difference was enormous. He considered himself an honorable man and in his mind there wasn't much honorable about piracy. Yes, he took Spanish ships, but only for the gold. He gave the rest, other than his share and that of his crew, to the same government that issued him the letters of marque—the papers that told him what he was doing was within the boundaries of the law.

He made a point of being fair, and he never raped women or murdered for the pure pleasure of it, even though some privateers used their papers as a licence to pirate. Though Blake knew the line between privateers and pirates was thin, he nonetheless prided himself on being on the right side of that line.

"I sail a privateer's vessel." He loathed that he felt the need to explain himself to this little chit.

She shrugged, pulled an envelope from the bag she carried, and dropped it on the table, directly under his nose.

"Then perhaps this will change your mind, Mr. Privateer."

He recognized the swirl of letters and knew who'd written his name.

"Where did you get this?" he demanded, all fuzziness gone from his head.

"I found it in my father's effects. There was a letter for

me as well. He was the one who told me that I should seek your help if I decided to look for Samantha."

"How is it ya don't know where she is?" Captain asked.

Though telling strangers the intimate details of her life wasn't something she relished, she hoped it would help them understand her need to find Samantha.

"We were separated years ago. I don't remember anything before I was twelve, and that includes Samantha."

Blake sneered. "Let me guess. Your *loving* father knew all along you had family out there, and he only decided to tell you after he'd died?"

She looked down her nose at him, her color returning. "That's right."

"Why am I not surprised?" he muttered.

"He also said you were a good man that I could trust."

Her tone left no doubt that she believed the complete opposite.

Blake didn't open the letter. It was too late for words or apologies or anything else that could be written on that parchment. And her sad tale didn't change that. If anything, it infuriated him further. He refused to let himself be used.

"Well?" Captain asked, his gaze darting between her and Blake. "What'll it be?"

Blake leaned forward, shoving aside the letter with his elbow. "I'll tell you what it'll be," he answered, his gaze piercing hers. "It'll be a cold day in Hell before I take you anywhere."

Her jaw clenched and her eyes hardened. She braced her hands on the table and leaned forward. "I don't know who you are, or how you knew my father, but clearly he was mistaken about you."

"That, my dear, is the first thing you've said that I agree

with." And because the truth of that haunted him every day, he raised his cup to his lips and drank.

Alicia wrenched open the door of Doubloons and stomped outside. It was no quieter there. Men whistled and yelled after women while the women taunted and shrieked at the men. Dogs barked and horses clomped through the streets. Pistols were fired skyward for no other reason, it seemed, than to add to the cacophony. Alicia envied these people their lack of troubles.

She, on the other hand, was now in quite a predicament. The ship that had taken her to Tortuga had sailed on once Alicia had confirmed that Mr. Merritt was ashore, and now the same blasted man refused to help her. She was stuck with no place to stay and no means of getting home. Kicking a rock down the cobblestone street, Alicia couldn't help but wish it was Blake's head.

"Arrogant, loathsome man," she grumbled. Because the weight of the bag she carried was beginning to hurt her shoulder, Alicia set it at her feet. She'd no sooner put it down than it was nearly trampled by a drunkard who'd stumbled out the door of Doubloons. His rancid breath washed over her and the odor of skin too long without a bath curled around her.

"'Scuse me," he mumbled before staggering away, a loud belch ripping the air.

Alicia wrinkled her nose, grabbed her bag, and decided to start moving. She needed to find a place for the night where she could rest and think. Because she knew one thing—even without Blake Merritt's help, she wasn't giving up. If she had family, she was going to find it. She simply didn't know at the moment how that was going to be possible.

Just then, the door opened again, spilling the din of the tavern into the river of debauchery that was the streets of Tortuga. If Alicia hadn't decided it already by the light of day, she did now. Tortuga was not a place she ever wanted to see again.

"Ah, good. I was afraid ya'd be long gone."

Alicia turned to the voice and smiled ruefully. "I would be if I had a place to go."

The giant grinned. "That's easily solved. I 'ave a place ya can stay until mornin'."

Alicia nearly swallowed her tongue. "And Charles thought *I* was mad."

His smile twisted into a snarl. Alicia took a step back.

"I'm not mad, missy. But ya need a place to stay, don't ya?"

"Well . . ."

"Yes or no?" he asked.

"Well, yes, but—"

"Then let's go."

He made to leave, assuming Alicia would follow. She grabbed his arm.

"I can't go with you. I don't even know you."

"Well, how long does that take? I ain't sittin' out here with the drunkards all night, missy. We're likely to either get shot or trampled."

Even as he said it, two brawling men came tumbling around the corner straight for them. The giant simply shook his head, extended one meaty arm in front of Alicia, and shoved both men to the ground with little more than a push.

"Well? 'Ave ya made up yer mind yet?"

She sighed. "It's not that I don't appreciate the offer . . ."

"Captain. And I don't see ya gettin' any better ones."

"I don't think I'd accept them even if I did."

"Ya can trust me." He smiled and Alicia was happy to see his eyes were neither full of rum nor evil. "I can tell ya what I know of Samantha."

Alicia gnawed on her lip. Well, she had bartered passage with a stranger. And had Blake been willing to help, she would have gone off with him, another stranger. Was Captain really any different?

Suddenly a pistol shot rang out so close it shrilled in her ears. She yelped and hunkered down. Before she knew it, the giant had her by the arm and she was sailing back onto her feet.

"Are ya comin' or not?"

She couldn't speak, her heart was thudding too fast and loud against her chest. She nodded instead.

"Good. And if ya can cook, we'll consider breakfast yer payment. Come, missy, 'tis this way."

He led her through the smoke-filled air, past all the ruckus of the taverns to the back edge of town. His home was nothing more than a rough shack thrown up between some trees, which was a good thing as the poor structure looked as though any sort of significant wind would topple it to the ground. However, it was a shelter, and despite Captain's size, she sensed she had nothing to fear from him.

Captain lit a fire in the tiny hearth and it helped chase away the smell of mildew that clung to the walls. From a trunk he drew out thick blankets and set them before the hearth. Alicia was glad, once she sat on them with a cup of tea in her hands, that they smelled relatively clean.

The giant had chosen the only chair in the cabin and sat upon it now with a contented sigh.

"When was the last time you saw Samantha?"

"I've only met her twice. First time, she walked into Doubloons when I was talkin' to Luke."

"You mentioned Luke before. Who is he?"

Captain choked on his drink and had to thump himself on the chest to clear it.

"Ya never heard of Luke Bradley?"

"No, why?"

"Blimey, missy, he's only the best pirate the Caribbean has ever seen!"

"But you said Samantha is with Luke. Are they . . . they can't be . . . she married a pirate?"

He set his mug down hard on the rickety table near his left elbow. "Now don't be lookin' so shocked. Luke's a damn good man, and last time I saw 'em, they looked right happy enough."

"All right, sorry. So, Samantha came into Doubloons . . ."

He nodded, a smile softening his face. "She was a sight. All dressed in red, she had every man, includin' meself, in her net. It was when I said somethin' that Luke took exception. Said he'd seen her first. I did, methinks, manage to charm her nonetheless. Said she was lookin' for another pirate named Dervish. 'Course right after that, Luke took her outside. I didn't see her again until a few months ago."

"In St. Kitts?"

"Yep."

"Did she ever find that other pirate?"

"Hmm," he said, swallowing more rum. He wiped his mouth with the back of his hand and set down his mug. "Luke killed him."

Captain said it as easily as if he were discussing the weather. Alicia bit her lip. What was she getting into? She was searching for a woman she didn't know who was married to a man that could kill another person. And their mutual friend, a friend she'd agreed to spend the night with, didn't think it was wrong. Charles was right—she was mad.

"Now, before ya pass judgment, let me tell ya somethin'. Luke was a great pirate, but he wasn't mean. Loot was what he was after, but he didn't do it like some do. He liked to use his brains and play around a little. Come to think of it, I think he preferred the hunt. But from what I know of Samantha, she wouldn't 'ave married 'im if he wasn't a good man. He's one of few that I'd give me own life to save."

"You said 'was.' He's not a pirate anymore?"

"Nah. Applied for his pardon." Captain's face split into a grin as big as his belly. "'Course when yer the best shipbuilder to be found in these parts and ya sell the Navy the fastest and strongest, they tend to forgive ya right fast enough."

Alicia tasted her tea, which was more like swamp water, and set her full cup aside.

"It doesn't matter, really. Mr. Merritt won't help me and I don't know where else to look. Being a woman alone, I can't simply hop on to any ship I please. I was lucky to get here as it was."

"What ya need to know about Blake," Captain began, while rubbing his belly, "is that he can be very stubborn. And when he gets mad, it only gets worse. Fastest way to get Blake to go north is demand he go south."

"He's not a pirate, too, is he?"

"A privateer, but 'tis all the same, really. Only Blake has the Navy on his side, not trying to hang his backside, see?"

"Either way, I need to think of another plan."

Captain leaned forward and gray eyes fixed on hers. "Ya know what I think? I say ya don't give him the choice."

"But the only way would be to—"

"That's right, missy." Captain nodded. "That's the only way."

Alicia's stomach twittered. "Why would you tell me to do that? You like Blake."

"Aye. I do. But Blake needs some fun in 'is life. He's too serious."

She didn't see how Mr. Merritt seeing her again would change that.

"Tell me, Captain. My father clearly thought that Blake was a good man whom I could trust. That's not been my experience so far. What do you think of him?"

"Missy, if I didn't like the man or trust 'im, I'd hardly send you after 'im. Me only advice? Stay hidden until yer well away from port."

Five

Lewis Grant smiled in the darkness. He no longer felt the rocks that pushed into the soles of his shoes. He didn't bother swatting away the bugs that buzzed around his face and gnawed on him until his skin crawled. All he felt at the moment was a glowing sense of satisfaction.

Thanks to the big oaf's habit of keeping the windows open, Lewis had heard every word. Now, not only did he know where Samantha was, but he had a means of getting to her. Lewis licked his lips.

All he had to do now was get onto Blake Merritt's ship—it would cast less suspicion than following him—and follow the little chit until she led him to Samantha. Oliver had given that whore more of his time and attention than he'd spared for his only son. Lewis intended to see that Samantha paid for that as well.

He crept from his hiding place under the window and walked out of the woods, back to the tavern. He'd find her, threaten to turn her over to the authorities unless she gave him back not only his father's ship but also everything she'd acquired as Sam Steele.

And once he had the ship loaded with untold wealth and he was back in Port Royal, he'd gladly let the Navy know exactly where she was. It was the least she deserved.

Blake rolled out of his berth as the sun pushed itself out of the sapphire water and into the purple sky. He took a moment to look, but his usual enjoyment at seeing the sunrise was ruined by the same thoughts that had plagued him throughout the night and the one before. He pulled on his trousers and drew on his shirt, leaving it unbuttoned. Barefoot, he padded to the table and stared down at the sealed envelope. He should have burned it. At the very least, he should have left it in Doubloons, where it could have been used to sop up spilled rum or to wipe the floors. He didn't know what demon had possessed him to jam it into his pocket, but he wished the little beggar had left him alone.

Looking down at the wrinkles that lined the envelope, owing to its unceremonious journey in his pocket, Blake was just as angry as when he'd first had it placed under his nose. Who the bloody hell did she think she was anyway?

"Alicia Davidson."

He said her name like a curse. For him, it was one. Ever since he'd first heard she'd been found and taken in, she was a festering wound that wouldn't heal. And seeing her, talking to her, had only made matters worse. Especially knowing who it was that had sent her to begin with. Help her? Sure, he'd help her, the same way Jacob Davidson had helped him. By turning his back and pretending she didn't exist.

It took a full hour of stewing, he figured, before he pulled himself together. He would not dwell on the matter a moment longer. Already he'd spent two sleepless nights because of her, one anchored in Tortuga, reliving her little speech over in his mind until it had given him a blasted headache, and again last night after they'd loaded the ship and left Tortuga in their wake. He'd thought knowing he had left Alicia behind would have given him peace of mind.

"Well, it bloody hasn't," Blake muttered, buttoning his shirt and pulling on his knee-high boots. Hoping the quiet of the deck before the rest of the crew awakened would do the job, he went above.

The sea was still and silent and his ship slept like the rest of his men. Filling his lungs with cool air, Blake made his way to the helm. Vincent, one of his first mates, was at the wheel.

"Morning, Captain."

"Morning. Nothing on the horizon?" Blake asked, taking the looking glass. Far as the eye could see was nothing but a rippling blanket of green-blue water. Blake couldn't imagine anything better. The knots in his shoulders eased. Here was home. Here he didn't have to justify himself, explain what was in his heart. Here he could just be, and it was where he belonged.

"Nothing. She's quiet."

"Good. Go get some rest."

Vincent jumped off the crate he'd been standing on and moved it aside. As a dwarf, he needed the box to see over the helm, but that was the only thing he needed to be one of the best first mates Blake had ever had. Nate, his other, was currently belowdecks. Both had a natural talent for strategy, and many battles they'd won had been greatly due to Vincent's and Nate's cleverness. Because of that, the rest of the crew treated Vincent as an equal, and his size was never an issue. If it ever became one, they would have to answer to Blake.

Vincent yawned and rubbed his round face, looking more like a young lad than a man nearly the same age as Blake.

"Thank God. I tried to sleep last night, before my turn on deck, but that new whelp you hired on in Tortuga kept throwing up. I've never heard such a bad case of seasickness in my life."

Blake's hand froze midreach to the helm. "You hired one on. I didn't."

"The man I hired is named Lewis. I've never seen this one before. He came on board in Tortuga, said you'd given him a job."

Blake got a very uneasy feeling low in his belly, and the knots came back into his shoulders.

"Where is he?"

"Below, keeping company with the chickens."

Perfect. "Can you take her a little longer?" Blake asked.

Vincent simply moved the crate back into position.

"Thanks. I shouldn't be long, and then you can get some sleep."

"As long as you can keep that boy from heaving, I will."

"Well, depending on why he stowed away on my ship, I may just toss him overboard."

Vincent smiled. "You're not that mean."

Blake scoffed and slipped below. He passed the hammocks of snoring men and followed the smell down another level to where they kept their livestock. The goats stretched their necks when he walked by, reaching for anything they could nibble on. The chickens watched silently from their wire cages. He sidestepped the worst of the streams that crossed the walkway between the cages and pens, wondering why anyone who was seasick would choose to stay in the worst-smelling part of the ship. Unless he was someone who didn't want to be found.

Blake didn't have to search hard. He simply had to follow the moans of the sick boy. Blake found him sprawled on his side in a clean patch of straw, a thin boy wearing worn brown trousers and a cap, a bucket next to his face and his back to Blake.

"Having difficulties, son?" he asked without sympathy.

A long moan answered him, and the boy tugged the brim of his cap farther down on his head.

"A little late to hide now, boy." Blake kicked his boot. "Get up."

For a while, Blake didn't think the boy was going to comply. But finally he moved, keeping his back to Blake while he got to his feet, the bucket clasped tightly in his hand. He swayed slightly and Blake cursed. This wasn't anybody who would be of value on his ship.

"Turn around."

Lowering the bucket, the boy drew off his hat as he turned. A long braid fell over what should have been a boy's shoulder. Only it wasn't a boy looking out at him through a face pale as the canvas of his sails.

Blake felt as though he'd been punched hard in the stomach.

"Hello, Mr. Privateer."

"Alicia? What the bloody hell are you doing on my ship?"

Six

She didn't answer. He could see she wanted to, but each time she opened her mouth to speak, she slammed it shut again, closed her eyes, and swallowed repeatedly. She swayed and stumbled back against the wall, then slid down until her backside was on the floor. She settled the bucket between her bent knees.

"Take me ashore, you'd be doing me a favor," she muttered.

He'd be lying if he said he wasn't tempted.

"You snuck on in Tortuga?"

She nodded.

"You've been sick ever since?"

Another nod.

"Dammit, Alicia, that was a day and a half ago!"

She wretched again, though nothing was left to come up. Wiping her face, she leaned back, looking as frail as a newborn lamb.

"I'm well aware of the hours that have passed, since they've been dragging like a lame dog."

Judging from the pale cheeks and dark circles under her eyes, Blake had no doubt she'd counted every second. But he refused to be moved by it. Since leaving Port Royal behind seven years ago, Blake had always had a clear vision and goal. He'd wanted to be a privateer, and from the moment he'd acquired his ship and received his first letters of marque, he'd felt all the pieces of himself fit perfectly for the first time in his life. He'd had a purpose and it wasn't one his father had carved out for him, but rather one he'd chosen himself. Though certain this girl couldn't jeopardize that, he was nettled by her presence nonetheless.

"If I took you back to Port Royal, what would you do?"

Her eyes suddenly filled with more energy than he thought she had left.

"I'd try another way to get to St. Kitts."

"To find someone you don't remember? Are you that stupid?"

"Why are you asking?" she queried. "Haven't you already made up your mind about me?"

Sick or not, Blake glared at her. She'd stowed away on his ship; she should have been begging for his mercy, for his understanding. It's what he'd expected her to do. The fact that she hadn't the energy to hold herself up and yet could challenge him so easily showed gumption. And despite his annoyance, he'd always respected that trait in a person. He set his jaw.

"You'd likely die in the process. If dehydration didn't do you in, a pirate attack certainly would."

Her eyes closed. "Your concern is overwhelming."

He came to her then and kneeled down. He waited until her eyes opened. "I'll take you to my cabin, get some food into you. But make no mistake, it's not out of concern. I just don't want a dead body smelling up my ship."

"You mean more than it already does?"

"You don't like it, you're welcome to leave. I have no objection if you aren't willing to wait until we make the next port to do so."

"I assume you're not married." Despite her pallor and sunken cheeks, her mouth twisted into a sneer.

"No, I'm not."

"Shocking," she answered.

Because a part of him was impressed with her sassiness, he bristled. He shouldn't be impressed; he should be angry at her for being there and at himself for seeing anything in Alicia Davidson worth admiring.

"Are you always this ungrateful for help?" he demanded.

"Are you always this ungracious?"

Not usually, but seeing her over that grave, crying over a man who had no business being cried over, infuriated him. But then, she'd seen a side to Jacob Davidson that Blake hadn't been privy to.

"Cabin's this way," he muttered.

She struggled to her feet and followed behind him, the bucket still in her grasp. This time he didn't care where he walked. He took the steps two at a time and had climbed to the next deck before he heard her retching again.

"Good God." Since he was close to the galley, he strode inside and asked his cook to make up some tea and to have it sent with some dry bread to his cabin. Then he went back to fetch Alicia.

"Are you coming?"

She'd sat on the steps, and now that she'd moved farther up the ship, she'd caught the attention of some of his crew. They were watching over the railing, wondering how and when a woman had come aboard. Blake wondered the same thing.

Alicia, however, didn't seem concerned with the men gathered nearby. In fact, with her head tilted to rest against the wall, and her hands hanging loosely on her knees, she appeared to be almost—

"Bloody hell," he cursed, taking the steps down as fast as he'd taken them up. Sure enough, there she was, the bucket on her lap, sound asleep.

"We can put her in me hammock," one of his crew volunteered.

"Or mine," another said.

This was followed by a rowdy argument of just who should have Alicia. And that was the second time Blake knew he had trouble on his hands. The first had been seeing her and knowing the reaction she caused in him. He hadn't had time to think of what his crew would do. And now—thanks again to her, he thought gratingly—he knew just what her presence would mean. Feeling a headache brewing behind his right eye, Blake silenced his crew with nothing more than a glare.

"She'll be in my cabin, for the moment, and I don't want to hear another word about her. Nate," he called, when he spotted his other first mate coming through the crowd, "bring a bucket of warm water and a cloth to my cabin." Blake handed Nate the soiled pail and ignored his questioning gaze. "Clean that, too, please, and bring it back with you. The rest of you have duties to attend to. And don't forget to mop below. It bloody stinks down there."

They knew better than to argue or dawdle, and soon the way was once again clear. Despite his feelings toward her, as Blake looked down upon Alicia, he didn't have the heart to wake her. He couldn't imagine the long night she'd spent being sick, and knew if he wanted to get her off his ship with as little guilt as possible, he needed to have her well. Otherwise he'd never have peace.

He dipped low and slipped her into his arms. Cursing at how little she weighed, he carried her up the stairs, onto the deck, and across to the hatch that led to his cabin. Vincent's eyes looked ready to explode from his head.

"A woman?" he gasped. "How did I miss that?"

Blake didn't want to think about her gender, or the way she'd turned her head against his chest and snuggled in. He didn't want to notice the way the sun hit her hair and made it shine, or the freckles he saw across her cheeks when he looked down.

"I don't know, but we need to discuss it. Thanks," he added when Vincent opened the hatch for him. "Nate will be bringing me some water in a moment. When he does, I'd like to see both of you in my cabin. Get Billy to man the helm. Hopefully it won't take long."

"Aye, Captain." Vincent smiled, gesturing to Alicia, who remained sound asleep in Blake's arms. "You know, chivalry becomes you."

Blake scowled. "You really must need sleep, you're delirious."

Vincent's chuckle followed Blake into his cabin. Blake told himself he wasn't being deliberately gentle with her when he lay Alicia onto his bed, then covered her with a light blanket. It was simply common sense. As long as she slept, she wasn't bothering him, wasn't looking at him with those deep blue eyes.

She sighed, then turned her head onto his pillow, which allowed him to gaze fully upon her face. She was young, barely more than a girl, but even dressed as a boy, she was

undeniably pretty. His gaze moved from dark gold eyelashes
that fanned over her pale cheeks, to her slightly parted lips.
The fullness and the pale pink captivated his attention. Had
she been anyone else, he'd have been sorely tempted to see
if they were as soft and sweet as they appeared.

But she wasn't. He took a deep breath, shook his head,
and turned from her before his eyes could betray him any
more. Yes, indeed, the sooner she left his ship, the better.

Alicia awoke to the sound of hushed voices and no idea
of where she was. Opening her eyes, she looked around.
Light floated in through a small porthole to her left, shining directly onto the three whispering men. She recognized Blake. The second man was taller, and the third was
the dwarf she remembered seeing not long after she'd come
aboard.

The large table they were standing beside and the comfortable bed beneath her left no doubt she was in Blake's
cabin. And at the moment he was likely hearing every lie
she'd told to get on board his ship. Considering his feelings toward her, something she had yet to understand, this
wouldn't help him see her in a better light. Since she'd never
been one to avoid any task, even the unpleasant ones, Alicia
gathered her courage and threw off the light blanket that
covered her. She paused in the action. He'd covered her up?

A sensation she'd never experienced before fluttered
through her stomach and warmed the area around her
heart. Had Blake taken the time, had the compassion, to
place the blanket over her? She'd never had anyone treat
her so delicately before. Women mostly turned the other
way, even when she wasn't dressed for work, because she
wasn't "normal" in their eyes. The men's reactions varied.

Some resented her for doing a job she not only excelled at but bested most of them at as well. Others couldn't believe a small woman such as herself could do such hard work while the rest, those who were accustomed to her, treated her as a man since they didn't look past her clothes and her work to the woman beneath.

Raising her eyes, she met the cold expression in Blake's and all warm thoughts withered.

"Good, you're awake."

Both the dwarf and the other man turned to her, each with a curious expression on his face.

"It appears so," she answered, pushing the hurt aside and swinging her legs off the bed.

"I'll talk to you later," Blake said to his men.

"The men have seen her," the tall man said.

"I'm well aware of that," Blake muttered.

"There'll be talk."

Blake's stunned expression had Alicia biting her lip to keep from smiling. There was no cause to worry about that sort of talk, not the way Blake hated her. He blinked, looked from his crewman to her. Alicia didn't have to force away any traces of humor. It withered on its own when Blake's gaze locked on to hers. His disgusted look and the following snicker shouldn't have hurt, not with the quantity of such glances she'd had aimed her way over the years, but they did.

Blake turned his back on her.

"If they want to remain on this ship, they'll keep their opinions to themselves."

The tall man looked over at her, and concern lingered in his gaze. Because it was nice to be worried about, she offered the man a smile, silently thanking him for his concern over her reputation.

He nodded and made to leave, but paused at the base

of the steps to look at her one more time. He winked, and if she read his lips right, mouthed the words "good luck" before heading up onto the deck. The dwarf followed, offering a faint smile before leaving. Only when the hatch had closed behind them did Blake face Alicia.

"The bucket is beside your feet. If you're inclined to be sick again, I'd prefer it wasn't on my bed."

"I'll keep that in mind."

Because his gaze never wavered from hers, it allowed Alicia the opportunity to notice what she hadn't yet, that his eyes were nearly as dark as the hair he had tied back with a piece of leather. He watched her closely as she moved from his bed to the table, taking the pail along with her. She wondered what his eyes would look like when he wasn't angry. In fact, she wondered at the transformations that would take place on his face if he actually smiled. But seeing him now, solemn and hard, she had difficulty imagining that was even possible.

"I arranged for some tea to be brought," Blake said, reaching over to the tray she hadn't seen until then. "It's ginger tea, it eases seasickness. If that stays down, there's some bread here as well. It's dry, but it's best to start with that." He pushed the tray in front of her.

"Thank you."

No doubt the answer stuck in his throat, so he nodded instead. Rather than take a seat at the table with her, he leaned against a support post, crossed his arms over his chest, and continued to stare at her. Suddenly she was all too aware of the fact that she'd been sick for the last two days. Her clothes were dirty and wrinkled and she didn't even want to think about what she smelled like. She didn't dare, however, ask for a bath. Perhaps a change of clothes was in order, though.

"Where's my bag?"

"What bag?" he asked.

"The bag I had with me. It has my personal effects."

"It must be down where you were hiding. I'll get it later."

Later. When he was good and ready and not a moment sooner, she thought. But he had brought her some tea, and despite her feelings, she appreciated it. She brought the cup to her lips. It was cold and slightly bitter, but it wasn't undrinkable.

Silence reigned as Alicia sipped her tea and broke small pieces of bread between her fingers. Blake's low and even breathing was the only sound other than the footsteps and muffled voices from his crew above. The cabin itself was quite large, she noticed, with the rectangular table surrounded by eight chairs and the bed that filled a whole corner. But looking at Blake, taking in his height and the breadth of his shoulders, looking farther down his chest and the muscular arms that were crossed over it, to his narrow hips and the—

Alicia felt her ears burn. She licked her lips. Well, past *that*, to the long expanse of leg, he'd need a large berth. She cleared her throat and skipped her eyes back to his. Heat had turned his eyes nearly black. His jaw pulsed just below his ears. She didn't know what to do about the look in his eyes any more than she did about her unusual reaction to him. Heart tripping over itself, hands sweating, mind wandering. Why, she wondered, did it have to be Blake of all men who would finally make her wonder just what happened between a man and a woman?

"What do we do now?" she asked and was mortified when her question came out in a squeaky tone she'd never produced in her eighteen years.

"*We*," he said, coming to lean over the table until his

face was inches from hers, "are not doing anything. I've decided that the best place for you is here. It'll keep the men from getting distracted and acting like a bunch of idiots to get your attention."

"You want me to stay in this cabin, the entire time?"

"It's better than the alternative."

"Which is?"

He didn't blink. "The first piece of land I see. You can get yourself the rest of the way home by whatever means you can find."

"And if I agree to your terms, you'll take me to St. Kitts?"

"You don't know all my terms yet."

Alicia thought she'd better stand for these. The last thing she wanted was for Blake to think that he intimidated her. Pushing back her chair, she came to her feet.

"Very well, what other terms do you have?"

"During the day, you're to stay inside. At night, when the men have retired, you can go on deck. The bed is mine; I'll have Nate set up a hammock for you. And I brought you some water and a cloth. If you're going to share my cabin, I'd prefer you smelled better."

"Anything else?"

"When we get to St. Kitts, I don't see you again. Ever."

She smiled sweetly. "Is that all?"

He rubbed his right eyebrow. "Do we have an agreement or not?"

Alicia held out her hand. Blake inhaled sharply, his eyes moving from her open palm to her face. If he didn't look so formidable, she'd think he was afraid to touch her. But after a hefty pause, he grasped her hand in his.

If he felt the tremor that passed between them as acutely as Alicia did, he didn't show it.

* * *

You must be feeling better."

Alicia yelped, dropped the mug she'd been holding, which shattered at her feet. She spun around. The tall man from Blake's cabin filled the doorway to the galley.

"Lord, you scared me," she gasped.

"Sorry. I'm not usually known for my stealth," he said with a grin and pointed at his long feet. "They tend to announce my presence no matter how quiet I try to be."

Alicia felt her fear melt like candle wax, leaving a warmth in its place. The man was big; there was no question. His shoulders looked as though they could carry a full-grown man without a stitch of effort. The arms he crossed over his chest were corded with muscle. Combined with the low timbre of his voice, he should have come across as menacing. But peeking out of an angular face were the brightest, prettiest green eyes Alicia had ever seen.

"Well, you're quieter than you think. I didn't hear a thing."

He nodded at the shards of crockery that littered the floor around their feet. "What were you trying to make?"

"I wanted more of the ginger tea. As long as I sip it, my stomach stays settled."

He took another mug and handed it to her, then dug some ginger out from a small bag on the counter. Alicia watched so as to know where it was next time. The water she'd been waiting to boil began to bubble in the pot, and while the man removed it, she cleaned up the broken pieces from the floor. When she was finished, he handed her the steaming mug.

"Thank you. I'm sorry, I don't know your name."

"Nate."

"Pleased to meet you. Have you been on this ship long?"

"Long enough."

"And you enjoy what you do?"

"Mostly."

"I see you're a man of many words."

His smile came slowly. "As much as I'm enjoying your company, it'd be best if you went back up now. Not everyone's asleep. The men see you talking to me, they may get the wrong idea about you, and then you'd be swarmed by the mass of them."

She nodded, turned away, and mumbled, "I'm sure my mere presence would have every man swooning and throwing themselves at my feet. If they're not careful, they'll stumble overboard in their daze and drown." She knew by the chuckle behind her that he'd heard. Grinning, she stepped up on deck.

The wind was so light it was almost nonexistent. Nevertheless, Alicia savored the feel of the fresh air upon her face. It had been a long, dull afternoon below and she relished the whisper of breeze that brushed her face in a salty kiss. The ship itself was still, something else Alicia was grateful for. Lanterns glowed along the sides of the ship, casting more than enough light for Alicia to see the obstacles in her path. Holding her cup solidly by the handle, she stepped over coiled lengths of rope, all sorts of different lines, and made her way to the bow.

Alicia leaned against the side of the ship and watched the reflection of the half-moon ripple on the dark water. Mesmerized by the gentle movement, she studied the play of light, how the moon undulated with the waves.

"Lassy, ye'd best get off to bed, before yer mother realizes ye aren't in yer bed the way yer supposed to be."

"But, Joe, one more minute won't hurt anything."

Alicia gasped. She'd remembered. Tears stung her eyes. She'd had a real memory. Before reading Jacob's letter, she'd believed she'd never been at sea. Now not only did she *know* differently, she *remembered* differently. Excitement coursed through her and she closed her eyes, pushed for more memories.

None came.

Pressing one hand over her eyes, she fought the disappointment. It wasn't so bad, she told herself. It was more than she'd had a few minutes ago. And hopefully seeing Samantha would bring back more. She took a trembling breath, followed it with a sip of ginger tea. Maybe tomorrow she'd remember something else.

Feeling sad, she set her mug down and lay beside it on the deck. It was hard beneath her back but she didn't care. She needed something else to think about besides the fact that she had so many missing pieces of her past.

Looking between the triangle of sails, she had a clear view of the stars. The heavens seemed to twinkle just for her. She'd never seen anything so beautiful. The sheer quantity of stars was stunning, and soon her sadness eased and she was able to enjoy the night.

She heard footsteps approach and prepared herself for another match of verbal sparring, something that after the long day of being contained held more appeal than it should.

"What are you doing?"

She tilted her head back. Even upside down, she could see Blake's frown.

"You're the second man to ask me that tonight. I'm looking at the stars. There are so many."

"No more than you could've seen if you'd stayed in Port Royal."

"But I didn't, did I?"

He rubbed his eye. "Unfortunately, no."

"Have you ever tried it?" she asked when she remembered Captain's words about Blake being too serious.

"Lying flat on my back looking at something I could as easily see if I was standing?"

"Yes."

"No."

"Why not?"

His annoyed sigh had her smiling.

"I don't see the purpose."

She flipped onto her stomach, braced herself on her elbows to look up at him. "Wouldn't it be more comfortable lying down?"

Blake's mouth suddenly went dry as powder. Good God, he knew she was talking about stars, but his mind had taken a dangerous route into murky waters. She was wearing another pair of trousers and a man's shirt with the sleeves rolled up to her elbows. Her hair was tied back into a braid again. She shouldn't have stirred anything within him. But ever since he'd touched her that afternoon, he couldn't stop thinking about how soft she was, how she'd felt in his arms. And now, blast it all, with her lying on her stomach, with a few buttons opened at her collar, he could see just enough creamy skin to taunt him. Would it be as smooth as her hand had been?

"Well?"

He shook his head, cleared his throat. "Well, what?"

"Isn't it more comfortable lying down?"

He loosened a few buttons of his own so he could breathe easier. "It, uh, depends."

"On what?"

His gaze dipped to her breasts again. He'd never noticed

them before, thanks to the large shirts she wore and his feelings toward her, but he knew he'd never be blind to them again.

"Blake?" Nate's voice called from the stern. "Are you busy?"

Blake ran an unsteady hand down his face. "No, I'll be right there."

"Duty calls?" Alicia asked.

He nodded. "Go back to your stars."

"Thanks, I will."

And as easily as that, she flopped onto her back, dismissing him as though he hadn't even been there.

He strode away, everything inside him hotter than it should be, considering the temperature had cooled significantly. And he knew, even before he looked back, that he wouldn't be able to dismiss her near as easily as she had him.

Seven

Is there a problem?" Blake asked Nate, when he'd returned to the stern.

His friend leaned against a gun, arms crossed over his chest. "The hammock's ready."

Blake sighed. "We talked about this. She's safer there than in with the rest of the crew."

"I agree. But nobody said *you* couldn't sleep with them."

"Are you out of your mind?" he bellowed, then immediately lowered his voice. "I won't be thrown out of my own cabin by the likes of her."

"Everyone will assume she's your wench."

Because he couldn't remember Nate ever arguing with him over anything, let alone a girl, Blake paused.

"I can't help what they think, Nate."

"Sleeping in the same cabin will tarnish her reputation."

"What reputation? Nobody here knows her or will ever

see her again. Besides, I don't think a girl who stows away on a stranger's ship is the kind of girl that's worried about her reputation."

"You said she came for your help."

"Yeah."

"So that's all this is about? Helping her?"

"It's not by choice, Nate."

"Mmm."

Blake glared at him. "What?"

"I didn't say anything. I simply acknowledged your comment."

"Not likely. You meant something by that."

Nate laughed. "Did I? I'd be curious to know what it is, then."

A steady pounding, not unlike the Navy's drums, began beating behind Blake's right eye. He heaved a sigh.

"Hard to know which one of you irritates me more," he muttered.

"It had better be me," Nate answered. "I've been at it far longer."

Despite the burden Alicia's presence was putting on his mind, Blake smiled. "Well, now that you mention it."

Nate examined him a moment. "I was beginning to think that frown you've been wearing all day was becoming permanent."

"It was beginning to feel like it might."

"But my engaging presence remedied the situation?"

"Not likely."

"Shame. Seemed to work with Alicia earlier."

Blake went very still. "When did you see her?"

"I found her in the galley. We had a nice talk."

"About what?"

"Well, now, a gentleman never tells."

Blake frowned. "You're not a gentleman."

"She seemed to think so," Nate answered.

"A minute ago you were worried about her reputation," Blake growled, not quite sure why he was getting so agitated.

"I am. But she's pretty and she's virginal. That makes her doubly tempting."

Something slippery twisted in Blake's stomach. "Are you speaking for the crew or for yourself?"

Nate smiled lazily. "Either. Why? Are we going to have to duel over her?"

Blake moved to the helm, not because the ship needed steering but because he needed something to do with his hands. Something besides wanting to use his fist to erase the sure smile off his best friend's face. The fact that he even considered hitting Nate had his stomach in a knot. Nate was his friend—what the hell was the matter with him?

"I'm not dueling with you over a girl."

"Girl? Hell, Blake, she's a woman, and if you can't see it, I sure can."

"She's too young," he said between his teeth.

"A lot of women younger than her are married and having children of their own." Nate angled his head to the side. "Are you telling me you haven't noticed the temptation you've agreed to keep locked away in your cabin?"

Blake thumped the wheel. "She's not a temptation. She's green with seasickness, she smells like something you'd find lying in a street in Tortuga, and she dresses like a boy. Where's the temptation in that?"

"The *woman* I saw in the galley was clean, she smelled of soap, and even wearing a man's clothes, there was no doubt she wasn't one."

Blood pounding, Blake abandoned the wheel and stomped

to the gunwale. The ship wasn't making much of a wake and the silence was irritating. Where was a good storm when he needed one? Hell, he'd even take a pirate attack. Anything to keep his mind off Alicia and the fact that his best friend was interested in her.

"Stay away from her," Blake warned.

"I thought you didn't like her."

"I don't."

Nate leaned forward. "Why are you willing to help her if you clearly hate her so much?"

"We were heading in that direction anyway."

"We were going to St. Lucia, not St. Kitts."

"It's not that—"

They were interrupted when Vincent climbed on deck. He shuffled toward them, then grabbed his box and slid it beside Nate.

"What have I missed?" he asked, pulling himself onto the box. Even standing on it, his head didn't reach Blake's shoulders.

"Blake was about to tell us why we're taking a *woman* he despises to St. Kitts."

"Ah, the rest of the story. I knew there was more." Vincent rubbed his little hands together eagerly.

"I told you both earlier, I knew her family when I lived in Port Royal."

Vincent turned to Nate. "Do I look daft? Because I never thought I did."

Nate grinned. "Nope. You don't. And don't be commenting on her beauty either, it makes Blake twitch."

The dwarf turned to Blake. "Well, this just keeps getting better. Get on with it, then. Who is she really?"

Blake assessed his friends and sighed heavily. They deserved more than he'd given them earlier.

"Her father left her a letter. She found it after he died. In it he told her to look for me, said she could trust me to take her to wherever she needed to go, which happens to be St. Kitts."

"Where this Samantha woman is?" Nate asked.

"Yes."

"And who is Samantha to her?"

"Her sister. She didn't know she had one until she read his letter."

"How was that possible?" Vincent asked.

"Because she lost her memory when she was twelve. The man she called father isn't her real father and apparently he hadn't troubled himself to tell Alicia she had a sister either."

Both men's jaws slackened. Nate recovered first. He whistled.

"That's a nasty blow. How is it she came to be with him then?"

Because Blake had already left Port Royal before Alicia arrived, he couldn't say. The fact that Jacob Davidson had taken a stranger in so easily had been all he'd needed to know.

"I never heard the details. I was gone by then."

"Well, obviously he thought enough of you to send her your way. Is that why you're doing this?"

"I'm not doing that man any favors. And as I told you earlier, I'd already said no to her. But now that she's here"—he shrugged his shoulders—"I just want to get rid of her. Taking her where she needs to go seems the fastest way to do that."

Vincent turned to Nate, his smile so wide, his eyes nearly vanished into his cheeks.

"I'm not buying that pile of dung, are you?"

Nate, at least, tried to hide his grin behind one of his large hands. "Not for a second," he answered. "Besides, he nearly bit my head off when I told him I'd spoken to her in the galley."

"I did not," Blake argued.

"Yes, you did."

Blake shook his head, but he didn't argue any further. He did, however, cast a glance down the deck, but Alicia remained on her back, unaware they were discussing her.

"He can't take his eyes off her," Vincent teased. "It's that chivalrous nature coming out again. The maiden needs help and our Blake is riding in to save her."

"Remind me to give you more duties, Vincent. It'll give you less time to wag your tongue."

"It would take more than that," Nate chuckled.

Blake smiled at Nate, relieved the tension he'd felt earlier was gone. They'd been through too much to have a girl—or woman—come between them.

Vincent ignored the insult. "What is she like?" he asked Nate.

"I'll tell you later," he said, grinning. Then, standing, he set a reassuring hand on Blake's shoulder. "If you need any help dealing with her tonight, I'd be more than willing to give you a hand."

Blake watched Nate's long strides carry him to the main hatch. He knew Nate had said that last remark deliberately to taunt him and he was trying very hard to pretend it hadn't worked. He knew he wasn't successful by the mirth shaking Vincent's shoulders as he laughed silently.

"Go ahead, I know there's something left you're itching to say."

"Not me," Vincent answered. Still it took a few minutes before his humor died and he turned serious.

"Port Royal holds bitter memories for you."

Blake didn't bother answering. They'd known when he'd gone to Port Royal for Jacob's burial that Blake wasn't happy to be there.

"You've never said why, but Alicia plays a role in that, am I correct?"

Blake pressed a hand to his eye. "Not to the extent you think she does."

"But she's involved?"

"Yes."

"And she doesn't remember that either?"

Blake shook his head.

"Then perhaps you should tell her."

"Why, for God's sake, would I want to do that?" Blake argued.

"Because I think you have the notion that if you take Alicia to St. Kitts, you will not only be free of her but also free of the memories you're trying to forget."

With a last considering look, Vincent, too, slipped under the main hatch.

Left alone again, Blake returned to the helm and grasped the wheel tightly. His thoughts churned. He didn't want to talk to Alicia about her precious father. He'd left Port Royal behind for a reason and he didn't see the need to address that reason now. What purpose would it serve? The man was dead, after all. A little late to go back for explanations and apologies. And too damn late to change the past.

Blake was honest enough with himself to acknowledge the knot that settled in his chest was one of regret. He didn't like it, knew the man didn't deserve it, but it was there as surely as the smooth wood was in his hands.

Alicia moved then, walked to the bow. In the moon-light her shirt glowed, reminding him of Nate's words—

and Blake's reaction to them—that she was virginal. She reached for her braid and with deft fingers uncoiled the length of hair until it was a shiny enticement flowing down her back. In the moonlight it appeared almost white. His stomach did a slow roll.

He cursed himself all kinds of a fool even though his eyes never left her. Telling himself the reasons he should hate her only angered him more. He shouldn't feel anything, not one damn thing toward her, least of all lust. And despite his argument earlier, he shouldn't have been jealous either. But as sure as the breeze whispered over his heated face, he knew he'd felt both.

Damn her, he thought, slamming his palm on the wheel. Why couldn't she have stayed in Port Royal and left him the hell alone?

The hatch banged again and Alicia heaved a sigh of relief. Though she'd enjoyed the stars and the fresh air, Blake's hostility was a presence on deck and it made her anxious. It was why she'd remained at the front of the ship, watching the water fold away from the hull rather than asking Blake the questions that kept pulling at her.

How had he known her father? Why was Blake so angry with him, and with her? Had he known all this time that she wasn't truly Jacob's daughter? Had the whole town?

"May I join you?" asked a strange voice behind her.

Alicia spun, her hand at her throat.

"I'm sorry. I didn't mean to startle you," he said.

"No, no. That's all right." She took a calming breath, tried to slow her racing heart. "I hadn't heard you approach, is all."

He smiled, showing a large expanse of gums and small

yellow teeth. He held out a small, rather delicate looking hand. "Allow me to introduce myself. I'm Lewis."

There was something about the eagerness in his gaze that gave Alicia pause. His eyes were little daggers that stayed fixed on hers in an unnatural way. He stood too close and Alicia took a deliberate step back. However, since she'd been raised with strong manners, she took his hand. It felt much the same way she imagined a snake would feel, clammy and cold.

"Alicia."

"Pleased to meet you," he drawled, holding tightly to her hand. "I wasn't aware there was a woman on board. Is your husband a crewman, or perhaps the captain?"

She pulled her hand free, wiped it discreetly on her thigh. "Neither, actually."

"No chaperone either?"

She angled her chin. "My travel plans are my own."

His smile faded. "Of course. Please forgive my rudeness."

Feeling very uncomfortable, Alicia was thinking of how best to excuse herself when she was saved the trouble by Blake's arrival.

"Lewis, is it?" Blake asked.

"Yes," the much shorter man answered and Alicia was very pleased to see his boldness wither in Blake's presence.

"A little late to be about. The others are all asleep below."

"I was heading there myself."

Blake nodded and stayed where he was. Lewis looked back to Alicia.

"So nice to have met you, Alicia. Perhaps I'll see you tomorrow."

Blake's mouth flattened, giving him a very formidable look. "Not likely. She'll be in my cabin."

Lewis's eyes widened. "Well, then, perhaps another time. Good night."

Neither Blake nor Alicia talked until Lewis was below and they were once again alone on deck. Then Blake turned to her, eyes hard as his mouth.

"You're not here to dally with my crew. I thought I'd made that perfectly clear."

"It's not what I was doing!" Alicia gasped, caught as much off guard by his words as by the furious tone.

"I'm not blind, Alicia. I saw the way he looked at you, and from where I was standing, you didn't seem to be discouraging him."

"I only met him now!"

"I allowed you on deck for a reprieve. Had I known you were simply going to disobey me at the first opportunity, I wouldn't have been so generous."

She gaped and placed a fist on her hip. "You call keeping me in your cabin for hours on end 'generous'?" she demanded, forgetting it wasn't wise to antagonize him.

His jaw flexed. "You want to know what I normally do with stowaways?"

"I'd hope you'd treat them a might bit better than you have me," she answered, her gaze never moving from his.

"You ungrateful wench," he grated between his teeth.

Before she could stop herself, her hand flew to his face. In a lightning-quick move he grabbed her wrist and held fast. Alicia was stunned. She'd never hit another person, and she was mortified to have tried now. That it was Blake, the man whose help she was counting on, made her mistake that much graver.

"Don't ever raise a hand to me," he growled, his dark eyes flashing.

She knew she should apologize but his self-righteous attitude infuriated her. He'd assumed the worst, and rather than ask her what was going on, he'd insulted her.

"Then don't be attacking my character. I am well aware of your terms and I did not break any of them. It was he who came to me."

Blake dropped her arm.

"Yet you didn't step away. Seems to me you were enjoying yourself."

"Let me assure you, Mr. Privateer, there has yet to be a moment on this ship that I have enjoyed." With a final cutting glance, she swept past him and went below.

In his cabin, she cursed him as she paced the floor. He was insufferable! He was headstrong, stubborn, and arrogant.

"I'll be happy to see the last of you when we reach St. Kitts," she muttered, slipping into her nightdress.

Only when she'd changed did the reality of her sleeping arrangements sink through her fury. She stood in the middle of the cabin and gazed around, her eyes landing on the hammock that had been set up since she'd left. For her, no doubt.

She turned to the bed. It was large and soft-looking and far more inviting. She looked back at the hammock. It was swaying slightly. Oh, no, she thought, setting her teeth. She'd been sick all night and most of the day. She'd suffered Blake's wrath and his bad temper and had been kept in the cabin because the mighty captain didn't trust her not to turn his crew into a pack of blubbering idiots. She was exhausted and her eyes felt as though someone had thrown in a handful of sand. The least she deserved was a decent night's sleep.

Walking to the bed, she drew back the covers and crawled in, pulling the blankets up to her chin.

If Blake had such a problem with her, *he* could take the blasted hammock.

Eight

Blake awoke to three very noticeable realities. One, he wasn't alone; two, he was very much aroused; and three, if she moved any closer to him, she'd be sure to get a surprise she hadn't figured on when she'd decided to take his bed. But then, he hadn't figured on this situation either when he'd come down last night—still unsettled by Nate's barbs and Vincent's claim that Blake needed answers—to find Alicia in his bed.

Hadn't he gotten Nate to set up a damned hammock to avoid that exact possibility? He hadn't wanted her in his bed. But he'd been tired and frustrated. He'd already changed the direction of his ship, altered his cabin, and had to endure his friend's badgering because of her. She was bold, ungrateful, and had dared try to slap him. And then she'd had the nerve to take his bed. Well, he wasn't about to be put out of his own damn cabin, was he? So, stripping down to his underwear, he'd climbed into bed.

He knew now it had been a mistake.

Yet he didn't move away. Instead, lying on his side with his head braced on a folded arm, he watched her sleep and wondered at the tempest of emotions she brought out in him. Anger, certainly, though he knew that wasn't rational. What Jacob had done was not her fault, but what she represented was a sore that wouldn't heal.

Still, looking at her pale cheeks and soft mouth, he was tempted. He couldn't explain that either, as his taste in women ran to those that were experienced in pleasing men. None of them lingered in his thoughts the way she did, and unfortunately he couldn't blame it all on anger. At times like this, he could look at her and wonder.

His gaze slid down to her throat, where her nightdress revealed the creamy swells of her breasts. He lost his breath. They weren't the most voluptuous but they pressed together, creating a seam that made his mouth want to explore.

Breathing softly beside him, she slept on, unaware of his struggles. And he had more than one. Yes, she reminded him of his past, and yes, she stirred his needs, but it was the jealousy he'd felt biting him yesterday that bothered him. He didn't like her. It shouldn't matter that Nate thought her attractive, or that Lewis was interested in spending time with her. He shouldn't care. But the thought of that little whelp, or even Nate, touching her made Blake want to stand guard, protecting her from anyone who would take advantage of her innocence.

Blake grunted, closed his eyes. Some protector he was. Wasn't he, even now, yearning for her, despite her innocence?

"Blake?"

He felt her hand on his forearm and nearly jumped out

of his skin. His eyes opened, and he cursed himself a fool even as his gaze ravished her. She hadn't braided her hair the way he knew most women did when they slept, and it fell in a tangled mass around her face and over her shoulder. Clear blue eyes filled with concern looked down on him. She'd propped herself on her left elbow, and with her right hand on his arm, gravity did the rest.

Her nightdress gaped open. Her breasts swayed, unfettered by any of those womanly bindings. And if she took another deep breath like the one she'd just taken, he'd see everything he'd need to go straight to Hell. Yet he found himself unable to look away.

"Blake?"

She leaned closer and he saw what he'd both wanted and yet been afraid to see. A perfect nipple, pink and hard, ready to be plucked. His blood slammed into his groin.

Groaning, he threw an arm over his eyes and flipped onto his back.

"What is it?" she asked.

He knew by the dip the bed made that she'd slid closer to him. Nate was right—she smelled clean and fresh. It was taking all his will not to reach out and touch her. His hand fisted into the sheet. He didn't dare speak because he didn't trust his mouth not to betray him.

It wasn't until she grabbed the blanket and he felt cool air brush his navel that he realized what she was up to. He grabbed the cover as though it were a line tossed to a drowning man in the middle of a hurricane. His eyes flew open, and he strained to keep them on her face. Because if they dipped down again . . . He inhaled sharply.

"Don't do that," he growled, holding the blanket at his waist.

"Why, are you hurt?" Her gaze trailed over his chest

and he clenched his teeth, because in his mind he saw her do the same with her mouth.

"No, I'm not hurt."

Their eyes met and the concern in hers made him feel like a scoundrel. She was worried about him and all he wanted to do was get her naked and devour her like a ripe peach. He closed his eyes again. Hell, what was the matter with him?

"Are you sure? Because perhaps I can help."

She tugged on the blanket.

"Alicia, unless you want the surprise of your life," Blake said, eyes still closed, "I suggest you stop right now."

Silence reigned for a moment, and Blake thought he had himself under control until she asked, as innocently as she no doubt was, "Why? What's under there?"

The situation was anything but funny and yet he couldn't help chuckling. How did a man answer a question like that?

He opened his eyes, saw her serious expression. Felt a little tug around his heart.

"Nothing you're ready for," he answered.

She frowned, dark blond eyebrows slanting over stunning blue eyes.

"I don't understand."

"And that, Alicia, is why you need to sleep in the hammock until we reach St. Kitts." Blake slid up the bed, taking the blanket with him, and leaned his back against the wall. Alicia leaned the other way. Now that they were a safe distance apart, Blake sighed deeply, feeling more like the man he'd been when he'd gone to sleep last night.

Until she tilted her head to the side, eyes fixed on his, and said, "Are you saying you find me desirable?"

Hell.

His silence, however, seemed to please her and she smiled, bringing out deep dimples in her cheeks he'd never seen before. Coupled with the tousled hair and questioning look, Blake had never felt lower. Christ, she was but a child.

"You're too young, and I don't like you, remember?" he reminded both of them.

"I think you're changing your mind about that," she said matter-of-factly. "Besides, I'm eighteen. How old are you?"

"Twenty-five."

He eyed her warily, because the smile wasn't fading.

"What?"

She shrugged and Blake found himself drawn to the rise and fall of her breasts.

"What?" he demanded, louder this time because he'd never felt so out of control.

"I've never had a man find me desirable before. It feels . . ." She shrugged again. "Nice. It feels nice."

Nice. His hands were sweating and he didn't dare leave the bed for fear of embarrassing the both of them, and she felt *nice*?

"You need to get dressed and get out of my bed."

Her blue eyes widened. "I won't change in front of you."

He cursed. "No, of course not!"

She leaned forward, and this time he turned his head.

"Then what do you want me to do?"

Take off your nightdress. Kiss me. Touch me and don't stop, not even if I think you should. Thumping his head against the wall, he said, "Turn around. I'll get dressed."

"Sounds reasonable," she answered.

Yes, it did. Very reasonable indeed. Why, he was practically saintly.

Blake waited until she had slid back under the covers and turned away from him before he leapt from the bed. He couldn't remember a time he'd ever dressed as quickly as he did then. Only when the last button on his shirt was fastened and his boots were firmly on his feet did he speak.

"I'll have some breakfast sent down. Would you like some water to wash?"

Shifting to see him, she nodded. "I would. Thank you."

He nodded, turned to leave.

"I really do appreciate everything you're doing for me. And I'm ashamed that I raised a hand to you yesterday."

Not quite looking at her, but rather at a particular spot on the wall behind her shoulder, he said, "You can thank me by taking the hammock tonight." And before he dug himself any deeper than he already had, he raced up the steps and as far away from Alicia Davidson as he could manage.

It couldn't have worked any better. Smiling, Vincent took the breakfast plate from Billy.

"I can take it from here," he volunteered.

Billy was a short, hairy man. He had hair poking from the collar at his throat, small tufts coming from his ears, and, Vincent knew, a veritable carpet when the man removed his shirt. He frowned at Vincent, his brows making one long black slash over eyes nearly as dark.

"I think I had better take it like he asked me to. Captain is in a right foul mood this morning. I don't want to be doin' nothin' to make it worse."

Well, well. Vincent licked his lips, wishing with all his might he'd been a fly on the wall of Blake's cabin last night.

"Where is Blake?"

Billy pointed to the steps that led to the bilges. "Doin' somethin' down there."

Even better. "Well, go back to your duties and let me take this. If Blake gets angry, I'll be sure to let him know it was my idea."

Billy shrugged and stepped away. Humming now, the tray in one hand and a steaming mug of tea in the other, Vincent went on deck.

"Tell me you're not serious," Nate said, from his position at the wheel.

"What? I'm taking the lady her breakfast."

"Hmm. Then I'll expect to see you straightaway."

When Vincent stopped, Nate continued. "Well, it only takes a minute to set the food down. Shall I hold the hatch while you put it on the table?"

Vincent stepped forward, dropped his voice. "You know perfectly well I want to talk to her."

"Do I?"

"Just open the damn hatch, won't you? Make yourself bloody useful."

Nate looked out at the horizon, squinted his eyes against the blazing sun. "I am making myself useful. I'm steering the ship."

Vincent was considering setting down the food and shooting his friend when, smiling, Nate left the helm and opened the hatch.

"Remember, I'm not part of this."

"Bloody hard to forget when you keep reminding me," he muttered. He called down first, and when he heard Alicia's soft reply, Vincent started down the ladder. He nearly dropped the tea and fell when Nate slammed the hatch, narrowly missing Vincent's head.

"Good morning."

"Good morning," she answered.

He set the food and drink onto the table. "Sleep well?" he asked, throwing a sideways glance at the hammock. There were no blankets on it. Forcing all expression from his face, he turned to her, managing a quick glimpse at the bed as he did. The covers were rumpled and judging from the pillows, *two* heads had occupied the bed. He couldn't help but smile.

"I did, thank you. And thank you for breakfast. I was deciding if I should go up myself."

"Blake is allowing you on deck?" Hell, last night must have been something indeed.

She shook her head. "I don't think so. He'd said when he brought me the water to wash that he'd come back with food soon."

"He'd planned to, but he had something he had to tend to. He asked me to bring this down in his place."

"He did?"

Vincent watched in amazement as her cheeks flushed and her hands fluttered at her collar. Figuring his task had gotten much easier, Vincent pulled out a chair.

"Please sit and eat while it's hot. And may I be so bold as to ask to join you?"

Alicia's eyes sparkled every bit as much as the sea.

"Please do. It's nice to have some company."

Knowing his time was limited, Vincent didn't waste any.

"Blake isn't much of a talker."

She smiled around a bite of pineapple. "Not unless he's angry."

"He can be a bit brutish at times."

"I've noticed." She finished her fruit and began to eat the eggs.

"Is he not, uh, warming up to you a little?"

Alicia choked on her eggs. She coughed and her eyes filled with tears. Oh, hell! Vincent stood on his chair and thumped her on the back. She coughed harder. He was beginning to panic when she turned in her chair and caught his wrist with her hand.

"I'm all right," she wheezed.

Blowing out a deep breath, Vincent sat down. "Well, thank God. I thought I'd killed you!"

They faced each other and silence stretched between them until her laughter bubbled out, and deep dimples carved into her cheeks. Despite his embarrassment, Vincent joined her. Soon they were both wiping at their eyes.

"I haven't laughed like that in months," Alicia said, suddenly sobering. "Thank you."

"I enjoyed it as well. You remind me of one of my sisters, Vivian."

Finishing her meal, Alicia pushed her plate aside and sipped her tea. "You have many sisters?"

"Five. And one brother. But Cale's the oldest and was practically grown before I came along." He shrugged. "I didn't see much of him and spent most of my time with my sisters. Vivian is closest to me in age."

Alicia looked out the cabin window. "I envy you the memories you have. The only thing I remember of my sister is that she has brown hair and that I used to call her Sam."

"But you're going to find her and she can tell you what you want to know. Are you not excited?"

She turned to Vincent and her sad smile tugged at his heart.

"It feels like meeting a stranger, which is really what she is to me."

Hearing heavy boots above their heads along with a rumbling conversation, Vincent knew his time was up. Blake would be looking for him soon.

"Has Blake talked to you much about your family, well, the one that you remember?"

"I know he hated my father."

Getting somewhere now, Vincent shifted his chair closer to Alicia. "Have you never asked him why?"

"I don't think he'd tell me."

"Well, you won't know until you try, will you?"

And leaving her with that to ponder, he took her empty plate and left her to her thoughts.

Alicia was going crazy. She'd been contained in the cabin for all of yesterday and most of today, and she'd run out of things to do. The bedcovers were straightened, the chairs all evenly spaced and pushed against the table. Since no one had come down to fetch her bathwater, and since it wasn't very dirty, she'd used it to mop the floor of the cabin. There wasn't a speck of dust on any surface.

She was ready to scream.

In the blacksmith shop there was always a din of noise, from the clang of metal on metal to the chatter she and Charles partook in to ease the long hours of hard work. Alicia dropped her forehead to the glass of the small, round window, felt the warmth on her skin.

She missed the shop. From the sense of belonging that she felt each time she stepped into the smoky interior to the satisfaction of seeing a final piece gleam in the sunshine. And she missed her father.

Closing her eyes against the undulations of the sea, Alicia saw Jacob in the shop, his thick apron on over his clothes, his face sweaty, and his brown eyes warm as coffee when he looked at her. His voice and touch were always gentle when he wrapped an arm around her shoulders to ask her how her day went and then again as he guided her in her work, never judging and never impatient. His love had filled the shop as much as the heat from the forge.

He was such a good man, such a wonderful father. She wondered why Blake hated him so much. Vincent was right—she really should ask him. Her eyes flew open.

The letter. Blake had the letter.

If she could find it, perhaps she'd learn why Blake had such harsh feelings toward her father. And since this was Blake's personal cabin, if the letter was anywhere, it was bound to be within these walls. Excited, Alicia set off to find it.

It was surprisingly, and disappointingly, easy. She'd almost hoped it would have taken longer to find as it would have used up more hours in the day, long hours she'd have to spend alone and confined. But as it was, the sun was high in the sky and the letter was in the first place she'd looked. In the corner next to the table was a series of wide shelves where Blake stored his maps and travel logs. Beneath them were two small drawers, side by side. When she'd opened the right drawer, the letter stared up at her.

Heart pounding, Alicia left the drawer open and scurried to the ladder. She climbed up as much as she could before her head touched the hatch. She peered out. She could make out boots, nothing more. She recognized Blake's, as well as Vincent's. Since neither was heading her way, she ran back to the drawer and picked up the envelope. When she turned it over, her stomach plummeted.

He hadn't opened it; the red seal remained intact. Why the devil hadn't he opened it? She inhaled a sharp breath.

Her father had taken the time to write the man a letter, and Blake didn't see fit to even *read* it?

With it clutched in her right hand, Alicia tore up the steps, flung open the hatch. She saw Blake spin her way, saw the questions on his face turn to ire when he realized she was disobeying him by coming on deck in full daylight. She knew there were other men around, could feel their questioning glances, but her eyes were focused on Blake's.

"What are you doing on deck?" he demanded, stepping away from the helm.

Ignoring him, she slapped the envelope against his chest.

"You didn't even *read* it?"

Red crept from the last two open buttons of his shirt, up his neck, and suffused his face. She knew, despite the unrelenting beating of the sun, that it had nothing to do with the heat. Other than the creaking of sails and rope, the groan of wood, the deck was ominously quiet.

"Where did you find this?" He grabbed it from her hand.

"Why haven't you read it?" she countered.

"This has nothing to do with you," he growled between his teeth.

Her jaw slackened. "It was written by my father! He asked me to give it to you. It has everything to do with me!"

He snarled. Then, grabbing her wrist, he shouted a command over his shoulder and nearly flung her down the ladder to his cabin. His boots hammered the rungs. The hatch closed with a thunderous slam. The sound was still ringing in her ears, when she spun to face him.

"Why didn't you open it?"

"Because I don't give a damn what it says!"

"Why not?"

His eyes narrowed. "I allowed you to stay on board. I've altered my course, altered my cabin, and this is how you thank me, by searching through my effects?"

"I'm trying to get some answers, Blake. None of this makes sense. Why did my father send me to you? Why do hate him so much?"

"I'll only say this once more. I'll take you to your sister. I don't owe you anything else." He whirled around and threw the letter back into the drawer, slammed it close. This time he took out a small key and locked it. Pocketing the key, he came back to her. "Stay out of my things or you'll find yourself sleeping back where I found you."

His words hurt, especially after the closeness she'd begun to feel that morning, when they'd shared the bed. She didn't want their relationship to go back to the way it was, when they were constantly throwing scathing remarks at each other. But neither could she let this go. She didn't know his past, but it couldn't be worse than hers. At least he knew where he'd come from, *whom* he'd come from. He may have chosen to leave Port Royal but he remembered what he'd left behind.

"Are you scared of what's written in it?"

Blake's eyes turned cold. "I'm not afraid of anything that man has to say."

"Then read the blasted letter!"

"No! And stay out of it, dammit."

He tried to stalk past her but she caught his arm. He stopped, his eyes boring into hers.

"I can't stay out of it, this is my life! I have no past. I have one memory. One. The rest are disjointed pieces that come so fast they don't make sense. I'm never sure if it's a memory or a dream, or just wishing on my part."

Her hand clenched his arm. "I don't know where I came from. If, in that letter, my father explains some of that, then I deserve to know."

"Your sister will give you the answers you need."

"I can't wait that long!"

His eyes cooled. "That's not my problem."

She let go of his arm. "What do you have to lose by reading Jacob's words?"

"I don't care what he says, all right? Nothing that heartless bastard has written will change that."

Alicia gaped. "Heartless? You know nothing of him; the man had a heart as big as the ocean."

Blake's mirthless laugh bounced off the cabin walls. "He wasn't only heartless, Alicia; he was selfish. The only thing Jacob Davidson cared about was himself. The fact that he kept your past a secret from you should tell you that."

She swallowed, couldn't fully deny his words. His smirk said it all, and it made Alicia rush further to her father's defense.

"He told me he was afraid to tell me the truth, that he'd already lost his sons. Because I watched my father mourn for them each and every day, I know he was telling the truth."

"Don't," he rasped, "talk about things you know nothing of."

"I know, because I saw it with my own eyes. I don't remember them, I realize now it's because they had already passed away before the Davidsons took me in, but I know he loved them."

"The sun rose and set on Eric. Nobody was more perfect than Eric, and believe me, he let Daniel know it every chance he had."

"He never spoke of Eric in terms of being perfect, only

that he missed him and that it was tragic the way he died. You know how he died, then?"

Blake gave a crisp nod. "The ship he was on was caught in a fierce storm. One of the masts snapped, and he happened to be underneath it when it came crashing down."

Alicia frowned. "It wasn't a storm; it was pirates that killed Eric."

"Is that what he told you? That it was a pirate attack?"

Alicia thought back to what Jacob had told her. "He never actually said it was an attack, only that Eric's death was a result of being in the company of pirates."

"There were no pirates!" Blake roared. "Eric was on a privateer's ship at the time."

"Then where did Father get the idea it was pirates?"

Blake glared at her. "In his eye, they were the same." He turned away briefly, took a deep breath before facing her again. "Tell me, Alicia, did he ever explain what happened to Daniel?"

Alicia shook her head. "When his name came up, he'd close himself off, go down to the water. When I asked Anna about it, she'd get so sad. It got to be that I stopped asking. I assumed he went to the water because Daniel also died at sea, only they never recovered his body."

"Daniel didn't die. To this day he's very much alive."

Alicia gasped, tears filled her eyes. "If only Jacob had known that. He'd have been so—"

"He knew, Alicia."

"But he couldn't have. I saw the pain in his eyes when he'd stand on the beach. He looked so empty, so sad. If he knew Daniel was alive, he'd have gone looking for him; he'd have stopped at nothing for his son."

Blake exploded, eyes wild.

"He had the chance! He had years to find Daniel, and

instead he did nothing! I hope he went to the grave with that guilt rotting away at him."

Alicia's jaw went slack.

"He's the only father I remember and he was a good man. You have no right to talk about him like that."

"Oh, I don't, do I? Well, you know nothing of that man you called father! And Daniel is better off without him."

"You bastard! I watched *that man* enough times to see him wipe away tears he didn't think I'd seen. He and my mother both would sit at night and pray for their boys. He loved both of them. Don't you dare stand in judgment when you know nothing of how he felt."

Out of breath, hands on her hips, she challenged Blake as she'd never done before. He didn't seem to notice. He matched her stance and his voice wasn't any quieter than hers.

"I know exactly how he felt! Unlike yourself, I don't have to think I know what the man was feeling because he told me straight out just what he thought of Daniel."

"And what was that?" she demanded, jamming a lock of hair behind her ear when it fell over her face.

"That it was Daniel's fault Eric was dead."

Alicia paused, blinked. "What?"

Blake turned to the window, placed a hand beside it. He stood silent and brooding for so long Alicia didn't think he'd continue.

"Daniel had a love of the sea, and it called to him as nothing he'd ever experienced before. The sea, the endless horizon, the fresh air. It was all he wanted, to simply own a ship and command his own crew. But he was afraid to tell his father because Jacob had never hidden his dream of both his sons taking over the blacksmith shop. It took Daniel a long time to broach the subject to his father."

Blake slapped his hand against the wood. "And when he finally found the nerve to tell his father about his dream, Jacob didn't listen. Not really. He convinced himself it was a lark, that if Daniel went to sea, he'd soon tire of the water and come home. Because of that, he asked Eric to go along with Daniel when he found work on a privateering vessel, thinking a month or so would do it."

"Why would Jacob send Eric on a privateer's ship if he thought them no better than pirates?"

Blake's laugh was mirthless. "It wasn't until after Eric died that Jacob felt that way about privateers. Until then, far as I know, he didn't have any objections to privateers."

"Was Daniel on the ship when Eric died?"

Blake nodded. "Daniel saw it all. It was him who took his brother's body back to Port Royal.

"Daniel was a broken man when he carried Eric's body home. He felt responsible for his brother's death; it weighed like bricks on his shoulders. He couldn't eat, sleep. It took three days to sail to Port Royal, and he spent those days at his brother's side."

Silence fell heavily. In her mind, it was easy to picture. Easy yet heartbreaking. What must that have been like for Daniel?

Blake turned to Alicia and his eyes reflected an anguish the likes of which she'd never seen.

"What happened next?" she asked.

"The hardest thing Daniel ever did was carry Eric into the house. Anna wept, clung to Eric's lifeless hand. Jacob wouldn't even look at Daniel."

Blake turned to look out the window, but Alicia knew he wasn't seeing the water past the glass.

"Daniel tried to explain, but Jacob didn't want to hear it

and Anna was too devastated to listen. Her weeping broke Daniel's heart."

"It was an accident."

"Well, you'd never know it by Jacob's reaction. He told Daniel he'd destroyed the family and he'd never be forgiven for that."

"What did Anna say?"

"Honestly, I don't think she heard the argument. Her focus was on Eric at the time. She was weeping over his body, touching his face . . . " Blake pinched his eyes closed. "Daniel couldn't bear to see Anna so upset, and he went outside for air. Jacob followed. He told Daniel just what he thought of him and of what he'd done to them. He told him never to come back."

"And Daniel simply accepted that?"

Blake opened his eyes, latched onto hers. "No. He stayed for the funeral, though not in the house. Jacob forbid it. But he went to the funeral, paid his respects. He went to see Anna one night when Jacob was asleep. Daniel and Anna had a good talk. She never blamed him, but until the day he died, Jacob continued to blame Daniel. It's why he never went back."

Alicia's heart squeezed with the pain the Davidsons had seen.

"Anna missed him so much; she'd have given anything to see him again."

Blake turned to her, and his brown eyes were wet.

"It killed Daniel to be away from her. He missed her with his whole being."

Suddenly everything fell into place, and the missing pieces she'd hoped for were now a poison that was destroying what she'd held dear. Her stomach roiled with the truth.

"You changed your name."

"Daniel was never me, he was who my father wanted me to be. Jacob wanted to tie me to the blacksmith shop, wanted me to be like Eric, who loved the shop as much as he did. But I didn't, and he let me know that it was my self-ishness that had lead to Eric's death.

"So I took my middle name and my maternal grand-mother's maiden name. I wanted as little to do with Jacob as he did with me. I left and, other than his funeral, have never been back."

"Is that why I don't remember seeing you at Anna's burial?"

"Jacob knew I'd come back for her. He was waiting for me on the docks. He told me I'd broken Anna's heart and that I didn't deserve to go to her grave. He said there was nothing left in Port Royal for me."

"But you're his son," Alicia whispered.

The fury that had exploded was spent, and Blake's shoulders fell, as did his voice.

"No, I'm not. Not anymore. Even before Jacob died, he was as dead to me as I was to him."

Nine

After Blake ordered her out of the cabin, Alicia went to the helm. She dropped onto a crate and pressed her palms to her cheeks. Blake's words whirled in her head with a dizzying speed. How could Blake be Daniel Davidson? She looked up, caught Vincent and Nate watching her, and knew they'd heard. A strained laugh escaped her. She dropped her hands into her lap.

"Until my father died, I thought I was Alicia Davidson. Now I'm not sure where I came from or what my name really is. I was told to find Blake Merritt only to find out that isn't his real name either and he's my father's son. If your names aren't really Nate and Vincent, I'll ask you to tell me now so I can absorb it all at the same time."

Nate's lips twitched, and Vincent smiled. Alicia uttered a sigh. "It's not funny, I know that. My father never said a word in his letter. Did you know?" she asked.

"I have some things to tend to. I need to see to it that

the crew is kept busy." Nate offered her a warm grin and squeezed her shoulder before going to see to the men.

"He's efficient," Alicia commented.

"No, he simply prefers to keep his nose out of everyone else's business," Vincent said. A frown creased his wide forehead. "It can be a most annoying habit."

The weight of Blake's words sat like an anchor in her stomach. "I hurt him, Vincent. I never meant to hurt him."

The dwarf brought his attention back to her, the lines on his face smoothing out. He sat beside her, legs dangling, and patted her hand.

"I know you didn't. As I'm sure Blake will realize when he settles down."

"I doubt that." She hung her head, which was suddenly too heavy for her neck. "He isn't known for being forgiving, is he?"

"He'll forgive you; he'll simply need some time to work up to it."

A piercing crash resounded from Blake's cabin.

"I beg to differ," Alicia muttered and jumped when something flew against the hatch.

"I need to go—"

Vincent grabbed her arm. His hand may have been small, but there was strength behind it. "Leave him."

Alicia wrenched her arm away, ready to throw something herself. "He's upset because of me. I want to help."

Nate strolled onto the deck. He crossed to the hatch and opened it, then jumped aside to avoid being hit with a flying chair.

Holding up a bottle, he warned, "Hit me with anything, and I'll drink the damn rum myself."

The noise from the cabin stopped and Nate took a few steps down, passed the bottle into Blake's waiting palm, and slammed the cover into place. Then Nate strolled back, resumed the helm. His eyes held no judgment, but his tone left no room for argument.

"I don't think it wise to go down anytime soon."

It was the most time she'd spent on deck since coming aboard. However, she hadn't felt right about staying at the helm and distracting Nate and Vincent from their duties, so she'd moved to the front of the ship. Though the crew left her alone, she felt their stares like sticky fingers on her neck as they went about their tasks. Even Lewis, who was charged with scrubbing the deck, kept to himself.

She'd had hours to fret about Blake. Daylight was waning and now a thin veil of cloud spread across the horizon, catching the russet and golden tones of the sunset. A fiery trail of sunlight blazed on the sapphire water. There was enough wind to toss Alicia's hair against her cheeks, but not enough to soothe her mind.

She'd dwelled a good part of the afternoon on the fact that she'd upset Blake, and while she was sorry for that, she was now focused on another point. He'd lied to her. Perhaps not to her face, but he had neglected to mention his being Jacob's son and he'd had more than enough opportunity to do so. If he had told her from the beginning, they both would have been spared the ugly argument that had taken place earlier.

And then there was her father. Could he not have written, "If you need help, seek out my son"? Did that mean Blake was right, and Jacob hadn't considered him a son any longer?

"It doesn't make sense," she muttered into the breeze. Her father had, until the day he died, pined for both his sons. She hadn't lied to Blake about that; she'd witnessed the grief play across Jacob's face. There was no doubt both boys had been deeply loved. And since the son who claimed to hate his father had come to the man's funeral, Alicia knew that there was more to Blake's feelings toward Jacob as well.

Alicia slapped her hand against the side of the ship, her frustration simmering like a banked fire. She couldn't remember a time she'd ever felt so ineffective. If only she were back at the blacksmith shop, she could hammer and pound on steel, work out her distress until her muscles ached and her arms were too heavy to hold a hammer.

Here she was but a guest, and an unwelcome one at that. Alicia realized, with a tug of her heart, that was part of her turmoil.

She'd never shown a man any interest before because she'd never been interested. Blake was different. He was tall and strong, and from the little she'd been able to see, his crew was well treated and he had their respect. He was helping her despite the fact he didn't want to. But it wasn't enough. She wanted him to like her.

She'd tried to convince herself over the years that it didn't matter if men didn't look at her, that she was doing what she loved and that was more than adequate. But the hurt of their indifference would surface sometimes. Why couldn't they look past her dirty hands to the woman underneath? Did it matter so very much that she was scarred? That she didn't wear dresses every day and fuss with her appearance? Was nobody ever going to bother to get to know who she really was?

She'd begun to hope Blake would. She raised a finger, traced the uneven tissue of her scar. He'd never seemed bothered by it; she'd never caught him staring at it the way some people in Port Royal did. And yet, in bed, he hadn't wanted her to get any closer. Did he find her revolting? Surely not, surely she hadn't mistaken the desire she'd seen in his eyes.

"And what would I know of a man's desire?" she muttered.

The scrape of brush against wood suddenly stopped. She pinched her mouth closed, cursing herself for speaking aloud when she knew Lewis was never very far away. She glanced back and her stomach clenched when her eyes met Lewis's. He quickly resumed his deck washing but the damage was done. A cold, slimy feeling had settled over Alicia and she walked away, very much aware that his eyes never left her as she did.

She ate the evening meal in friendly silence with Nate. Vincent was sleeping in order to take the night watch later. From the back of the ship, she marveled when the sky darkened, turning into a black canvas filled with hundreds of sparkling white jewels. Not so very far away, she thought, her sister was under the same sky.

Sam. Fanny had said she would be thrilled to see her, but Alicia couldn't help thinking that Sam would also be sad her sister didn't remember their life together. For Alicia it was different. She was jubilant to have family and desperately wished she could remember them, but as she didn't, her heart couldn't be as easily bruised.

There hadn't been any noise coming from Blake's cabin in hours. It was a nervous kind of quiet. What was he doing? Had he fallen asleep? What would he do, if he hadn't, when she went below? As much as the light blanket Nate had fetched for her helped chase away the night's chill, she wasn't prepared to sleep on deck. She looked over her shoulder but, thankfully, saw nobody except Nate. For the first time all day, Lewis was nowhere to be seen.

"Do you think it safe for me to go below?" she asked, moving to Nate's side. Despite the hour, he didn't seem the least bit tired and his eyes were clear and alert when they met hers.

"You're always safe with him. He'd never lay a hand on you."

"How can you be so certain, considering how many things he threw and broke tonight?"

"He's furious, can't deny that, but he'd never take it out on you, or anyone else. It's not his way."

"You've seen him this angry before?"

Because her neck hurt from the effort of looking up at him, Alicia was glad when Nate settled his tall frame onto the crate, his long legs stretched out endlessly.

"He's been mad, but not like this."

She tugged the blanket when it threatened to slip off her shoulders.

"That doesn't make me feel any better."

Nate shrugged. "I can't change how you feel. I can tell you, he's been mad enough to throw things before." His lips curved. "Just not this many."

"You're enjoying this, aren't you?"

"I don't enjoy seeing my friends hurt, but I suspect he'll be back to his old self by morning. Blake isn't one to dwell for long."

"No, he cuts his ties and runs," she said, and a coldness settled upon her that had nothing to do with the air.

"Everyone has their own way of working through things."

"I'm not sure what to say to him."

Nate crossed his arms and ankles, studied Alicia.

"Stepping in the middle of things isn't what I enjoy. That's Vincent's territory. However, since I'm here and he's not, I'll offer you this. You can't go wrong with honesty."

Alicia frowned. "That's it?"

Humor danced in his eyes. "No, but the other way is a slippery road, and I won't be the man to go down it with you." He came to his feet, walked to her. Before she knew his intent, he'd leaned down and kissed her cheek. "More's the pity, too. Good night."

Not quite sure what he meant, Alicia nonetheless knew she'd been dismissed.

She whispered good night and, holding her breath, slipped into Blake's cabin.

Her way was lit by a cluster of candles he'd left blinking on the table. Shadows were long and the room smelled of burned wax and rum. The floor was a mass grave of chairs, books, and whatever else Blake had been able to get a hold of.

Alicia crept down as quietly as she could but she needn't have worried. He was wide awake, propped up in the far corner of his bed with his legs sprawled all over its surface and a nearly empty bottle resting drunkenly on his thigh. He'd torn the tie from his hair and dark strands fell in dangerous disarray around his face. His shirt was unbuttoned and gaped open. It wasn't the first time she'd seen his chest. There was no reason it should move her and yet seeing that expanse of gold skin made her fingers tingle.

"I'm not so drunk, Alicia, that seeing you look at me that way doesn't affect me."

She prayed the soft light would mask the flush that heated her cheeks. "I have no idea what you're talking about," she said and drew the blanket from her shoulders, busied herself with folding it until the corners matched perfectly. She set it on the bed next to Blake's booted feet.

The liquid swished in the bottle, followed by a loud swallow.

"I'm beginning to suspect differently," he muttered.

Her gaze snapped to his. His brown eyes were black in a lean face that looked both alluring and alone. It was the second fact that had her ignoring the first and walking around the bed.

He scowled. "Go away."

"I know what you're doing; it won't work."

"And what is it you think I'm doing?"

"You don't want to talk about your father and you're trying to distract me."

His grin was slow and seductive, as was the pass of his gaze over her body. Both tripped her heart.

"If I wanted to distract you, I could think of a much more satisfying way."

When she couldn't find her tongue to respond, he chuckled, a sound as rich as the rum in his bottle. "Fortunately, the only thing on my mind tonight is finishing this." He held up the bottle, then took a loud swallow.

"Fine. We can talk about Jacob tomorrow."

Blake leaned forward, swayed slightly. "Did nobody ever tell you you're supposed to listen to your captain? We're not going to talk about him. Not ever."

"Blake—"

"I said no, Alicia." He grinned crookedly. "I've never been on the receiving end of that word before."

His hair fell over his brow and his smile was slow. No, she realized, feeling her own blood moving sluggishly through her veins, she didn't imagine any woman would ever refuse a man like Blake.

"You're drunk," she said.

"Who me?" he asked, swinging his arms wide.

Clearly he forgot the bottle in his hand and it smashed against the wall. Glass exploded and the last of the rum slid down the wall in amber tears. The bed was covered in shards.

"Are you hurt?" he asked.

"No." She examined herself, but other than a few pieces of glass on her trousers, most of it had spilled around Blake. He had splatters of rum darkening his pants and slivers of the broken bottle in his hair, near his hands, and—

"You're cut," she said, seeing the angry line of red above his navel.

He looked at it, shrugged. "Looks harmless enough."

"That's because you're too drunk to feel the pain. It needs tending. Here." She offered her hand. "You need to get out of that bed so I can clean out the glass and have a better look at that cut."

"I've had worse."

"Be that as it may, the rest needs to be picked up before you cut yourself again."

"Just let—"

"Take my blessed hand, Blake."

"You're damn bossy considering this is *my* cabin."

She blew out a breath. "If you'd stop being stubborn and mule-headed, I wouldn't have to be, would I?"

"Women," he muttered, but he reached out and clasped her hand.

His touch was warm and strong, and it sent heat up her arm. His eyes widened and in them she saw the same expressions she knew were on her own face—wonder, desire, and a hint of fear. Neither moved. Awareness held her captive. Her heart skipped a beat, then leapt solidly behind her breast.

She saw the glint in his eye at the last moment. He tugged on her arm and would have sent her sprawling but she managed to dig in her heels in time. Working in a blacksmith shop had its advantages, she thought, as she was able to pull him off the bed. He managed to make it to his feet and send a shower of glass tinkling to the floor. Swaying, Blake put a hand to his head and groaned. Gently, Alicia guided him to a chair he hadn't destroyed yet.

"Sit. I'll get the glass out of the bed, then I'll have a better look at your cut."

"I have a better idea," he said and lay on the table, shoving the tray of candles perilously close to the edge in the process. "Let me know when you're done." He flung an arm over his eyes.

"Don't you dare fall asleep, Blake, or I'll leave you there."

"Mmm."

"Wonderful," she grumbled and yanked the sheets off the bed. "I'll take the bed. Suits me just fine." Bringing all four corners to the middle, she kept the pieces of glass inside the folds. She tucked the sheets into a far corner of the room and asked Blake if he had more.

"Under the ladder, in the chest."

When the bed was put to rights, and Alicia was certain he wouldn't be endangering himself by sleeping in it, she kicked more debris out of her way and went to fetch some water from the galley.

"You're alive," Nate said when she stepped on the deck. "Does that mean Blake is dead?"

"Not yet, but he may wish he was come morning. He managed to cut himself and I need to clean it."

"How much was left in the bottle before he smashed it?"

Alicia paused, angled her head. "How can you be so sure it wasn't me that smashed it on his head?"

Nate grinned, leaned on the wheel. "Because I'd like to

think you'd allow me the pleasure of witnessing such an event."

She laughed and felt a few knots in her shoulders ease. "I'll keep that in mind. Can you spare a little more rum? I'd rather not risk any infection."

"It'll hurt."

Now she grinned. "His own fault for behaving like a jackass."

"You're a pleasure to have on board. Here," he said and pulled her to the helm. "Mind the ship and I'll get what you need."

Alicia felt the blood drain from her body. "What? You can't do that! I know nothing of ships."

"You run a blacksmith shop, Alicia. And as much as that still amazes me, I have no doubt that if you can manage such a task, you can handle this ship. Besides, I won't be long."

Before she could argue any further, she was talking to his back. Her hands clutched the wheel and she was envisioning all manner of catastrophes before her mind began to work properly. The wind was light, the sea calm. They were in the middle of the ocean—therefore, running into rocks was unlikely. Nate wouldn't have left her to it if there were any chance of her destroying the ship. She took a deep breath and eased her grip on the wheel. She would have preferred, now that she was calm enough to think about it, to do this in daylight when she could really appreciate what it was she was doing.

Though the moon and lanterns were bright enough, they couldn't show her the horizon, the endless ribbon of blue. As Nate came up the stairs, holding a bowl and a bottle, she found herself wishing for another chance at sailing, one in daylight.

"Thank you. I enjoyed it very much. I never would have thought to ask for such an opportunity."

She took the items from his hands.

"Well, now you don't have to, I'm offering. Tomorrow night. I'm sure if you tell Blake I've offered, he'll be agreeable to the idea," he said, his eyes twinkling.

"Well, then, I will. Good night, again."

Nate lifted the hatch. Her boots crunched on glass as she made her way to the table, where Blake seemed fast asleep. His breathing was low and even, and he hadn't moved. Setting the bowl down onto a chair, Alicia took a candle and brought it closer to his cut. It wasn't long, but there was a sliver of glass protruding from the cut. She normally kept her fingernails short due to her work, but they'd grown a little since the funeral and were just long enough to pull the glass out.

Blake's breathing didn't break rhythm. She dipped the cloth in the water, not surprised to find it cold, and pressed it to his wound. He mumbled something, then all was quiet again. Smiling, Alicia pulled the cork on the rum and poured out a large stream directly onto the cut.

"Mother of Christ!" he yelled and jolted upright.

From directly above she heard Nate's bellow of laughter followed by a soft tap as he closed the hatch.

"Sorry," she said sweetly, "couldn't be helped."

Blake frowned. His breathing, she noted, was no longer low and even. "What the hell did you do to me?"

"I cleaned your cut. You're welcome."

"Hell, feels worse now than it did before."

Alicia crossed her arms. "Are you going to sleep on the table or are you going to bed?"

He swallowed, blinked a few times. "Bed." He swung his legs off the table, but when his feet hit the floor, his knees forgot their purpose and his legs buckled.

Alicia threw her arm around his waist. "If you can't handle your drink, then perhaps you should do it in moderation next time."

Blake swung his head around and nearly took them both down when he lost his balance and staggered. "I can handle my rum."

"Of course you can." Grunting, Alicia managed to walk him to the bed. When the backs of his knees hit the mattress, he fell back and took her with him. She landed soundly on his chest, her hands on his shoulders. His breath hissed out, but when Alicia went to move, his hands tangled in her hair, keeping her there. His gaze suddenly sharpened.

"I didn't want you here."

"I know."

"I'm fairly certain I still don't."

"I know."

The cabin grew warm and Alicia could swear his skin heated under her palms. Everywhere they touched burned. Her breasts pressed into Blake's chest and she felt their peaks harden. Between her legs a strange but thrilling heat uncoiled. He watched her silently and steadily. She wished she could read his mind, hoped he wanted what she did. To touch and be touched in return.

"Blake."

His hand clutched her hair, not painfully but enough to keep her from moving.

"I don't know what to do about you, Alicia. And my head's spinning too much to think about it just now. I just know I can't wait any longer, not for this."

He brought her mouth down to his and kissed her. Not chastely as she'd seen Charles kiss his wife, but with his tongue and his lips all working together to send her senses reeling. Her heart started pounding, her blood crashed in her ears like waves ramming against rock, and yet she yielded, gave Blake everything she felt in that moment.

With one hand in her hair, he ran the other down her back, took the kiss deeper. Alicia sighed into his mouth, clutched his shoulders. Though he kept her solidly in his embrace, he rolled her to her side, slowly eased from the kiss so they could breathe. His eyes closed but his breathing was as ragged as hers. He threw a leg over her, buried his face in the crook of her neck. He moaned her name.

And then he fell asleep.

Ten

Blake had never been one to ease from sleep slowly. He went from buried in layers of dreams to full alert. The problem was it wasn't only his mind that awakened ready this morning. And through a tortuous twist of luck, he wasn't alone.

His arms were full of woman—considering their kiss last night, he could hardly pretend she was otherwise—and his senses were drowning in her. Silky hair tickled his neck where her head nestled and from it came the faint scent of oranges. Her arm crossed his bare chest, keeping him in place.

He'd never imagined her arm banded across him would feel so right.

As he held her close, Blake's mind went through the events of the previous night. It wasn't difficult to remember what had taken place. A headache drummed behind his closed eyes; his stomach smarted where the glass had cut him, and his throat felt as though he'd swallowed sand by the bucketful. He'd expected all of those things.

What he hadn't planned on was Alicia. He hadn't planned on liking her. Hell, he'd tried hating her, had, in fact, managed it since he'd heard of her coming to live with his parents. But that all changed when he'd come to know her. He knew by the calluses on her hands and the strength in her arm when she'd made to slap him that she worked hard. She was fiercely loyal and stood up for her beliefs. His feelings about Jacob hadn't changed, but Blake could appreciate Alicia's unwavering support of someone who was dear to her.

He wondered what it would take for her to support him that way.

And that, Blake realized, was what was weighing on his mind. She'd slipped beneath his guard, and it wasn't only because she felt so bloody good in his arms either. He'd come to look forward to having her on deck at the end of the day, so he could share a part of it with her, to see her face fill with wonder when she watched the sunset or the dolphins that frolicked in the wake of the ship. She'd come, in a disturbingly short amount of time, to matter to him.

If only he knew what to do about that.

He dared to open one eye and was rather proud of himself for not whimpering when it felt like someone smacked his head with an oar. Blackness prevailed outside his window; the lack of sound above suggested the majority of the crew had yet to awaken. It would allow him time to think without distraction. Alicia shifted, drew a deep breath, and snuggled in closer. The softness of her breast rested against his side.

This time there was no withholding his whimper.

If regret were gold, the ship's hold would be bursting

with it. Easing from Alicia, Blake tucked the blanket around her. Darkness prevented him from seeing her clearly, which was a blessing. His willpower only went so far.

Buttoning his shirt, he fumbled around the chairs, feeling for his coat. Luckily he remembered where he'd left it, and the ruckus he made kicking aside last night's debris didn't last more than a few seconds. The bed creaked and Blake hesitated, but Alicia's breathing remained even and he knew she'd only rolled over. It would be easy to go back, to slip in beside her and taste her again when his senses weren't dulled by rum.

He also knew—gauging from their previous reactions to each other—that if he gave in to the temptation of kissing her, it wouldn't stop there. Because that wasn't a step he'd take lightly, he shoved his lust aside and went above.

The first thing he noticed was nobody was manning the helm.

"Where the hell is Vincent?" he muttered. By the glow of lanterns, Blake made his way around the cannons, over the rigging lines. The plump moon guided him around to the main hatch. Pale light and Vincent's whistling poured from the opening. Pots clanged and the smell of tea rose to Blake. Knowing Vincent would be up in a moment with a hot drink in his hands, Blake went to the bow, sat, and leaned against the gunwale.

At that level, even the faintest of breezes vanished. Around him curled the smell of damp wood steeped in seawater. There wasn't a smell he loved more.

Except possibly oranges.

His life had been wonderfully uncomplicated the last eight years. Not perfect, he'd admit. There were always trials involved in being at sea—sickness, boredom, fierce storms, and merchant ships who fought lethal battles to keep their wares. And, as Captain had reminded him earlier, he'd had a steady inflow of marriage proposals.

Blake didn't put much stock in those. When women flocked to him, flaunted their bodies, and whispered in his ear, he chose carefully. He'd steered away from the young ones, often slipping money in their hands even as he declined their invitations. Sure, there were a few who cried a sprinkle of tears over his ability to walk away, but usually within an hour or so he'd see them back among the crowded tables, smiling sweetly as they tried to lure away the coins that jingled in the sailors' pockets.

If only Alicia had slapped him when he'd kissed her. If only she wasn't so damn sweet in her innocence. If only he didn't want her with every breath he took.

He thumped his head against the gunwale. What a damn quandary he was in. He gazed up at the stars, recognized a few constellations, and knew in a handful of days they'd be in St. Kitts. He'd be rid of Alicia. Dammit, shouldn't it be what he wanted? Yet the thought left him anything but happy.

He didn't want her to go. And he wasn't getting anywhere, he realized. Might as well keep Vincent company. He headed for the helm but stopped after a few steps, wondering why Vincent wasn't singing or whistling. Vincent always made noise when he was alone. Nate figured it was because of all the sisters Vincent had been raised with; he was used to constant racket.

Blake crept steadily to the stern, eyes casting side to side. He missed Vincent completely on the first pass. A second look found his first mate on hands and knees near the hatch that led to the captain's cabin. Blake stopped momentarily to decipher what exactly Vincent was doing. When he figured it out, he swallowed his curse and strode silently toward his friend, keeping a steady eye on his target. He reached Vincent just as the man seemed ready to lift the hatch.

Blake gave him a firm kick to the backside.

Vincent yelped, jumped, and managed to spin so that he landed on his arse, wide eyes facing Blake.

"Jesus, man, trying to scare ten years off my life?"

"If you'd been steering my ship, I wouldn't have had to."

Vincent wobbled his head in agreement.

"Fair enough. Give me a hand?" he asked, extending an arm.

Blake chuckled. "You managed to get yourself down there all by yourself, you can manage to get back up again."

At the helm, Blake took the compass, double-checked his heading, and satisfied the stars hadn't lied, left the wheel to watch the sunrise. There wasn't much to see, just the black of the sky fading into blue.

"I thought you'd be asleep yet," Vincent said from his side.

"And you had a keen desire to watch me do it?"

"Well," his friend said slowly, "it was more the sleeping arrangements I was after discovering."

Blake rolled his eyes. "What you need is a woman. A good strong one, someone who can keep you out of trouble." He paused, made it appear as though he were thinking. "I know just the woman," he said, snapping his fingers. "Maybe a quick stop in Barbados is in order once we leave St. Kitts."

The color drained from Vincent's face.

"Are you mad? The last time I saw that woman, she almost strangled me!"

Leaning back against the gunwale, Blake crossed his arms over his chest.

"Beatrice was only being affectionate."

"Affectionate?" Vincent's voice squeaked. "I was lucky to get away alive."

"Now you're exaggerating. She told me herself she wanted to bear your children."

Blake nearly took pity on the man when Vincent stumbled.

"You head that way and I'll jump overboard." Vincent shuddered. "Anything's better than Beatrice."

"Keep that thought in mind next time you decide to meddle." Blake put a hand on Vincent's shoulder. "Now get some sleep. I've got the ship."

It took Alicia three tries to fasten the last button on her gown. She ran her trembling hands down the front of her bodice, only to discover the buttons weren't aligned. Chiding herself for being nervous, she began again. She had no reason to tremble; it wouldn't be the first time Blake had seen her in a dress. However, it would be the first time she'd worn one *for* him.

Alicia fussed with her hair, tying it in various configurations of braids before deciding on a style that swept most of the tresses in a twist that she secured at the nape of her neck. She pinched her cheeks for color, then put her belongings back in her bag and set it underneath the stairs. She'd put the cabin to rights when she'd first awakened, and a quick glance confirmed there was nothing left for her to do below.

She took a deep breath, then another. Blake had kissed her last night. He'd kissed her and held her even after he'd fallen asleep. When she could have slipped away, she'd chosen to stay in his arms. Alicia pressed a hand to her fluttering belly. It was time to see just what he thought of that.

The hatch, like the rest of the ship, was well maintained and barely made a noise when she raised it. She stepped onto the deck and her eyes connected immediately with Blake's.

He was so handsome. His hair ruffled in the morning breeze, and she had a moment of regret because she had no idea what it felt like. His brown eyes were clear and steadily watched her approach.

"Good morning," she managed, wishing she knew what was going on in his head. Did he find her pretty? Was he happy to see her? Did he want to kiss her as desperately as she wanted to be kissed?

"You're awake early."

The fluttering died. She raised her chin. "I cleaned the cabin and straightened the bed. I didn't touch any of your effects, I just thought that perhaps—"

"Alicia," he interrupted, his mouth twitching.

"What?"

"It wasn't an accusation, only an observation."

She dropped her hands when she realized she'd placed them on her hips in defiance. "I wasn't sure if you'd be angry with me this morning."

"I could say the same thing."

She smiled. "Yes, I suppose you could."

"I'm not proud of my behavior last night. I owe you an apology."

It wasn't what her heart yearned to hear, but it was a start.

"Are you sorry you kissed me?"

Blake sighed. "Alicia, it's not that simple."

"It is to me. Are you sorry?" she asked again, closing the distance between them by one step, then two.

"Stop." His voice held no conviction.

"We're alone, we're both old enough to make our own decisions." She halted when her shoes touched his boots. "I want you to kiss me again."

His eyes went molten. "It's not a good idea."

"I think it's a fine idea."

"No, it isn't. You're too young."

"Do I look young?"

Her blood heated as his gaze glided over her. When it lingered at her breasts, a heaviness settled upon them and the peaks drew hard. She had no doubt, since she hadn't brought along a corset, that Blake could see them through the thin cotton of her bodice. He muttered a curse and his eyes flew back to hers.

"That doesn't change the fact that you are."

"If I were older?"

He ploughed his fingers through his hair, while his eyes once again skimmed over Alicia until her skin burned. Then he trudged to the back of the ship, braced his forearms on the side of the ship, and with his mouth set, stared out to sea.

"You don't still hate me, do you?"

He scoffed. "No, that would be easy. That's not the way my life usually goes."

"Is it my scar?"

"Don't be ridiculous," he growled, looking at her.

"Then kiss me."

"You don't know what you're asking," he rasped.

She slid between him and the side of the ship, knew a sort of victory when he didn't back up. She had to arch her neck to look in his eyes, but it was worth the effort to see the desire wage a war with his chivalrous nature.

"Actually, I do," she whispered. "Kiss me, Mr. Privateer."

Pressing onto her toes, her hands braced on the solid mass of Blake's chest, she reached for his mouth with her own.

Blake couldn't have moved if a hurricane blew in. Nothing was as strong as the want—the need—that raged in his blood and drowned out every other sound but that of her breathing. It was essential to his very being that he know the flavor of her mouth again. For the first time since he'd acquired the ship that rocked beneath his feet, something else mattered.

"Alicia."

Cradling her face in his hands, he gently took what she offered. Last night's kiss had been hard and fast; he'd been unable to control the need. He wasn't in a hurry now, Blake thought, his lips moving over hers in a gentle caress. He wanted to savor her. Nothing had ever tasted sweeter than Alicia's mouth. Her movements were uncertain, definitely not practiced as some women's were. But it was that innocence that touched Blake. The woman in his arms was precious and he aimed to see she be treated as such.

Her palms swept up his chest, curled into his hair. Blake's knees trembled when she opened her mouth under his. Desire hummed in his ears. A fog curled in his brain, tried to obscure his logic and reason for not pressing Alicia into the gunwale and ravishing her. If he didn't slow down, he'd soon be lost in the thick of it. But he couldn't pull away either. One more taste, he promised himself, and he traced her lips with his tongue. As he moved his hands to the back of her neck, the fog thickened. She was so bloody soft.

"I'm surprised you're awake. Thought for certain you'd be in bed nursing a dreadful headache."

Alicia startled, her body stiffened, and she drew back. Blake pressed his forehead to hers, cursed Nate's timing, while he tried to steady his breathing. Although perhaps it was good that they'd been interrupted as neither he nor Alicia had had the sense to stop.

Blake heard the man's steps coming closer and knew by Nate's misstep the moment he realized his captain wasn't alone. Blake took Alicia's hands from around his neck, kept one firmly grasped in his, and turned.

Nate grinned like a child given a shiny new coin.

"Ah, now I see," he said. "Good morning, Alicia."

Despite the color that rode high on Alicia's cheeks, she returned Nate's greeting.

They stood there like idiots until an itchy feeling settled between Blake's shoulders and the headache he'd forgotten about while holding Alicia resumed its pounding. He pressed a hand to his eye.

"Head hurt?" his first mate asked, his knowing smile telling Blake he already knew the answer. "Why don't you go below? I promised the lady I'd teach her all about the ship."

"What?"

"Well, that's not exactly—"

Interrupting Alicia, Nate continued, his eyes on Blake's. "She asked me last night and who was I to refuse? The lady wants to know about the ship." Nate gestured down the length of the deck that gleamed in the morning sunlight. "Since we're up early this morning, it's the perfect time."

Blake wanted to flatten Nate when the man winked at Alicia.

"*You* take the helm," Blake grumbled. "*I'll* show Alicia around."

Nate shrugged, moved to the wheel. If Blake wasn't

mistaken, the man was biting his cheek. Blake didn't appreciate being herded, but Nate was right. It was the perfect time. The sun was warm, the wind was stronger than it had been but still enjoyable, and it would afford him more time with Alicia.

"Let's start at the front," Blake said. With her hand entwined in his, they moved to the bow, the canvas billowing above them.

"Do you know much about ships?" he asked when they'd reached the front.

Alicia smiled. "I know they float, have sails, and the front is the bow and the rear is the stern. And," she added, holding up a finger, "they all have names." She frowned. "Captain told me what yours looked like, but I don't remember him giving me its name."

"Captain?"

"Oh." Alicia's eyes widened and she gnawed at her lip. "He, um, well . . ." She shrugged. "He encouraged me to come aboard."

At least she looked sheepish. Blake doubted he'd see the same expression on Captain's face next time they encountered each other.

"Or course he did," Blake mumbled. "Don't know why that surprises me."

"He's a very nice man," Alicia reminded Blake.

"I'll try to remember that when I see him. Anyway, my ship's called the *Blue Rose*." He didn't tell her he'd named it so because his mother's favorite color was blue and she preferred roses. "We'll start with the basics," Blake said instead.

"The larger the ship, the more it can hold. But the more supplies, the more guns it has, and the slower it moves. The smaller ones go faster for two reasons. One, they have less cargo encumbering them, and two, because they are shallower on the draft."

"The draft?"

"The amount of ship that's below the water, is the easiest way to say it. Captain said your sister was in a sloop.
It would be smaller than this one, but also a little faster.
This one's a schooner," he said, trailing his hand along the
smooth gunwale.

"Is it only the size that tells you what kind of ship it is?"

"Usually it's a combination of the ship's size—its number of gun decks—as well as the number of masts and the
manner in which the sails are attached to those masts.
Take mine. She's a two-masted schooner, so those two long
poles you see are the masts. The larger ships can have up
to four."

"Is that also a mast?" she asked, pointing to the pole
that extended over the water at the bow.

"In a manner of speaking. We call that the bowsprit.
The smallest sail at the end of it is called a—"

"A flying jib." Alicia gasped, her hand at her throat.

"You know its name?"

"I—the name, it just came to me. Give me a moment."

She squeezed her eyes shut, her pretty mouth pinched
and the hand that remained entwined with his shook. After
a few silent minutes passed, she pulled her hand from his
and moved to the gunwale.

"Alicia?"

Her heavy sigh had him moving closer to her side. His
hand caressed her shoulder.

"What is it?"

"It's these bits and pieces of my past that creep up on
me. Once, sitting in the sun outside the house, I had this

fleeting feeling of sitting in water and being so cold and afraid that I remember shivering despite the heat. There were a handful of times growing up that I used to wake up at night with my ears full of cannon blasts only to find myself in my bed with Jacob and Anna asleep downstairs.

"But there were never enough to these glimpses for me to remember anything significant. It's always these random thoughts and scraps of information and then nothing. No matter how much I focus on remembering more, nothing comes to me." She kicked the gunwale. "It's so frustrating!"

He rubbed her shoulder. "We can stop, if you want. I can show you the rest another time."

She turned, placed her hand once again in his. Sadness lingered around the edge of her smile.

"No, let's keep going. Maybe I'll remember more."

Her spirit amazed him. He couldn't imagine not knowing his past. The fact that she could forge ahead despite the pain and frustration of not knowing her own history was a testament to the woman's strength.

He guided her along and was relieved when the last of the sadness slipped away. Soon she was once again looking at him, her eyes bright.

Seeing that she was truly interested in what he was saying had pride settling warmly in his chest. He loved his ship, every board and every rope. Eric had never understood that and his father even less so. He'd tried explaining it, several times, but neither had realized what it meant to Blake. It got to be that he'd stopped trying to make them understand.

For years he'd longed to be able to share his ship with someone who would look at it with the same wonder he had the first time he'd clapped eyes on it. Eric had enjoyed the water, but Blake had known by the look on his brother's face that he didn't understand, didn't feel the same connection. Neither had his father. The only times he had come to the water were to see Eric and Daniel off and to forbid him from attending Anna's funeral. Blake would never forget the look on Jacob's face. He had looked at the ship with resentment, and the youngest of his sons standing on it with disappointment. Shoving the hurt away, Blake continued.

"Everything on a ship has a name and a purpose."

Alicia tilted her head to the side. "How long did it take you to learn it all?"

He shrugged. "I don't know. Even when I was a young boy, I'd spend as much time at the harbor as I could. I'd ask any sailor that happened by about ships. Most were happy enough to tell me, and my presence became so commonplace that soon they let me onto the ships, showed me everything." He sighed. "I couldn't learn it fast enough. By the time I left home, even though I hadn't spent much time on the sea, I knew what was needed to sail a vessel."

"And you bought this ship straightaway?"

"No, I had no money at the time. I've only had the *Blue Rose* for three years."

Alicia squeezed his hand. "And you love her."

It wasn't a question. It was said with affection and understanding and not a hint of recrimination or disgust. He drew her into his arms, felt his heart pull when she lifted her head and met his gaze. Her hands went around his waist. He smiled, then lowered his mouth to hers. It was a kiss to show what her understanding meant to him. He took his time about it, and when her mouth moved under his, opened for him, he forgot the reason for the kiss and simply lost himself in the wonder of it.

When it ended, her smile was every bit as wide as his.

He brought their joined hands to his mouth and pressed a kiss to hers.

"You don't have to go below today."

Eleven

The day was a glorious wonder for Alicia. It reminded her of walking through Port Royal in the early morning and watching the town slowly come to life. The crew trickled up, by twos or threes, until the deck was full of men. She had no idea of their duties but enjoyed watching the activity nonetheless. When a few began to climb the rigging, she watched in fascination until they'd climbed so high Alicia's stomach clenched. Since she hadn't been sick in a while, she decided it best to look away before she changed her good fortune.

Despite her asking, neither of the three men that alternated keeping her company—Blake, Nate, and Vincent—would assign her a task of her own. Instead she passed the time asking questions and trying to keep all the different words straight in her head. Mainsail, foremast, bilge, fore and aft, topmasts. There were two of those but at the moment she couldn't think of the difference. She did know that the side of the ship she was leaning against was actually called a gunwale.

Blake came to stand beside her. They'd had such a marvelous day. If he hadn't been with her on the quarterdeck, he was on the main one, and more than once he'd turned to catch her watching him or she'd feel his gaze on her and turn to see she was right. Always a warmth settled around her when his eyes connected with hers. But times like these, when he was close enough to touch and she smelled the ocean and wind as well as his heat, every nerve in her body went on alert.

"Do you ever tire of it?" Alicia asked.

"Of what?"

"Of the endless water, days at sea. Of not having solid ground beneath your feet."

"I did the first few weeks. Now I can't imagine being anyplace else."

"I think I would. I enjoy being able to walk the streets, to smell the earth after a rain, to sleep on a bed that doesn't move."

Blake shrugged. "I can do all those things when I make port."

His eyes crinkled against the glare of the sun reflecting off the steel blue water. Small creases folded out from the corners of his eyes. Wind whistled between the canvas, snapped the sails when a gust blew through. After a day outside, Alicia was now used to the shouts hollered between crew members if someone needed help or if one man annoyed another. The crew was often annoyed.

"You really don't miss it, do you?"

He looked at her. "Miss what?"

"Port Royal."

"There's nothing there for me, Alicia. Hasn't been for quite some time."

Because she feared he'd leave, she placed a hand over his. "There's the house. The shop."

"Alicia." His eyes grew solemn, lost the warmth they'd held all day. "They mean nothing to me."

"You're wrong. If they didn't, you wouldn't look so sad. You wouldn't have been so angry last night."

"I'm entitled to be mad. It doesn't mean I'm ready to turn the ship around and go back."

"You came to his funeral. You were mad at me for years, and you hadn't even met me. You refuse to read the letter. That tells me it means something to you."

He sighed, pressed his free hand to his eye. "I'd really hoped we were past this."

"I may have been their daughter for a time, but their sons, *both* their sons, were everything to them. I didn't replace you in their hearts. I couldn't have."

Blake yanked his hand back and he moved away. He gave Vincent some instructions on his way past and disappeared below. She counted to thirty and then she followed.

"Alicia, I really don't want to repeat what happened last night," he said from the table.

He was sitting on a chair with his booted feet propped on another. Restrained anger rippled in the air.

"Good, neither do I." She kneeled at his side, fixing her gown so she wasn't stepping on it. "Blake, you've come to mean something to me and I don't want to hurt you. But I really think we need to talk."

He sighed deeply. "I'm not talking."

"Fine, then I will." She grasped his hand, squeezed it within her own, and began from the beginning.

"From the time I woke up at the Davidsons', I never felt

anything but love. Even without memories, I felt their affection. I never doubted what they told me about my memory loss because I had no reason to. They always treated me as their daughter.

"And as much as they loved me, I always knew a part of their hearts was reserved for Daniel and Eric. I saw that every day in the little things, such as when Anna cooked. She'd place a piece of pie before me and say, 'Apple was always Daniel's favorite.' Sometimes she'd add an extra blanket to my bed and say, 'Eric always got a chill when it rained.' She prayed every night. She'd say a prayer for each of you, and though Jacob pretended not to hear or care, he always rose as Anna was finishing, and more than once I heard him murmur 'Amen' as he walked out the door. He never changed the name of his shop. To this day the sign above the door says 'Davidson and Sons.'"

"He was just too lazy to change it," Blake murmured, though his voice held some of the emotion she knew he was feeling.

"There was nothing lazy about a man who worked long hours in a sweltering blacksmith shop six days out of seven, and I know, because it's hard work. If he'd wanted to change the sign, he could have."

Blake cocked his head. "Why do you work in the shop? Doesn't Charles still work for him?"

"He does. But I'm not there because I have to be, nor have I ever been. I adore that shop. Soon as I was recovered, I followed Jacob there every chance I had, much to Anna's dismay," she added with a laugh.

"I can't explain why I went, only that there was something about Jacob that drew me. I loved watching his hands work, listening to the rhythm of his voice when he spoke. From the first time I walked into the shop, he began to teach me about his work. I don't think he did it really believing I'd take over for him, but more because I listened. From there it became habit. We walked there together and he heard my ideas. He never dismissed them if they were wrong, but rather encouraged me to consider doing it another way."

"You love it," he acknowledged.

"I do. And it didn't take Anna long to realize that either. She knew there was no prying me away. I'm good at what I do, Blake, but more than that, I love what I do."

"It can't be an easy place for a woman to be."

"The shop is easy, it's everyone's reaction to me being in it that's difficult."

He arched a brow. "Then why do you stay?"

She shrugged. "It's who I am. I'd never be happy hosting tea parties and socials. Your parents knew that and your father was just happy to have me by his side."

"Yeah," Blake grimaced. "I'm sure he was."

"He was, because all he ever wanted was to work with his family, to have them beside him. His face lit up when I walked in. I think that's why he never cared what others thought, because to him, family stayed together."

"Please," Blake scoffed. "He sent me away. That's not indicative of a man whose family means the world to him."

Alicia considered him a moment. "Did you know Jacob carried a rock in his pocket? It was a small thing that had been polished smooth by time and water. It was gray with specks of pink. It didn't seem remarkable but he never went anywhere without it. I imagine it came from one of you."

Blake's sharp breath and the look in his eyes nearly broke her heart. His eyes were shining; his teeth were clamped together. Within her hand, his trembled and she knew it had been Blake's rock that her father had carried.

"I found that when I was a boy. I gave it to him one year for his birthday."

"I buried it with him. I figured if it meant enough for him to carry it around for years, it should go with him."

He nodded, looked away.

She said nothing more. What could she say? It was up to Blake now. For long minutes, sounds from above trickled in to alleviate the silence. Vincent was bellowing at someone and whoever it was wasn't happy because he stomped across the deck as though wearing boots filled with mortar. Blake didn't utter a word, but Alicia took comfort in the fact that he hadn't demanded she leave either.

Finally, after a long sigh, Blake moved. Shifting to one side, he drew a small key out of his pocket and held it to Alicia. She pressed a hand to his stubbled cheek.

"Are you sure?"

"It's what you wanted, isn't it?" he asked softly.

"Yes. But is it what *you* want?"

He dropped his feet from the chair, eased her aside so he could pace. "I'm not sure. Part of me agrees that I need to or it'll haunt me forever."

"And the other?" she asked, standing.

"The other thinks it's best to leave it unread. I already know he blames me for Eric's death, do I really need to read about it?"

"I can guarantee you those won't be his words."

Heart racing, Blake passed her the key. "I guess we'll find out."

The letter was as he'd left it, and she smoothed the envelope before passing it to him. He took it, but made no move to open it.

"Do you want me to leave you alone?" she asked, already taking a step to the ladder.

"No." He reached out and grasped her arm. "Stay."

She did, but while he sat on the edge of the bed, she took a chair at the table. Funny, he thought, how she'd pushed for this, and yet when the time came, she was generous enough to give him some space. Regardless of what his father's words were, he was no longer angry at him for taking in Alicia. Jacob had treated her injuries, loved her as his own, and because of that, Alicia's memories were happy ones. Knowing what he did now, Blake was ashamed of how he'd resented his father for that. Wouldn't it have been worse if his father had let her die? Or if once she was healed, he'd left her to fend for herself at twelve years old?

Blake looked down at the writing on the envelope. He traced the letters with his finger. By the time he started the "M" for "Merritt," his hand was trembling. The paper rustled in his grip. Annoyed with himself, he turned over the envelope and broke the seal. He was twenty-five years old, for God's sake, he could read a blasted letter without shaking like a virgin.

Ripping the letter from the envelope, feeling Alicia watching silently from the table, Blake read his father's final words to him.

To my wonderful son,

I'd hoped you'd never have to read this letter. I'd hoped we could talk face-to-face before it came to this, before stubborn pride kept us apart. If you're reading this letter, then it means I failed.

I want to make it clear, Daniel (you'll always be Daniel to me) that this is my failure, not yours. I saw, much too late, that in order to be your own man, you needed to be at sea. I never understood that. Perhaps I never wanted to. I was selfish, son, and I wanted you and Eric at my side, in my shop.

When Eric died, your mother and I were devastated. And yes, I'll admit for a time, I blamed you. When Anna died, I was still blaming you. It was easier than accepting the truth. But I was wrong, Daniel. I was at fault. Had I left you to follow your heart, Eric would be alive and your mother wouldn't have died brokenhearted. She never stopped loving and missing you. And neither did I.

I know I gave you the impression that I didn't love you enough to accept your dreams, or the man you were, but that couldn't be any further from the truth.

I love you, Daniel. I'll never forgive myself for depriving your mother of having you in her life and at her burial. I'll always be ashamed of that and of the last words I spoke to you. I don't know if you can forgive me, I'm not sure I have any right to ask. Please know I died being so very proud of you. You're my boy, Daniel. You'll always be my boy.

I know you hate the shop, but it's half yours. Yours and Alicia's. You don't have to take it, Daniel, but I wanted to give you the opportunity to have it, and to work it, without the pain of the past in the way nor any expectations on your shoulders. I don't want you there if your heart's not in it. I won't make that mistake again, even in death. Know that I'm looking down upon you and am proud of whichever decision you choose to make. You're a good man, Daniel, and I'm sorry I wasted years not letting you know that.

Your loving father.

A sorrowful wail filled the cabin, echoed off the walls. It wasn't until Alicia rushed to his side that Blake realized the sound had come from him. He buried his face in his hands, his shame pressing heavily around his heart.

"He's sorry."

Alicia's hand rubbed his back. "I know, Blake. He loved you."

"Why didn't I—" He choked on the words, on the truth of them. "Why didn't I see that?"

But he hadn't and now it was too late. His father was gone and the opportunity to make amends was gone with him. Jacob wasn't the only one who'd had time to go back and make things right. Why hadn't Blake tried again? Why hadn't he fought harder to make his father understand?

"I can't say I'm sorry." His eyes blurred. "I'm too damn late."

"No you're not. You can go to his grave, say it there."

But it wouldn't be the same. It wasn't only Jacob who had failed; Blake had as well. And believing that to the depths of his soul, Blake bowed his head and let the tears flow.

Twelve

The sound of wood scraping against wood drew Alicia's attention from the fiery sunset. Turning, she saw Vincent maneuvering his crate toward her, his face set with concentration. There were times, like these, when she wanted to scurry over and help him. She'd learned, however, that the crew made little concessions for his size and that Vincent preferred it that way. Instead she watched and smiled.

"I thought you could do with some real companionship," he said once he'd settled onto the box.

"Nate will be along shortly, then?" she teased.

He placed a hand on her forehead. "Are you feverish?"

Alicia laughed. "Not at all."

"Well, something must be ailing you if you prefer that big lubber's company over mine. And whatever it is, we should treat it immediately," he added with a grin. "The last thing we want is for something like that to spread around and infect the crew."

"What makes you think it hasn't already?"

"Because if it had, Nate's head would be so swollen he'd be unable to get through the hatch."

Alicia laughed and some of the sadness that she'd carried from Blake's cabin drifted off her shoulders.

"Thank you, Vincent," she said.

"For what, darling?"

"You make me laugh. You remind me of home and of Charles."

"Who the heck is Charles?" he demanded.

"A friend. A friend," she added when Vincent frowned, "that is happily married with four children."

"Good," he nodded. "That'll save Blake the trouble."

"The trouble of what?"

Vincent grinned. "Of battling the man for you."

"Don't be ridiculous," Alicia protested, though the thought of two men dueling over her was fascinating.

"It's not so ridiculous a notion. He's become very possessive of you. I'm sure if Nate decided to court you, he'd be shot for his efforts."

Alicia knew Blake would never do such a thing, but she remembered how angry Blake had been when she'd spoken to Lewis and how he'd rushed to be the one to show her the ship when Nate had offered to do it. Her smile bloomed before she could stop it. Vincent's blue eyes glowed, and he looked very pleased.

"Speaking of the devil, is Blake still in his cabin?"

"Yes." He'd been down there since reading the letter, long enough for the sun to begin to fold into the sea.

"Then I think he's wallowed long enough. Why don't you go take him some supper?"

"He must be hungry by now," Alicia agreed, trying— with absolutely no success—to look serious.

Vincent chuckled. "I'm sure he is. And don't worry about the ship. Tell Blake we don't want to see his face until daybreak."

Because Blake had missed the evening meal by hours, all Alicia was able to put together for him was some salted pork, a few pieces of fruit, and a cup of water. But since all she really wanted was an excuse to see him, the food was of little importance.

"You didn't need to bring me anything," Blake said from where he sat across the bed. "I was going to come up shortly."

Alicia set the plate on the table. She had no map for what she was about to do and could only hope she wouldn't make a mess of it, or that Blake would reject her. That, she wouldn't be able to stand.

"Alicia?"

She swallowed her nerves and moved to the side of the bed, where his booted feet rested. She felt his eyes on her and dared meet them with her own. Then, before doubts could steal her courage, Alicia placed her hands on Blake's right boot and tugged it off. She held fast to the other foot when he pulled, and though he managed to reclaim his leg, she succeeded in removing his other boot.

She let it fall to the floor with a thud.

Blake was on his knees on the bed. "What are you doing?"

Burnished light seeped through the window. A spear of it crossed over Blake and drew out some copper tones in his brown hair. He'd rolled the sleeves of his shirt to his elbows; broad hands rested on narrow hips. She had to work to create enough moisture in her mouth to answer.

"I thought you'd be more comfortable."

"I need my boots, Alicia. I can hardly walk the deck without them."

"You won't be going on deck tonight," she said. Then she raised her skirt to her knees and knelt on the bed. There was plenty of room between them yet, but as there was resistance in Blake's eyes, Alicia didn't move any closer.

"I have a ship and crew to tend to." His voice slid underneath her skin.

"I think you have something here that needs tending, don't you?"

Blake's eyes widened, and he drew a deep breath. "This is not a good idea. You can't mean . . . You don't know . . . Oh, hell," he managed, looking tortured.

Because he didn't move, Alicia did. It was difficult with the material of her gown tangling in her legs, but she managed to close the distance between them. Then, with no idea what to do next, she simply followed the voice in her heart.

She lifted both hands to his face and skimmed her fingers over the coarse whiskers that darkened his chin and jaw. His cheeks were smooth, especially under his eyes and at his temples. With her fingertips, she eased the creases that lined his forehead, then brushed her hands over his lips.

"You're very handsome," she whispered. Leaning in, she replaced her fingers with her mouth. His hands clutched her arms, dug in the sensitive skin as his mouth moved under hers. Empowered by his response, she flicked her tongue over his.

He yanked his head back, breaking the kiss.

"We need to stop this now. I promised myself I wouldn't touch you."

"What? Why?"

"Because," he scowled, running a hand through his hair. "You're not some tavern wench, Alicia, and you deserve better than to be treated as one."

"I'd be happy to simply be treated as a woman for once in my life," she snarled. Fighting the gown that was determined to twist itself around her legs, she scurried backward off the bed. She'd been afraid of rejection, hadn't thought she'd be able to stand it, but it went past that.

She was furious.

"Why is it so hard for a man to see me? I care about you, Blake. I fussed with my hair, put on a dress, and you're telling me that it's still not enough? You won't touch me for fear of treating me like a wench? Well, Blake," she raged, yanking the pins from her hair and letting it spill down, a task he watched intently, "maybe I'd like to be treated as one. At least then it would let me know that I'm attractive enough for a man to bother with!"

Before she could blink, he was standing before her. He took her hands, grasped them when she tried to yank them back. If he thought he could spew a few trite words that would calm her, he was in for a nasty surprise!

"Stop fighting me, woman, and let me speak. You're beautiful. I thought so from the first time I saw you."

"You hated me, Blake. It was written plain on your face. Just like now it's pity." She shoved at him with her shoulder. "Let me go. I need some air."

Keeping their hands together, Blake took two steps and backed her into the wall, pressed his weight against her. "You'll get some air later. For now, let me talk."

Because her cheeks already burned with mortification, Alicia kept her tongue. The sooner he said his piece, the sooner she could escape this debacle. Nodding at her when she said nothing, Blake continued.

"You tempt me, Alicia, more than you know," he muttered. "But I don't want to take your innocence and hate myself for it in the morning."

"Your sacrifice is duly noted," she growled. "Now let me go."

He sighed. "You'll thank me for this later." He released her, took a step back.

Alicia saw red. With both hands she came at him and shoved hard.

"What the hell was—"

"You don't know anything about anyone but Blake Merritt, do you? You think I'll thank you tomorrow for taking the moral road? Well, I won't. And don't you dare," she rumbled, "look at me with compassion."

He scowled. "Well, how the hell would you have me—"

"Stop being selfish! Your father didn't see eye to eye with you so you walked away for eight years? Now you turn your back on me because you think it's what's best for me? I'm surprised you haven't run on deck yet. Why, surely Nate and Vincent are going to run the ship to ground without you there to guide them."

"You'd better stop now," Blake warned.

"Or what?" In fine fighting form, she stood before him, chin raised. "Shall I find you a bottle to throw?"

Blake prided himself on his fairness. He'd never treated a crewman unjustly and always tried to take a quarry with the least amount of violence. But dammit, standing there, her golden hair in tumbled disarray, her face flushed, and her breasts heaving, she was pushing him beyond his boundaries.

"I'm not throwing anything, I'm leaving." And the sooner the better. Shoving his desires aside, Blake nearly choked on regret. He headed for the stairs.

"Fine, Mr. Privateer," she yelled at his back. "Tuck your tail and run away. You're good at that."

Her words hit him like a bullet and he froze. He'd been fighting his desire for days, and he wouldn't have thought anything could be stronger than that, but now his anger came to the forefront. He spun around.

"You yell at me for not knowing anything, but you're no different, are you? You think I walked away from my father easily? You think I didn't think about him and my mother every damn day? You think I didn't bleed when I heard she'd died?" He walked, she retreated, until she was once again being pressed into the wall by his weight.

Through the swirl of anger, Blake felt her softness against him and he went hard.

"You think I don't want this?" he questioned, his hands tangling in her hair. "You have no idea how much I god-damn want this."

He shoved with his hips, telling her just how much he did. Her eyes widened and she gasped. Blake swept in and plundered.

Need flashed through his body like lightning. He kissed her until his lungs burned and his hands shook. Her whimpering drove him on. He couldn't get to her skin fast enough. Why did women wear so many blasted layers? He buried his face in her neck, acknowledged the scent of oranges through the lust that pounded in his veins while his hands fumbled with the buttons on her bodice. He didn't know how many attempts it took—he was distracted several times—when Alicia's clever hands slid underneath his shirt and dug into his chest.

Finally the buttons gave way, and with all the finesse of a staggering drunk, he managed to push the bodice and sleeves to her waist. The thin cotton underneath was amazingly sensual. Through it, Blake saw the shape of her breasts and the nipples that crested the generous swells. His mouth watered.

"You don't know how much I've wanted this," he said, then he bent to worship. His hands took in their fullness, molded them to his palms. Beneath them her heart hammered. Perfect, Blake thought, before he drew the cotton aside and tasted.

"Oh," she gasped, and her whole body shuddered against him. Blake held her waist with his hands so she couldn't move. He suckled and teased, his teeth toying with her nipples until she moaned and her head rolled back against the wall. Her hands clenched in his hair when he tugged, then blew to ease the slight pain.

"Blake," she murmured.

Hearing her voice, thick with desire, speak his name was the best sound he'd ever heard. Coming back to her, he tasted her mouth as completely as he had her breasts. She held him tightly, slid her tongue around his. Then she was ripping at his shirt, and before he knew how it happened, she'd gotten rid of it and her hand slid down his stomach. His belly clenched.

"Mother of God," he groaned as her fingers brushed his arousal. "No, don't!" he ordered when she pulled back. With his hand, he guided hers back, showed her how to please him. Only when his eyes began to cross did he ease away from her and drop to his knees, where he finished undressing her.

When she was gloriously naked, he dragged his palms from her delicate ankles up the length of her legs to where he most wanted to taste her.

"You can't mean to—" she stammered, pressing her thighs together and pushing at his shoulders.

"Trust me, I can."

And he did. He kissed her knees, nibbled his way up her thighs. Beneath his mouth her muscles quivered and her hands fell to her sides. Slipping a hand between her legs, he eased them apart. With his thumbs, he parted her, then with a slow pass of his tongue, he tasted her. Her moans poured over him, slowed him when he ached to find his own release. He tormented her with his hands and mouth until she gasped his name, clutched his shoulders, and her legs collapsed.

He held her until she was strong enough to support herself, then he stood up. Lord, she was a vision with her half-lidded eyes and lips swollen from his kisses. Her breasts had small abrasions from his beard. He'd done that.

He wanted to do it again. Throbbing, Blake threw off his clothes, watched her eyes widen when she took in his desire.

"It's your first time, Alicia. It may hurt a little, but I promise you, it'll be worth it." He teased her breasts again until her eyes fluttered. "Let me have you," he pleaded.

She nodded and Blake lost the last of his rational thoughts when she opened her arms to him. That she wanted him in that moment as badly as he wanted her was all that mattered. She melted in his arms, her curves fitting against him in all the right places. Her nipples pressed into his chest, her hands fisted in his hair when he slanted his mouth over hers. With his finger, he played with her until she was wet and her hips rocked against his hand.

"Wrap your legs around me," he instructed and nearly sobbed when she did. She was ready.

With all his blood between his legs, he was hard as stone. Taking her mouth in his, he thrust his tongue against hers and pushed inside her.

Alicia gasped and the haze of desire vanished in a flash of discomfort. Blake was pressed deeply inside her, stretching her uncomfortably. She hadn't thought of how her body would accommodate him and it seemed it couldn't. She suddenly wanted nothing more than to get dressed and pretend she hadn't thrown herself at him.

With his hands on her buttocks, he pushed a little more and Alicia winced.

"Blake, I think it's best if—"

"This will only hurt for a moment," he said and thrust until Alicia felt a sharp stab of pain.

Alicia froze, then pushed at his shoulders. "Let me down."

"Trust me," he promised and slid a hand between them.

While Blake murmured loving words in her ear, his fingers touched her until she once again felt the desire warming in her blood. The pain was easing and her body, it seemed, could take him after all. Soon his fingers were teasing her until she felt the slickness where their bodies joined and an urgency that demanded she concentrate on nothing else but what her body was feeling.

Blake had never felt anything as wonderful as Alicia taking him into her body. She was wrapped around him and his own desire was raging. He slid inside her one long stroke after another until his teeth ached from the effort of going slow. When they were both wet with sweat, he began to pump until his vision blurred.

Capturing her mouth, he kissed her as he increased his rhythm. He felt her legs tighten around him, heard her breath catch.

"Alicia," he moaned.

Cupping a breast, he plucked at her nipple.

"Oh, God. Blake."

She snapped like a bow and liquid heat spilled over him. Squeezing her buttocks, he pulled her hard against him. Then, with her muscles milking him, he poured himself into her.

Alicia was sprawled on the floor of Blake's cabin, naked as the day she was born. Blake was beside her, eyes closed, his breathing not quite back to normal yet. There was still enough light in the cabin to see without candles. She should have been mortified and reaching for something to cover herself with. She should, she imagined, feel ashamed.

She'd never felt better.

"Is it always like that?" she asked, turning onto her side to see the man she'd given herself to. She smiled, looking at him. She'd given herself to a very handsome man.

He opened his eyes, looked at her. His hand came to caress her cheek and his voice was as soft as his touch. "It's never like that, sunshine."

She slid over, curled around him, and placed a hand on his warm chest, her fingers toying with the dark curls. He placed a hand over hers, stilled the motion. He balanced on one arm, looked down at her with eyes that brimmed with concern. "Did I hurt you?"

"No. It was beautiful."

"I wasn't very gentle."

She grinned. "I don't remember asking you to be. You gave me everything I wanted and more."

He shook his head. "You deserve better than to be taken up against a wall."

"No, I don't. I didn't know there could be that kind of passion. We couldn't get to each other fast enough, you needed me so much that you couldn't wait to get me in a bed." She rose up, touched her lips to his. "That's the best thing you could have done, Blake."

His lips twitched. "You sure know how to make a man feel good."

She laughed, fell back with arms stretched over her head.

"And you're stunning," he said as his eyes took a leisurely stroll over her.

"I feel it," she whispered. "With you."

She held out her arms, but this time Blake shook his head.

"We should talk."

"We just did."

"No, I mean really talk. We'll be in St. Kitts the day after tomorrow."

Alicia sat up, her heart diving. She'd just found something special and she wasn't prepared to let it go.

"Blake, we have tonight." The cabin was darkening quickly now. Night was settling in. "Vincent has the ship. Can you stay with me? For tonight, will you lie with me? I promise we can talk in the morning."

He'd never imagined a woman would ever be on board his ship, and gazing at Alicia now, naked on his floor with her heart in her eyes, he knew he never wanted there to be another.

Standing, he held his hand out to her. She slid hers into his, and Blake felt the way he had when he'd bought the *Blue Rose*. Like a piece of himself had come home. When she was in his arms, he did what he felt she deserved. He kissed her gently, coaxed a reaction rather than demand one. Her hands sliding into his hair, she pressed her body against his arousal.

"Hmm," she murmured against him.

"That's just the beginning," he whispered. Then he swept her off her feet and lay her on the bed.

Where before he'd been acting on a fierce need to possess, this time he was swept by an equally strong need to cherish. His fingers did all the things they'd done before, but at a much slower pace. He took his time to rub her delicate feet, to kiss the amazingly sensitive skin behind her knee. Her softness captivated him and his hands explored all of it.

"You taste as sweet as you look," he murmured as he nuzzled her neck.

Alicia arched, lost in the sensations of being desired. She hadn't really given lovemaking much thought in the past. Yes, she'd wanted someone to find her pretty, but she hadn't imagined what the actual act would entail. She was certain, however, that had she imagined it, it would have paled in comparison to making love with Blake. In her innocence she'd believed it was more about the man seeking pleasure, that it was what was asked of a woman. Never would she have believed it to be so pleasurable for her.

Nor would she have believed that she could want it again so soon afterward. Or that he'd be ready to so quickly as well. He was lying half over her, just enough for her to feel the pressure of his weight and the evidence of his need.

Blake continued to kiss around her neck, lower to the base of her throat. Her heart kicked and her breasts became full and heavy. Everywhere he touched, she tingled. She knew now how soft his hair was, and her fingers kept coming back to tangle in it.

He was thorough, not leaving any part of her unclaimed. She smiled, closed her eyes, and tightened her grip on his head when he suckled her. Her legs opened, inviting him to join her again.

"Not yet, sunshine," he said, though he did press a hand to where she throbbed.

Alicia's hips jolted off the bed. She wanted him with a fierceness she couldn't explain. It wasn't only that he was the first man to find her desirable; indeed, she couldn't imagine ever letting another touch her the way she allowed Blake. It went beyond the lust of the flesh, she thought, though his flesh did feel fine. She trusted Blake. He made her smile, made her feel beautiful. He was headstrong but then so was she, and she knew she'd never be able to settle for someone who wasn't. His strength was part of what appealed to her.

Aware he'd stopped touching, Alicia opened her eyes, found him staring. There was tenderness in his gaze, there was affection. He shifted fully onto her, moved between her legs.

"Alicia," he whispered. Then, cupping her cheek, he kissed her with such care it brought tears to her eyes.

And as simply as that Alicia knew she loved him. Privateer or pirate, it didn't matter.

He entered her slowly, twined his hands in hers as he did. She rocked with him, her heart bursting with emotion. Using her whole body, she told him without words just how much she loved him.

Alicia awoke in the arms of her lover. A lover, she realized smiling, that was snoring lightly in her ear. She didn't dare move because she wasn't ready for him to awaken, but could see by the pale light outside the window that morning had come. She hoped to lie tangled in memories and sensations before life interrupted them.

Blake would want to talk about what had happened. She

bit her lip. There was no doubt in her mind she loved him, but was he ready to hear it? The last thing she wanted was for him to feel obligated to say the same, and yet she knew she'd be devastated if he didn't return her feelings.

Before she could think on it any further, the hatch opened, and noise spilled into the cabin. Blake was instantly awake and bolted upright.

"What is it?" he demanded, pulling the blanket to Alicia's chin to keep her covered.

"It's me," Nate called. He remained on deck and only his shadow stepped into the cabin. "Ship on the horizon, Captain."

"Colors?" Blake asked, sliding out of bed.

"Red and gold."

"Prepare the crew. I'll be up in a minute."

Nate shut the hatch and Blake had his pants on before he turned to Alicia.

"It's a Spanish ship and we're commissioned to go after them. I'm sorry, but you'll have to stay below. It's safer that way."

"I know how to shoot a pistol, Blake. In fact, I brought my own."

"Is that so?" he asked. He smiled as he drew on his shirt. "You've been armed this whole time?"

"Yes."

He peered at her from under his brows. "Ever thought about using it?"

"Many times," she admitted, then laughed when he looked surprised. "But I'm very glad now I didn't."

His fingers stopping on the top button, he slowly lowered his hands. She held out her palm. The blanket slipped and nearly exposed her breasts before she caught it in her other fist. Blake's eyes lingered on her flesh and she heard his breath catch. He raised his gaze after a moment and placed his hand in hers. His heat swept into her.

"I can't tarry, Alicia. I'm needed on deck."

"I know. And I'll give you my promise that I'll stay here."

"Thank you. Sometimes taking a ship can be fast and easy and other times they put up a struggle. It can be very dangerous. If you hear the guns, hide under the bed. Stay low. I'll come down as soon as it's safe."

Alicia let the blanket fall. She wrapped her arms around Blake and opened her mouth over his. His hands spread over her naked back, and he sighed into her mouth as his lips mated with hers.

"Be careful," she whispered when they pulled apart.

"I will," he said, his eyes as hot as the hands on her back, "as I have a very good reason to come back."

Keeping his eyes on hers, he pulled the blanket up around her shoulders, brushed her breast with the back of his hand.

"Get dressed." He kissed her again. "If I know you're down here naked, I won't be able to concentrate."

"Then I hope they surrender immediately."

He grinned. "Me, too, sunshine."

Thirteen

The sails snapped and the ship cut through the white-capped waves. Wind whipped Blake's hair as he stepped onto the quarterdeck. Because he couldn't afford even the smallest distraction, he tied his hair back.

"Guns loaded?" he asked.

Nate was at the helm, two hands on the wheel and a grin on his face.

"Double round being loaded now as well as some with roundshot. Muskets, blunderbusses, and pistols ready, and I've got men fetching every cutlass and axe we have."

"Swing guns?" Blake had added two when he'd bought the ship, one at the stern on the quarterdeck and one at the bow. Since most merchant ships had his schooner out-gunned, the swing guns could fire upon an enemy without exposing the ship to the firepower of a broadside.

"Loaded. Vincent's down getting the powder flasks, and he's concocting some stinkpots. If they decide to fight, we can launch a few when we get within distance. The smoke and stench will slow them down."

"Provided the wind doesn't turn and push the foul odor onto us. I've choked on the stuff Vincent puts in those pots, kept me coughing for days afterward, and I couldn't rid the taste from my mouth."

"But we captured the ship."

They had, but that didn't mean it was something he wanted to repeat. Blake took out the looking glass and lost his breath when he saw what it was.

"Hell, Nate. Spanish galleon with a flotilla of three, no wait, four ships."

"Did you think I was amassing all our firepower for show only? We may very well need it all."

Blake thought of Alicia below, dropped the glass, and ran a hand over his face. His stomach clenched.

"I hope they surrender," he muttered.

Nate glanced over, eyebrows raised. "You've suddenly lost your appetite for this? Was a time you'd practically be dancing when a ship was spotted."

"That was different. It was only us then. Alicia's below today; that changes everything."

Nate's smile withered. "We haven't lost a battle yet. Today won't be any different. She won't be harmed, Blake."

Blake slapped Nate on the back. "Not if I can help it."

The mood was buoyant when Blake stepped below deck. Off-key voices sang the song of a wench and a sailor; some feet stomped to the music while a few men whistled along with the tune. Blake didn't begrudge the singing as there was time yet. Instead he ignored them, moved along the guns, double-checked to make sure there was extra ammunition at each. The guns gleamed as did the other weaponry that was either tucked into the sashes of his men or lying at their feet.

Blake stepped onto a crate, drew the crew's attention. The singing stopped and the air became heavy with anticipation.

"Men, I know we've been fortunate in the past. We've taken a great deal of Spanish treasure without sustaining much loss or damage. We accomplished that by keeping our heads and today is no different. Be prepared for any eventuality, don't let down your guards. It's still a battle."

There were nods of agreement. Some muttered, "Aye, Captain." Satisfied there was nothing left for him to do, he made his way to the galley.

The odor brought tears to his eyes.

"Bloody hell, Vincent, those are supposed to make the quarry sick, not us."

Vincent threw him a grin. "I think they're the best ones I've made yet."

"How the devil would you know that?"

"I can't feel my nose."

Despite the seriousness of the situation, Blake chuckled. "Are you about finished?"

"This is the last one." He set the pot in line by the others. There were ten altogether.

"I'll help carry them up."

There was no singing on deck. The wind gusted the sails and the lines moaned, but the men themselves were quiet. Some manned the guns; some climbed the rigging. Water splashed high up the hull and splattered the deck.

"Deck's slippery," Vincent commented before taking his five pots to the bow.

Not a good thing, Blake thought, taking his share to the stern. Slipping on deck was always dangerous, but in the midst of a battle, it could be disastrous. Not only could it waste precious time, but a pistol could discharge and hit the wrong man.

"We're within hailing distance, Captain. Sails have been trimmed accordingly."

Through the glass, Blake could see the galleon clearly. He counted thirty guns on the starboard side, two more mounted aft, and another dozen swing guns along the gunwale. There were men stationed at each and they didn't look friendly. Blake closed his eyes. If anything happened to Alicia . . .

"Captain?"

He forced himself to look again, to block Alicia from his mind. It was as he'd told his crew. They'd done this before and had come away victorious because they'd kept their heads. He couldn't stop himself, however, from glancing at the hatch and offering up a quick prayer that nothing happened to her.

"They're armed and ready; I don't think this will be a quick capture," Blake said.

"Awaiting your orders."

"Shift the helm, Nate. We need to get a little closer to launch the pots." Blake went to the edge of the quarterdeck and yelled, "Keep a lookout on the main and foremast, they'll have archers up there. Vincent?"

"Aye?" he answered midship. He had two pistols tucked into his pants and a musket strapped across his chest.

"Run a shot across her bow."

"Yes, Captain," he replied.

Vincent lit the fuse and jumped out of the way. The gun shot back with the explosion, a cloud of smoke blowing from the end of the cannon. The smell of burned gunpowder and expectancy rode on the wind. The men who weren't manning the guns raised their muskets. Blake was among them.

The flotilla, as Blake expected, altered their direction with the *Blue Rose*'s warning shot. They were sailing out of range.

"Avast!" Blake yelled. "Surrender now and no further shots will be fired."

With the sails adjusted, the *Blue Rose*—the faster of the two ships—stayed slightly back of the galleon, just out of range of a broadside.

It didn't stop their enemy, however, from opening fire.

With a shout from the opposing captain, arrows rained down from the platforms that rode the sails of the other ship.

"Archers!" someone yelled before pistols began firing in rapid succession.

Deafening sound carved its way across the deck. Curses and threats came from every direction. Blake's ears rang from the motley of artillery being fired.

"Fire the swing guns!" he yelled. "But hold the cannons!"

Blake was among those who took aim at the archers, switching pistols with each shot. Enemies fell from their perches on the platforms, twisted, and tumbled their way to the deck. Blake had men designated to reload pistols and they did so now, with a flurry of activity and steady hands. All except for Lewis, who Blake saw was cowering behind the gunwale, the extra ammunition lying useless at his feet.

A thundering boom rent the air, and the *Blue Rose* lurched from impact. The galleon had fired its swing guns. Blake staggered, grabbed the gunwale for balance. Water slewed up the hull with a fierce wave and slapped Blake in the face. He sluiced the water from his face with his hand, turned.

"Reload with roundshot!" Blake called to Nate, who was at the swing gun closest to him. "We need to cripple that ship before she cripples us!"

Blake discharged another shot, then threw his weapon to the deck. He grabbed a stinkpot and almost dropped it when it slid within his hands. Tightening his grip, he pitched it across. It exploded on the quarterdeck of the other ship. Men yelled when the foul smoke blinded them and the mixture of chemicals Vincent had thrown in burned their eyes and throats.

"Vincent!" Blake hollered.

"Already at it," he answered and Blake saw another two pots launch across. One landed midship, the other behind it.

"Firing roundshot," Nate called, but he never had the chance.

A cannonball screamed over them and they hit the deck. It shattered the main mast of the *Blue Rose* with a piercing scream, sent shards of wood spearing every which way before crashing to the quarterdeck. The impact shook the wood beneath their feet violently. It was a sound Blake had only ever heard once before. For a brief moment, the memory of seeing Eric beneath the mast blasted over him and sent a sharp stab of pain straight through his heart. He shook it off, opened his eyes, and grabbed his musket. That was when he saw Nate on the deck. And he wasn't moving.

"Nate?" Scrambling toward him on his hands and knees, Blake slipped on the slick surface. His hands spread wide and his cheek slammed into the deck. Pain rippled across his face even as he lunged to his feet.

Jagged slices of wood were everywhere. With the mast broken in half, the boom swayed dangerously. Blake had to stay low to keep it from slamming into his back and knocking him flat.

He dropped to his knees when he reached Nate. The big man was on his stomach; his eyes were closed. Blake blinked as sweat poured into his eyes, stinging them. His hands shook when he reached for a heartbeat.

"Nate? Nate, are you all right?"

"Quit bloody yelling, would you, and see why my leg's burning to beat Hell."

Blake's breath came out in a long whoosh when he heard his friend's voice, then he turned to see what Nate was talking about. There was a piece of wood, about the length of Blake's foot and the width of two fingers, sticking out of the back of Nate's thigh. Blood pooled on the deck beneath it.

Another shot shook the *Blue Rose*. Blake set his jaw. He hated to do this, knew Nate was in pain by the paleness of his skin, but they didn't have a choice.

"Hell, Nate, can you manage the way it is? They're killing the ship and we need all the hands we can get."

"Bloody sure I can, just help me, will you?"

Blake ripped off his shirt, tore it into strips, and wrapped it around Nate's leg to slow the bleeding. Then he grabbed him underneath the arms and pulled. Nate groaned, leaned on his good leg. Blake helped him hop back to the gun.

"I've got it. Go!"

Nodding, Blake turned and yelled. His crew was fighting hard but there were a few unmoving on the deck. He put that aside for now. There'd be more lost if they didn't turn the tide soon.

"Fire the guns!"

Blake took a loaded pistol that was passed to him and fired it at a man who was lighting the swing gun on the galleon. Beside him Nate fired. The roundshot exploded out of

Nate's gun and destroyed the mizzenmast of the other ship. Men threw up their arms to protect themselves as the mast collapsed to the deck with a roar.

Beneath Blake's feet, his ship trembled as the guns below deck opened fire. The galleon screamed as the shots blew holes into her sides. Blake threw down his spent pistol, wiped at the sweat on his brow, and grabbed two stinkpots. Cringing at the smell, he tossed them over.

The taste of gunpowder burned in Blake's mouth as he reached for another stinkpot.

"Blake?" Nate hollered.

"What?"

"They're surrendering. They've hoisted the flag."

Relief poured over Blake as surely as the sweat that ran down his back.

"About goddamn time," he muttered and set the pot down. He grabbed a musket for good measure, then moved to the gunwale.

The galleon looked ravaged. Long tears and larger holes had the canvas limping amid the rigging. With one mast down, the ship looked like a drunk with a missing front tooth. There were holes in the hull from the *Blue Rose*'s guns. Though the bilge pumps would be busy, the holes weren't severe enough to sink it. She'd make it to port.

Along its gunwale its crew lined up, hands up as they yielded, their captain among them. Blake kept his musket pointed nonetheless.

"Vincent?"

"Here, Captain."

Blake shifted his attention long enough to ensure that Vincent was all right. He had a scrape on his forehead that left a thin trail of blood running down his cheek. His shirt was torn but otherwise he appeared fine. A knot of tension eased in Blake's shoulders. His friends were all right.

"Nate's hurt. Take the helm and get us in closer."

"Aye, Captain."

The wind hadn't eased—it continued to swirl around the deck—but after the roar of battle, Blake couldn't even hear it. He did, however, retie his hair as it slapped at his sore cheek. Looking over his shoulder, Blake called to the men nearby.

"Prepare to board."

They moved in next to him, each taking a grab hook. All but one who stood frozen near the bow.

"Lewis!" he called. "Come and help."

The young man didn't move. His eyes didn't shift in his ashen face. Blake cursed, but there was nothing he could do at the moment. The *Blue Rose* was within reach of the galleon.

"Stand back," Blake warned, "we're coming over."

The men on board the other ship stepped back and Blake gave the command. Grab hooks arced through the air and dug into the galleon's side. When the ships were close enough, planks were set down to make walkways between the vessels.

"How's Nate?" Blake asked when Vincent ran toward him.

"Cursing, so I figure he's right as rain. Commanded me off the quarterdeck, said if he couldn't handle the ship, then we may as well shoot him and throw him overboard." His mouth curved. "I was sorely tempted."

Smiling, Blake slapped Vincent on the shoulder. "There'll be time for that later. For now, let's see what she's carrying."

*   *   *

"Holy mother of God," Vincent gasped, "do you think they're all like this?"

Blake was beside him, looking into the barrel they'd pried open. They'd found the treasure room on the lower deck of the galleon. It was chock-full of sealed casks. They lined the walls, were stacked onto each other as much as three high.

He reached in and took out a handful of silver coins. They were both smooth and cool and gleamed in the light from the lantern he held in his other fist.

"We won't know until we get them aboard the *Blue Rose.*"

"We can take that much weight?"

"Our hold is mostly empty. And we don't have far to go before we arrive in St. Kitts."

"Is that where we divide the treasure?" someone asked from behind.

Frowning, Blake turned. Seeing Lewis standing there, suddenly looking fit and healthy, with a sparkle in his eye as he looked at what Blake held in his hand, didn't sit well with Blake.

"What are you doing here? You weren't given the order to come aboard."

Lewis shrugged. "I didn't know I wasn't supposed to. Besides, I wanted to see what we captured and how much of it I can expect."

Blake's eyes narrowed. He passed the lantern to Vincent, which wasn't a good idea. Considering how much he desired to hit Lewis, he should probably keep his hands full.

"You'll know when everyone else does, and seeing as

how worthless you were during the battle, I wouldn't be expecting as much as the others."

"That wasn't the agreement when I signed on, was it?" he asked, a smug smile on his clean face.

Blake's heart rate leapt. He was sore and knew he was filthy. Vincent had blood on his face and tears in his clothes. Nate had a goddamn piece of mast sticking out of his leg and this little whelp was standing him down, clean as the day he boarded, demanding an equal share?

"Then feel free to stay with the galleon if you're not happy with the arrangements, or I'll give you the longboat and you can get yourself to the nearest port. But I guarantee you this, you will not be seeing what the others will. You have to earn your keep on my ship and you haven't."

Lewis's face went scarlet. Behind him Vincent chuckled. "I think you've made him angry, Blake."

"I scrubbed the deck until my back hurt and I had blisters on my hands. I've done everything asked of me, ask your dwarf or the giant, they'll tell you."

Blake's hands curled to fists.

"My men have names and will be addressed with the respect their ranks demand. And you," he said, pointing a finger at the whelp's chest, "are done on board the *Blue Rose* as soon as we make port."

"I was planning on leaving anyway. Everything I need is in St. Kitts."

Lewis's smile sent a shiver of foreboding down Blake's spine. Blake took a steadying breath before he did something truly stupid. This wasn't the time. He had treasure to move and he'd yet to check on Alicia, though he knew she was fine. None of the shots had pierced a hole in his quarters; he'd checked that immediately before boarding the galleon.

"Now," Blake continued, "if you want to earn a little more of this, you can help move these barrels."

Lewis looked around the room and it gave Blake great satisfaction to see his smile fall.

"All of these?"

"Every last one," Blake added. "Vincent?"

"Yes, Captain?"

"The deck looks to be in poor shape as well, does it not?"

"Indeed it does, Captain. There's debris everywhere. It'll take work to clean it up."

Hatred bloomed in Lewis's eyes but Blake didn't mind it. There wasn't anything Lewis could do to him, and in the meantime seeing the man miserable would go a long way to making Blake's day brighter.

"Then let's get to these barrels. Lewis has work to do and it would be a shame to hold him up."

I'm fine, dammit," Nate cursed when Blake insisted he lie down so they could see to his leg.

"Unless you want your leg to be used as a coatrack, you're not. Now stop being a baby and let's get it out of there."

Nate growled but complied. He sprawled on the quarterdeck. The barrels were in the hold and Blake had made sure Lewis had cleaned his deck first. He'd all but spat fire, but he'd gotten the job done, which allowed Nate to lie down on a clean, uncluttered surface.

Vincent appeared, carrying what Blake needed and whistling a lively tune. His face had been washed but the tattered clothes remained. It wasn't easy for Vincent to find clothes that fit; therefore, he didn't own a large range of extra items.

"What do you have there?" Nate asked, lifting his head to see.

Vincent passed him a bottle. "Here, drink this. The last time you were hurt, you whimpered like a baby."

"The hell I did," Nate grumbled but he took the bottle nonetheless and drank a hefty mouthful before lying down again. "Make it quick."

Since the carpenter was busy with repairs and their surgeon was one of the four who had been killed, Blake was taking it upon himself to see to Nate's wound. Had it been a gunshot, he would have demanded the carpenter do it. Since carpenters were sometimes called upon to perform surgeries, he would have more experience. But as it was, the bleeding had mostly stopped and Blake felt confident he could do a clean job of it.

"It's going to hurt," Blake warned.

"So don't scream," Vincent teased.

"Kiss my—holy hell!" Nate roared when Blake yanked the wood out.

Setting his jaw against the pain he knew he was causing, Blake grabbed the cloth Vincent passed him and pressed it to the wound. Nate's body jerked and blood seeped through the cloth, which soon became sticky beneath Blake's hands.

"You were lucky, it didn't go in too deep." Still he had to make sure all the splinters were out and he cringed when his fingers probed and Nate moaned. Satisfied it was clean, Blake nodded to Vincent. The dwarf passed Blake a bottle, then moved to Nate's head to bring another bottle to his lips. When Nate had drunk a healthy gulp, Blake tipped the bottle he held directly over the wound.

"Jesus Christ!" Nate roared.

Vincent patted him on the shoulder. "There, there. We're

almost done. And even better, as the crew's busy with the ship, hardly anyone heard you wail like a baby."

"You won't be laughing when I punch you for that."

"I'm trembling," Vincent laughed. He took Nate's rum and drank some himself.

Blake smiled as he listened to the banter, then he threaded the needle and set to work.

The sun was at its highest peak in the sky before Blake finally had a moment to take a breath. From the instant Nate had called to him that morning, the work had been endless. He'd helped transfer the barrels, tended to Nate, and put his back into getting his ship clean and assessing the worst of the damage. If what Blake had seen from that one barrel held true for the rest, they stood to make a hefty profit, even after the ship was restored.

"It could have been worse," Vincent said, stepping onto the crate he'd pushed next to Blake.

Blake stared at the churning water behind his ship, his mind as agitated as the sea.

"Thankfully it wasn't."

"A shame we lost Billy and the others."

"We did our best."

Vincent eyed Blake, knew by the strain around his mouth his friend was in pain.

"Doesn't make it hurt any less, though, does it?"

Blake ran a hand down his face, exhaled heavily. "No, it doesn't."

"It's been a hell of a day so far. Why don't you go down and see Alicia? There's nothing going on here I can't handle."

Indeed there wasn't. The mood on the ship, despite the

treasure, was woeful. Sadness prevailed and even the smell of the delayed midday meal being prepared didn't offer any encouragement. They'd lost four men and everyone felt the loss.

Blake nodded. "All right, you know where to find me."

When he opened the hatch and began down the stairs, the sense of home wrapped around him and eased some of the weariness from his shoulders. Here he wasn't captain, wasn't the man the others turned to for guidance. Here he could be Blake and he could take the time to mourn the men he'd lost. He could hold Alicia until he felt settled again. Alicia, he thought, shaking his head. Who would have thought that the girl he'd hated would become the woman he needed?

His smile vanished when he reached the bottom and she wasn't there. Where was she? The battle had ended hours ago; she wouldn't still be hiding under his bed. His chest clutched. She hadn't gone above in the midst of the chaos, had she?

"Alicia?" He spun around, eyes scouring the room. "Alicia!"

From behind the steps he heard a sob. With his heart in his throat, he raced around the ladder. He found her behind the chest, back pressed to the wall, curled into a tight ball. Her knuckles were white where they held her legs close.

"Alicia?" he asked, bending to one knee. He placed a hand over hers, shocked to find it icy cold. "Sunshine, are you hurt?"

A mewling sound came from her throat.

His stomach fell. He'd checked the hull, hadn't seen any holes, and had assumed she was fine. Then, he'd had so much to do. Why the hell hadn't he taken two damn minutes to check on her?

"Can you talk? Please tell me if you're injured." He ran his hands down her arms and legs but felt nothing but her trembling.

She raised her head and Blake felt as though he'd been punched. Her hair was disheveled, her face was pale as dawn, and the look in her eyes knocked his breath away. She seemed completely shattered.

"Did someone hurt you?" His vision reddened at the edges. If anyone had laid a hand on her . . .

She shook her head, and Blake's vision cleared.

"It's all right. We're all fine. Nate and Vincent, we're all here." He didn't tell her about the deaths; there was no point in distressing her further.

"It's not that," she said, and her eyes spilled again.

Feeling utterly useless, Blake wiped away the tears with his thumbs.

"I remembered," she rasped, squeezing her eyes shut. "I remembered everything. It was pirates."

It took a moment for the full meaning of her words to become clear, but when it did, he cursed. She'd remembered her family being murdered and she'd been alone when she had. Her shoulders shook with her sobs, and he couldn't keep up with the flow of her tears. Not knowing what else to do, Blake moved beside her on the wall and drew her onto his lap. He wrapped his arms around her, kissed her head.

"I'm sorry I wasn't here," he murmured as his hand smoothed over her back.

"I thought I wanted to know," she cried. "But now I wish I d-didn't."

Blake had never heard such despair and had no idea how to ease it. Since he hadn't been through anything as unspeakable, he could offer no words that would bring comfort. He wished a thousand wishes: that he could've spared her this or that he'd been there sooner. That he could reach within her and take her pain as his own. Instead he held her and let her tears slide down his chest. He could only hope his presence was helpful.

Alicia felt like a clam who'd been ripped open and scraped until she was raw and empty. Everything hurt. Her head throbbed from crying, her throat chafed when she swallowed, and her chest felt as though someone were sitting dead center over her heart. The torrent of tears had passed—considering she'd cried for the last few hours, she was surprised there were any left—and only the occasional one trickled down her cheek. Exhausted and spent, she leaned into Blake and welcomed his support. At least she was no longer cold and shaking. Her hand rested on his chest, and beneath her palm was the calming rhythm of his heart.

He said he wished he'd been there when her memory returned, but Alicia was glad he hadn't been. With the first blast of the cannons, when the sound had howled from both overhead and below, she'd been pelted with images from her past. Only this time they weren't disjointed bits. They were complete and clear and they'd caught her unprepared.

"The noise was the same as that awful night. I'd forgotten how loud it was."

"That's what brought the memories back?" Blake asked.

"It must be. One minute I was sitting on the bed and the next I was on the floor and my head was bursting with images."

Blake leaned to the side, placed a hand under her chin. "Can you tell me?"

Her chin trembled and she bit down hard on her lip.

"I'd heard the noise first. Before I had time to figure what it meant, my mother was running into my cabin. She was so scared, Blake. Her face was ashen, her hand shook when she grabbed my arm. I knew whatever was happening was dire because she was holding me so tightly," Alicia said and rubbed at her arms. It was as though she could feel her mother's fingers digging into her flesh.

"I didn't know fear could have a smell, but it did that night. It hung heavy in the air, and with each breath I took, it filled my lungs until I was choking on it." She looked into Blake's dark eyes. "Your father was right—it was pirates. I caught a glimpse of one when we ran from the cabin. My mother hid us in the bilges, and we sat in that stinking water while they destroyed our lives. While my mother held me and cried, they laughed and cheered.

"That feeling I told you about, of being cold and wet? Now I know what it meant."

Blake took her hand, uncoiled her fingers, and laced his with hers. He squeezed gently. "How did you and your mother get off the ship?"

Alicia sorted through the newly found memories. "It seemed hours that we waited while they ran up and down the stairs, stripping the ship bare. They never came as low as we were, but we didn't move until the ship fell silent. We'd thought they'd left. But then we heard voices and movement again so we stayed longer. Only when we were both shaking from the cold and it had been another long while since we'd heard anything, did we move. We waded through the water—it had gotten much deeper since we'd been below—and made our way up the decks."

"Had they gone?"

"Yes. She told me not to look, to keep my head high, but I couldn't miss the blood, Blake, it was everywhere. We were stepping over dead bodies and severed limbs and slipping on the blood." Alicia pressed a hand to her mouth, breathed deeply until she knew she could continue without throwing up.

"She screamed for Sam and my father. The one blessing was that we didn't see my father that night. I'm not sure either of us could have taken that."

"Is that when you left the ship?"

"She was thinking of how best to do that when something exploded. I remember a searing pain, like my face was on fire, and then I was falling." Alicia had to take a steadying breath. "I saw her as I fell; she was hurt as well. Her nightgown was torn and there was blood on it. Her eyes filled with horror and she screamed my name." Alicia looked down at her hands. "That's all I remember before waking up in your father's house. She must have taken me from the ship and swum us to shore. She was hurt. I don't know how she managed to get us to shore."

Blake said nothing, simply drew her back against his chest. His lips pressed to her head, his arms held her closely. Safely.

"He should have never done it," Alicia said, her heart squeezing. "If he hadn't, they'd still be alive."

"Who shouldn't have done what?" he asked.

"My father. If we'd stayed in London, none of this would've happened."

It was strange how the memories came after six years of being lost, but Alicia could see her old home in London, could remember the words and the tones from the line of people who'd tried to talk her father out of selling his home and most of his possessions for the sake of an adventure.

"He thought it would be such fun for me and Sam to see more of the world, to be able to come back with such grand stories." She scoffed. "I think it was he who yearned for those things, but we weren't sad to leave London either. Especially Sam. She loved the ship. I remember wanting to play with her, but all she was interested in was being at the helm."

"You remember your sister?"

Alicia nodded, felt the flicker of excitement through the despair.

"When I went to the plantation where Sam had been, I remembered her hair being brown. Now I remember the rest. And I'm sure the Samantha that Captain talked about is her. Didn't he say she was building boats with her husband? That sounds exactly like something Sam would do."

"Sam?"

"Her pet name. Only my mother called her Samantha." She pressed a hand to her heart. "I miss my mother. I miss her so much, which sounds stupid because until a few hours ago, I didn't even remember her."

Blake eased Alicia away, looked her in the eye. "Doesn't change who she was, Alicia."

"It's Alicia Fine, by the way."

He smiled, kissed her hand. "Either name you go by doesn't change who you are. And you've every right to miss your mother."

She sniffled. "I know, and yet I feel that I'm disrespecting Anna at the same time. Blake, your mother was wonderful to me. I loved her, I truly did."

"And knowing her, I'm sure she felt the same. Likely tickled to have had a daughter for a while."

"I know I should be happy I was blessed with two sets of parents, but I feel cheated. They're both lost to me, and unlike Jacob and Anna, I never was given the chance to say good-bye or the opportunity to give my real parents the burial they deserved."

Blake leaned forward, pressed a kiss to her cheek. "We can do something for them in Port Royal. We can have a service, you can make some fancy markers out of steel. They won't be nameless anymore, I promise you that."

Love for Blake surged through her.

"They'd be proud of you, Alicia. Just as I know my parents were."

Tears filled fast, blurred her vision. "Thank you. And I know they were proud of you as well."

"I'm not sure I believe that, but I'd like to think so." He took her hand, pressed a kiss into her palm. "So, now what?" he asked.

Alicia took a deep breath. "Let's go find my sister."

Fourteen

We're almost there," Blake said.

Alicia had been at the bow all morning, watching the horizon. St. Kitts had begun as a speck in the distance, and now, as they approached, she could see houses and businesses, people moving about, and ships in the harbor.

"The sand is so white. Even from here it's sparkling."

Blake put his arm around her shoulder. "You can't possibly be thinking about the color of the sand at a time like this."

She turned her face to his, forced a smile.

"I was so sure Captain was sending us to the right Samantha, but now the doubts are crowding my head. What if it isn't her? What if it is and she isn't here? Maybe she's left. I don't think I can take much more, Blake. My stomach is in my throat. I just want to see my sister. A delay now would be torture."

"If she's not here, we'll keep looking until we find her."

Alicia wrapped her arms around Blake, drew in his scent and his strength. He'd been her rock yesterday. With memories swirling in her head, both the good and the bad, he'd been the constant she'd needed. His presence had allowed her to go into the past, to revisit her newly remembered life and all the emotions that went along with it, knowing that when she resurfaced, he'd be there to hold her, to wipe her tears.

They hadn't made love, nor had they talked, but Alicia knew what was in her heart. Staying within the circle of his arms, she pulled back to look at him. His eyes squinted against the glare of the sun, but in them she saw all she needed. He was a good man, an honest and fair man. She placed her hands on his freshly shaved cheeks and felt the heat from the sun on his face. Her heart did a quick jump when the words formed, but she let them come.

"I love you, Blake."

His hands clutched on her back. Since she wasn't sure if that was a good sign or a bad one, she kept talking.

"I didn't expect this and I'm not saying this with any expectations. But you've given me something I've never had. Because of you, I feel beautiful. Because of you I'm going to find my sister." She pressed a kiss to his lips, lingered when he took it over and turned a simple kiss into a sensual banquet that heated every part of her.

"You've no idea," he murmured, pressing his forehead to hers, "how much hearing you say that means to me."

"Really?"

"A man would be foolish not to want you to love him." He smiled, kissed her again. "I'm no fool."

She laughed. "No, you aren't. You're handsome and stubborn"—she giggled when he scowled at that—"and a wonderful man. Whatever happens, Blake, I've no regrets."

His eyes took on an edge of steel. "I should hope not or it'll make the next twenty years damn uncomfortable."

Her stomach, already jittery, quivered. "W-what?"

His smile came slow and sure. "I love you, Alicia, and as you've already admitted to feeling the same, then I think we have a better beginning than most."

Blake watched Alicia, felt rather smug about the fact that she couldn't seem to find any words.

"Blake, man, surely you can do better than that," Vincent said as he strolled closer. "After all, it isn't every day a woman is proposed to."

Blake sighed, bowed his head. When he'd come to the conclusion last night that he wanted Alicia as his wife, he hadn't envisioned Nate and Vincent around when he asked her.

"Much as it pains me to say it, Vincent's right, Blake," Nate said. "A woman should be wooed and have all sorts of fancy words bestowed upon her. Alicia, darling, if you allow me, I could do so much better than this pathetic display."

Alicia giggled, and Blake turned to his friends—though that distinction didn't apply at the moment—while keeping an arm across Alicia's back.

"Don't you two have work to do?"

"I don't, do you?" Vincent asked Nate.

Nate shrugged. "Can't think of anything."

Neither man moved. They simply stood there expectantly, arms crossed and smiles on their faces as though they had every right to witness this moment.

"We're approaching port, I know there's work to be done," Blake reminded them.

"We've gotten as close as we can. The anchor's been dropped." Vincent grinned at Nate. "The man's been too distracted to notice we've arrived at our destination."

"Well, Alicia *is* quite a distraction. I know she's turned my attention a time or two."

Blake hissed. "I'll shoot them, one day I'll shoot them," he vowed.

"They love you, Blake."

"It's what's kept them alive," he muttered, then he deliberately pushed them from his mind.

"Alicia, you're brave and strong and loyal. You say what's on your mind, and you fight for what's in your heart. I admire you." His voice lowered. "I want you in my bed, on my ship, and in my life. Will you marry me?"

Alicia's eyes filled with tears as surely as her heart filled with love. They'd found each other through a twist of fate, and she was thrilled that good had come from tragedy. That Jacob would finally have his wish. She and Blake would go home and run the shop together. Nothing could be more perfect.

"I'd be honored to be your wife," she agreed before Blake swept her off her feet and kissed her soundly.

When he set her down again and she was able to hear through the desire that filled her head, she heard Nate's applause and Vincent's cheers. Her soon-to-be husband received pats on the back before she was once again swept off the deck.

"That's my wife," Blake warned when Nate deliberately held her a little longer.

"Not yet, she's not. And if she has any sense, she'll change her mind and come to see I'd be the better choice." Still, after a kiss on the cheek, Nate set her down. "I'm happy for you, darling," he whispered into her ear, for no other reason than he knew it would irritate Blake.

"Thank you," she said, taking in the three men around her. She loved them all, she realized.

A movement caught her eye and she saw Lewis watching them. It was like a cold splash down her back and she shuddered.

"What is it?" Blake asked, taking her hand.

"I don't like him," she said and was further disconcerted when Lewis kept staring. Usually when she caught him looking, he immediately pretended to be doing something else. It unsettled her that he was no longer hiding the fact that he was watching her.

"You don't have to worry about him, sunshine. He's been dismissed of his duties. He won't be coming back with us."

"Good," she acknowledged and turned to the beach that beckoned off the starboard side. Though the uneasy feeling remained between her shoulders, she tried her best to ignore it. After all, she thought, hands digging into the gunwale as her eyes raked the beach where her sister might even now be walking, she had more important things to think about.

There it is," Alicia whispered. She stopped dead, her shoes sinking into the sand. Her heart thudded louder than the hammering coming from the shell of the boat being built. Wood of different lengths was spread about the sand and the various tools were lined up neatly within easy reach of the man who was hard at work.

It hadn't taken more than two people to find someone who knew where Sam and Luke's ship building was located. If those people's excessive chatter was any indication, the whole island was proud as parents to have them there. Now, here they were, at the far end of the harbor where there was much less activity, watching a man with golden hair hammer a board over the skeleton of the hull.

"Do you suppose that's Luke?" Alicia asked.

From behind, Blake wrapped his arms around her. His chuckle filled her ear. "You're not going to find out waiting back here, are you?"

Alicia inhaled deeply. The air was rich with a mixture of salty sea and freshly cut wood. The humidity was heavy, and Alicia was glad she'd pulled her hair back into a simple braid as it allowed the breeze from the water to cool her heated neck. She dried her hands on her skirt.

"All right, then. Let's find out." Blake moved in beside her and she clasped his hand.

The man must have been used to being watched because he didn't stop his work when Alicia and Blake stepped up. He did, however, cast them a glance before taking another curved board and setting it into place. Over the thudding of the hammer, Alicia studied this stranger. His hair was long and grazed his shoulders. Though he wore a shirt, it was unbuttoned and revealed both golden skin and at least six gold chains around his neck. Combined with the black patch over his left eye and a cut of mustache over his lip, Alicia was certain she was looking at Luke Bradley. If anyone ever looked like a pirate, to her eye it was this man.

"Luke Bradley?" she asked when he'd finished with the plank.

He lowered the hammer, looked at her a little closer this time.

"Maybe," he answered, stepping to the front of his ship and kneeling. He angled his head, checked his lines. Satisfied it looked good, he went for another board.

"I'm looking for Samantha Fine. I mean, Bradley, I guess." Alicia fidgeted when he dropped the hammer and it sank silently into the blanched sand.

His right eye narrowed. "Why?"

"I'd rather tell her myself," Alicia answered. "It's a long story."

"She's come from Port Royal to find her," Blake added.

He turned his attention to Blake. "And who in blazes are you?"

Blake raised his chin. "Blake Merritt."

He shrugged. "Never heard of you."

"That's what I said when I heard your name."

"No need to be insulting," the man grumbled.

"Please, if you can just tell me where Sam is. I've waited a long time for this."

His spine stiffened. He took a step toward them, not a speck of warmth in his gaze. "Sam? Who are you and what do you want with her?"

Blake moved in front of Alicia. "We only want to talk to Samantha."

Luke had to look up to meet Blake's gaze, but Blake was impressed by the determination he saw there. This wasn't a man easily cowed. But then, a notorious pirate wouldn't be.

"Are you in the market for a ship?"

"No, we're—"

"Then tell me what you're after."

Alicia stepped around Blake. "This is going to come as a huge shock to Sam. I think it's best if I tell her."

He scowled. "What in blazes are you talking about?"

"Luke?"

Alicia spun around at the sound. Her heart jumped to her throat, preventing her from saying anything. She may not have seen Sam in years, but her memory was fresh. Though Sam had turned into a beautiful woman, there was enough of the girl she used to be for Alicia to recognize.

Luke strode to Sam, pulled her close to his side while

Alicia's eyes feasted on her sister. Sam's hair was long and flowed around her shoulders. It was darker than Alicia's, but with the sun reflecting off it, she could see several strands that were the same color as her own. Questions swirled in Sam's eyes as they darted from Luke to Alicia and Blake.

"Hello?" she said.

Sam's smile was friendly and familiar and it knocked Alicia's breath from her chest. Her legs shook and she grasped Blake for support. Oh, God, it really *was* her!

"I'm Blake Merritt and this . . ." He turned to Alicia. "Sunshine?"

Alicia nodded, licked her dry lips. She placed a hand to her racing heart. While Luke scowled, Sam waited patiently. If she was curious, she wasn't unfriendly about it the way her husband was. The waves of mistrust rolling off Luke were as real as the waves that rolled into the beach.

Letting go of Blake's hand, Alicia took a shaky step toward Sam.

"This will come as a shock. I don't know how else to say it but to simply tell you outright. It's me, Sam. Alicia."

Sam took a step back. Her face lost all its warmth and color. Her eyes turned icy.

"I don't know how you came to learn of my sister, but that's a cruel thing to say. She died years ago."

"No, Sam. I didn't. I made it to Port Royal. Our mother swam me to shore."

"Liar," Sam said waspishly. "My mother never made it off the ship. Neither did my sister."

Alicia reached for Sam, but her sister flinched and stepped out of range. The action tore Alicia's heart. Her hand fell to her side. Blake lay his hand on her shoulder and she drew strength from that. She had to remember that for Sam this was an impossibility. Sam had no reason to believe her sister had survived and it only made sense that she didn't believe the truth the first time she heard it.

"We were in the bilges while the pirates attacked. We stayed until they'd looted the ship and were gone."

Tears shone in Sam's eyes. "Nobody else survived. I know because I was in the water and went back after the pirates had left. There was nobody alive."

Alicia gasped. "That was you?" Her own eyes pricked with tears. "When we thought it was safe to come up, we heard footsteps and voices so we remained below." Her voice cracked. "If we'd gone up, we wouldn't have wasted all these years." She turned to Blake. "It was her. She was there and we didn't even know it."

"Luv?" Luke asked Sam. "Is it possible?"

"I—I don't know. I didn't think so, but she does have similar features."

"Look," Blake interrupted, "there must be something she can tell you about your past that nobody else would know."

Alicia nodded, wiped her tears with her palms.

"Our father was Edward, our mother was Helen. We left England when I was twelve and you were seventeen." Alicia scrambled for a memory that would prove beyond a doubt who she was, something that wouldn't be known or couldn't be learned from anyone else. Her sister was so close, and all she wanted was to hold her and know they'd never be separated again. She had to rid Samantha of any doubts.

"Remember that boy you liked, Adam? Before we left England, you wanted to say good-bye, and I lied to Mother and Father and told them you were sick and couldn't come down to dinner. You promised if I lied for you, you'd let me—"

"Have my dessert for an entire week," Sam said, her face crumbling. "Alicia, it really is you?"

"Yes," Alicia sobbed, "it's me."

They raced for each other, arms wrapped tightly around shaking shoulders, and held on.

"I thought you'd died," Sam cried and her arms held Alicia like a vise. For a time they simply clung to each other, then Sam pulled back and pressed her palms to Alicia's cheeks, tenderly traced the scar. She ran them over her arms as though to convince herself Alicia was real.

"I never dreamed it was possible." She turned to Luke, her smile as wide as the beach. "This is my sister."

Luke grinned. "Yes, luv, I see that."

Alicia laughed, then Sam pulled her back. Her voice broke again. "My baby sister, I've missed you."

"I missed you, too, Sam. We've lost so much time."

Sam sniffled. "Then we won't waste another moment. Let's go home. I can make a nice dinner." She grinned. "We have so much to talk about."

"Would that include your husband?" Alicia asked, laughing.

"Oh!" Sam blushed. "I didn't introduce you. Alicia, my husband, Luke Bradley. Luke, this is my sister!"

Luke's smile was humorous but Alicia didn't miss the love in his gaze as he looked at his wife. "It's good to meet you," he said to Alicia.

Sam turned to Blake. "And is this . . . ? Oh, are you married as well?" Sam's eyes, which hadn't a chance to dry, once again spilled over. "I missed your wedding."

"It's good to meet you, Samantha. My name is Blake Merritt," he said, coming to stand near Alicia. He grasped her right hand as Sam still held claim to the other. "You didn't miss the wedding. She only accepted my proposal today."

Alicia shoved him with her shoulder. "He only asked me today."

"We haven't missed it?" Sam's chin trembled. "I'll get to see you married."

Emotion clogged Alicia's throat. She'd given up hope of ever getting married, and now here she was. Not only was she going to marry a wonderful man, the sister she'd lost so long ago would be there. She sniffled. "Yes, you will. But in the meantime, can we go somewhere, where we can talk? I want to know everything I've missed."

"Oh, yes," Sam agreed, "let's do that. Our home is just over that small rise. Luke, Blake, you'll join us?"

"You go, luv. We'll catch up in a while." He stepped to Sam, wrapped an arm around her waist, and kissed her thoroughly. "That'll hold me," he grinned when he released his wife. Turning to Blake, he asked, "You good with a hammer?"

"I am."

Luke pulled it from the sand, tossed it to Blake.

"Good. I can use an extra pair of hands."

Sam's house was beautiful. It wasn't exceptionally large with its two bedrooms upstairs and a parlor and kitchen downstairs, but it was welcoming. Large windows in the parlor took advantage of the stunning view. Standing in the kitchen while Sam fixed some sweet tea, Alicia marveled at the way the transparent green water of the bay turned darker and darker blue as it made its way farther out to sea. The sand was amazingly white, and Alicia knew before the day was out, she'd be digging her toes in it.

"It suits you," Alicia said, once again looking at her sister. "This house, the location."

Squawk. "Sam's house. Sam's house."

Alicia giggled. The parrot had already greeted her upon her arrival with a low whistle that had flustered her.

Sam turned from the counter, smiled. "I'm working on his language. Carracks used to be a very well-spoken bird until Luke decided to teach him some new phrases."

Squawk. "Luke's in charge. Luke's in charge."

"See what I mean?"

As though the parrot knew he'd said the wrong thing, he turned on his perch and buried his red head in his yellow and crimson feathers.

"And he has a nasty habit of repeating things."

Smiling, Sam passed Alicia a glass of tea, then sat at the wooden table. She looked over Alicia's shoulder to the water outside.

"I wasn't sure, after the attack and then the plantation, that I'd ever find someplace where I'd feel whole, where I'd belong." Her eyes fell to the glass that she turned within her hands. "I always tried to believe life would be good again, but there were times when that faith was hard to come by."

"I know you escaped the plantation. What happened?"

Sam lifted her head and Alicia was taken aback by the pain that clouded her sister's eyes. "We had nothing when we landed on the beach. When Oliver Grant found us and offered medical help as well as lodging and work, it was more than we'd dared hope for."

Alicia gasped. "I forgot! I heard Joe and Willy also survived. Are they here?"

Sam clutched Alicia's hand to keep her from launching out of her chair in search of more family.

"No. Willy stayed in Barbados. He's working there. Joe

stayed with me. He's out now with Aidan fetching supplies for Luke. I expect them for dinner."

"Who's Aidan?" She pressed a hand to her heart. "Is that your son? Do I have a nephew?"

The blood drained from Sam's face, leaving her cheeks as white as the sand outside. "I don't have any children."

Her voice trembled and Alicia could see it was costing her to keep her emotions under control.

"I'm sorry, Sam. I didn't mean to make you sad."

"No, it's all right. I try not to think about it, but it's impossible not to." She smiled, but it didn't reach her eyes. "I can't conceive, Alicia. I've tried everything I can think of, more rest, no spirits, not getting out of bed for days after making love, nothing works. But that's a discussion for another time." She drew in a choppy breath. "I didn't think there was a person alive as vile as the captain of the pirate ship that attacked us, but I was wrong. Oliver Grant was."

Alicia pushed aside her tea, took both her sister's hands in her own. Sam gave her a watery smile.

"He tortured people, Alicia, and not only adults. He used food as leverage, whipped his slaves, regardless of their age, and raped the women." Her gaze fell to the table. "I was one of them."

"Oh, Sam," Alicia gasped, her stomach in a tight knot. "I'm so sorry."

"I vowed after he did that I'd make him pay, and the next time he came for me, I was ready."

"I'd have killed him," Alicia said, shuddering at what her sister went through.

"I thought I had. I hit him with a hammer. He was bleeding and not moving when I ran. Before I left, I freed as many of his slaves as I could. Then I took Joe, Willy, and

Aidan—he was one of the children that had been abused—and we took Grant's ship."

"So Grant died that night?"

"Not then, not as I thought. He followed me for years and finally caught me in Barbados. He tried to hurt me again but Luke came in time. Grant shot Luke, but before Grant could touch me any further, his heart stopped and he died." Her eyes met Alicia's and in them were both regret and conviction. "I'm not sorry he's dead."

"Nor should you be, but I can see it weighs on you."

Sam sighed. "It does. I know it shouldn't, but I can't help how I feel. I wasted four years trying to get revenge for our family and all the time Grant was doing the same to find me." She shrugged. "So much time and energy lost."

"Captain said Luke killed the pirate that killed our family?"

"He did. I tried to avenge them, but when the time came and I had Dervish in my sights, Luke made me see that killing Dervish wouldn't bring back our family. So I turned my back. Unfortunately Dervish was armed and would've killed me had Luke not shot him first."

"He saved you twice," Alicia realized. If she hadn't already liked Luke for making her sister happy, she would for knowing he'd saved her sister's life.

"Luke saved me in every way that matters. He's my life. Well," she amended, wiping a lone tear, and patting Alicia's hand, "he's most of it. I still can't believe you're alive. It seems like a dream."

Alicia had to blink away her own tears, but the guilt that pressed against her heart wasn't so easily dispersed.

"God, Sam, I'm so sorry."

"For what?"

"For being a fool. I only remembered our past yesterday. Up until then I thought I was Alicia Davidson from Port Royal, daughter of a blacksmith."

Sam gasped. "You lost your memory?"

Alicia explained about the scar and how she'd been told she'd fallen as a child. She told of the letters she found that led her to search for Sam and the battle that brought the memories back.

"I was feeling sorry for myself because I'd lost two sets of parents. I felt cheated out of time with both of them, and with you. But now I see how lucky I was. I was loved and cared for. I had food and water, shelter and family, even if they weren't my own. And all along you were fighting a daily battle just to survive. God," she said, pushing up from the table, "I can't believe I was so selfish."

Sam's chair scraped the floor. She grabbed Alicia by the arms and turned her from the window.

"Don't ever feel guilty for having had the Davidsons. I'm glad you didn't suffer through what I did and I would never hold that against you. I wouldn't have wanted anything for you but what you had. I didn't have a choice with what Grant did to me, but I can't regret it all as it brought me Luke."

"He's very taken with you."

The sadness faded from Sam's face. Her smile sparkled as bright as her eyes. "Yes, he is. And I'm pleased to say I feel the same about him. He makes me very happy."

"I see that. I'm happy for you, Sam."

Her eyebrows rose. "And Blake?"

Alicia grinned. "It seems too soon to feel what I do, but I love him, Sam. He's the man I want."

Sam spun Alicia in her arms. "We need a party. We can have everyone over and celebrate—"

"Celebrate what?" Joe asked, lumbering into the kitchen, bringing with him the smell of sea air. A young man with blond hair followed beside him.

Squawk. "Aidan bring food. Aidan bring food."

"Joe!" Alicia called and ran, throwing herself against his chest. His girth was wide and her fingertips barely touched at his back.

"Do I know ye, lass?" he asked. The fact that he didn't recognize her didn't stop him from patting her awkwardly on the shoulder.

Alicia laughed, drew back. She studied the man she'd known for the first twelve years of her life. He was older, the lines beside his eyes and mouth were more deeply gouged by the weather, but the familiar cigar smoke clung to him the way it always had. Neither the warmth in his gaze nor the gentleness of his touch had changed with time.

"It's me, Joe. Alicia."

His eyebrows furrowed. "Alicia who?"

"Joe," Sam said, coming to stand beside them. "Alicia survived that night. We weren't the only ones who made it to Port Royal."

Unlike Sam, Joe didn't need convincing. His eyes instantly filled and tears ran unabashedly down his ruddy cheeks. He yanked her back into his arms and clung hard enough to squeeze the breath from Alicia's lungs.

"Ah, lass." He sobbed openly while fat drops fell on her head. "I've missed ye. We all thought ye'd died."

He rocked her like a baby and together they wept. It was amazing, Alicia realized, just how many tears a body could produce. Finally he eased his grip and stepped back.

"Yer all grown, lass. Last time I saw ye, ye were about the same age as our Aidan."

At the mention of the boy, Sam pulled him from the

cage where he was feeding the bird some nuts and brought him closer. Though she and Aidan were the same height, she absently combed his hair with her fingers. His cheeks flamed but he didn't stop the action.

"Alicia, this is Aidan. Aidan, this is my sister, Alicia."

He watched her carefully, saying nothing. His brown eyes were solemn and looked far too old for a boy who, despite approaching manhood, had a cap of windblown blond hair and holes in the knees of his trousers.

"Aidan," Sam prodded, placing a hand on his shoulder.

"Pleased to meet you," he mumbled.

Sam gave him a playful shove. "You can go until supper. Maybe that stray dog will be down at the beach."

His head shot up. "Can I have him?"

Squawk. "No bloody dog. No bloody dog."

Sam glared at Carracks but softened her gaze when she met Aidan's. "The answer hasn't changed from the last twenty times you asked me. It's enough you bring him food. The mutt lives here half the time as it is."

"Luke gives me the food," Aidan argued.

Squawk. "Luke's innocent. Luke's innocent."

"I am so," Luke said, strolling in with Blake behind him. He walked to Aidan, wrapped an arm loosely around his throat. "Quit getting me into trouble, boy, or it's the dungeon for you."

"You'd have to catch me first," Aidan taunted.

"Don't think I can't," Luke said, removing his arm, though he left his hand on the boy's shoulder. "I only let you win those last few races."

"Ha!" Aidan said, his eyes dancing. "You're just too old to catch me."

"Old, is it?" Luke growled. The boy ducked away and went to stand by Joe.

"Don't come lookin' to me, boy. I won't be savin' ye."

Since he was closer to her now, Alicia caught his attention and said, "I'm happy to meet you, Aidan. We have quite a family, don't we?"

She took Blake's hand in hers and felt the warmth from him wash over her. Aidan's eyes bounced over everyone in the room. His smile mirrored Alicia's.

"Yeah," he said. "I guess we do."

Fifteen

Blake stepped through the door, found Alicia up to her naked shoulders in suds, and promptly dropped the bag he'd been holding. It landed on the floor with a plop. Alicia, seeing who it was, lowered the arms she'd brought up to shield herself and leaned back against the rim of the bathtub.

Bubbles lapped over the mounds of her breasts. Blake's blood moved south and left him a little dizzy.

"Could you shut the door, you're letting in a draft."

He tried to swallow, succeeded on the third attempt, and closed the door with a kick of his boot. Because he'd never seen anything as arousing as Alicia naked in a tub of water, he couldn't take his eyes off her.

"Blake?"

"Mmm?"

"Are you all right?"

"I'll let you know when my brain starts working again."

The flush created by the warm water crept up into

her face. Blake grinned, completely charmed by her. He crouched at the side of the tub, trailed a finger over her shoulder and across the back of her bare neck. A few pieces of golden silk that had escaped the twist she had created to keep her hair dry grazed his knuckles.

"Is there room in there for me?"

Even as her eyes widened, her lips curved. "I don't think so. Besides, what would Luke and Sam say if they knew you were here with me?"

"Sam's busy with Aidan and his lessons. As for Luke, who do you think told me where you were?"

Alicia's mouth dropped open. "Luke told you to come while I was bathing?"

Blake's fingers slid down her arm, swirled in the water. The bubbles dissipated, enabling him to see her breasts and the reaction his nearness was creating. It created an equally strong response in him. Leaning in, surrounded by the tang of oranges, he kissed the sensitive area at the side of her neck.

"He seemed to think the fact that you were naked would interest me. He was right."

Sighing, she tilted her head. Blake braced his hands on either side of the tub and swept in. He kissed the base of her neck where her heart pounded; he nibbled his way along her jaw; he whispered in her ear what he wanted to do to her while at the same time he plunged his arm in the water and cupped her breast. Alicia jolted and a surge of water rose up and over the lip of the tub, splashing Blake. He barely gave it a thought as he was intent on the pleasure that bloomed over Alicia's face when he moved his hand between her legs.

"Blake," she sighed.

He changed his position and her eyes fluttered closed.

He didn't stop until Alicia had collapsed against the tub. Through it all, Blake watched her and marveled at how much it seduced him to see her lost in passion. He wanted to see it again.

Standing, he took off his drenched shirt, kicked off his boots, and peeled his pants off. Alicia's eyes shot open.

"Blake—"

"Just lean forward. I'll sit behind you."

She did as he asked, and when he sat down, water over-flowed and sloshed to the floor. Blake drew her against his chest, filled his hands with her breasts. Despite the fact that his knees poked out of the water, there wasn't a place on earth that he'd rather be.

"Are you sure you don't want to come back to the ship tonight?"

"It's not that I don't want to," Alicia explained. "But Sam went to the trouble to prepare the room for me."

"And?"

She took a deep breath. "And as silly as it sounds, I sim-ply want to be close to her." She arched her neck to look at him. "Does that make any sense?"

"It does, but that doesn't mean I won't miss having you in my arms."

He lowered his head and kissed her. His thoughts scat-tered like ashes in the wind when her mouth responded with undiluted passion. He'd been ready for her since he'd walked into the room, and having her backside pressed against him, her mouth tantalizing his, sent a lightning strike of lust to his loins.

"You could stay," she whispered. Boldly she slid her arm between them and took him in her hand.

Blake grasped her by the waist and turned her until she straddled him. Her breasts were out of the water now and his eyes drank their fill. She was rosy everywhere. He tweaked her nipples, murmured his appreciation when they hardened between his fingers.

He brought his gaze to hers, felt an overwhelming sense of possession at seeing her like that, with her eyes locked onto his, her hands on his shoulders. Her smile was sweet and the dimples in her cheeks were endearing. He noticed the scar in passing, not because it drew from her loveliness, but because it was a part of her.

Leaning forward, he suckled her, felt her body bow in his hands. With his hands on her hips, he eased her onto him, holding his breath until he was completely within her. He held the position as long as he could stand, loving the connection he felt when they were joined, the sense of rightness.

As he began to move and Alicia leaned forward to accept his thrusts, he had but one logical thought.

If they were to live on the ship, he was going to have to buy a bigger bathtub.

She's not the *Freedom*, but she comes in a close second," Luke said, slapping a hand to the newly repaired mast.

Blake scoffed. "The *Blue Rose* will take your *Freedom* any day."

"You know," Luke drawled, leaning negligently against the gunwale, the sun glinting off his chains, "it's a fine ship. Don't you think you could've managed a more fitting name?"

"Such as *Freedom*? That's not very original," Blake reminded him.

Luke shrugged. "Wasn't my choice, it was a name Samantha chose. Besides, she's the best ship we have."

"You have more than one sloop in your bay. What makes her your favorite?"

Squinting, Luke looked to the beach and to the two women sitting there, their toes dug into the sand. Blake didn't know Samantha and Luke's story, but he knew from the four days they'd been in St. Kitts that there wasn't anything Luke wouldn't do for his wife.

"The *Freedom* is Samantha's ship. It's how we met. She's our flagship and doesn't have an equal."

"You didn't build it?" Vincent asked.

"No," Luke answered, his eyes shining with affection, "but that doesn't make her less valuable to us."

"Is she for sale, then?" Nate asked.

They were all at the gunwale—Nate, Vincent, Blake, Joe, Luke, and Aidan. It had taken four solid days of work and their combined efforts to repair the *Blue Rose*.

"Not enough money in the Caribbean for that, mate."

"Well, we do have a hold full of treasure," Vincent added.

Luke scoffed. "I've seen my fair share."

"Not like this one," Vincent said. "Must beat any treasure you ever found."

Luke looked insulted. "I'll have you know there was no better pirate than myself. Even," he added with a pointed look at Blake, "if some of you have never heard of me."

"I don't know about that," Nate added lazily. "Blake here's a pretty fine pirate."

"I'm not a pirate," he argued.

"What's the matter with being a pirate?" Luke asked. "It's nothing to be ashamed of."

Blake had gotten to know Luke these last few days, and everything he'd seen of Luke so far, he'd not only liked but he'd respected. Still he knew, and what had happened to

Alicia's parents was a prime example, that not all pirates had Luke's disposition. But he didn't want to offend his future brother-in-law either.

"I'm sure you were a fine pirate," he said.

"Sam Steele was better," Aidan chimed in.

Joe roared, his belly shaking and his blue eyes glinting. "Ye got that right, me boy."

"He does not," Luke frowned. "I was every bit as successful as Steele."

"Far as I know, Steele was never captured and thrown in prison," Nate said.

"Bloody hell." Luke turned to Joe. "Is there anything you didn't tell them?"

"Well, I didn't tell 'em about the time ye were shot in the arse."

Blake choked. "Were you really?"

"Oh, shut it, the lot of you." Luke scowled at Joe, but the big man's answer was to grin in return.

"Tomorrow," Luke said to Blake. "The *Freedom* against the *Blue Rose*. We'll see which ship is faster."

Blake grinned. "Suits me. What's the wager?"

Luke mulled it over. "If you win, you don't owe me for the fancy new wheel we put in."

Blake whistled, looked over at the item in question. He'd been awed when Luke had offered him one of the key pieces that made a Bradley ship recognizable. The wheel wasn't as large as most, but it was made of mahogany and was polished to a smooth shine. There wasn't another piece on deck that was the same reddish brown and yet it suited the *Blue Rose*. Blake was honored to have it and he'd made his appreciation clear.

"That's a steep wager. What if I lose?"

"You cook the meat for the party tomorrow night. I

bloody hate that job, and," Luke added, sneering, "you forget you ever heard I was shot in the backside."

Blake? Someone's here to see you," Nate called down the hatch the following morning.

Before Blake could answer, the hem of a blue dress came into view. His stomach tightened, something he was slowly getting used to when he saw or thought of Alicia. Not having had a chance to be intimate with her in the last few days had only heightened his awareness of her.

"Couldn't stay away any longer?" he asked, turning to the bed where he'd left his shirt.

"As a matter of fact, I couldn't," Samantha said.

Blake spun around, his face burning. He jammed his arms into his shirt and fumbled with the buttons.

"Sorry. I thought you were Alicia."

Samantha smiled. "She's with Aidan. Since he learned she's a blacksmith, he's been nattering her with questions."

"He's very bright. He has an inquiring mind."

"That he has. Some days he gives me a headache with all his questions. Usually it's about ships and sailing as Aidan is ravenous when it comes to the sea, but he's taken a very serious interest in blacksmithing." She smiled. "I'm sure Alicia's head will be pounding by the time they're through."

"It's nothing she can't handle," Blake assured her.

"I agree. After all, she is a blacksmith." Samantha shook her head. "I must admit I have a hard time imagining my little sister doing such work, but it seems to agree with her. Her face shines when she mentions it."

"She was worried, you know, about what your reaction would be to that. She was scared you'd think less of her."

Samantha frowned, her gaze hardened. "Of course I wouldn't. And not only because she's my sister, but because no person should be judged by anything less than who they are at heart."

He smiled. Determination was obviously a fine trait. "I just wanted you to know, your acceptance meant a lot to her."

Blake moved to the table, offered Samantha a chair. When she'd sat, he took his own seat.

"You do know you'll be losing the race today?" she asked, grinning.

Blake laughed. "Sure of your ship, are you?"

"And sure of Luke." She turned serious. "What I'm not sure of is you."

"Oh?"

Samantha rested her arms on the table, linked her fingers. "I realize this sounds strange coming from me, but as Alicia's sister, and the last of her family, I feel it's my duty to ask what your intentions are toward her."

Blake frowned. "You know I've asked her to be my wife."

"I do. But you've only known each other a short time. You're sure of your feelings?"

Leaning forward, Blake matched her pose. "I've never been more sure. I don't take marriage lightly, Samantha. I've never asked another woman to be my wife and I don't see anyone in my future but your sister."

"I'm glad. I don't want to see her hurt, Blake."

"Then let me assure you that I have no intention of hurting her. I know how special she is."

"Any chance you'll live in St. Kitts?"

Blake shook his head. "My ship is my home. I can't be a privateer on land."

"I was afraid of that." She bit her lip, sucked in a deep breath. "Can you promise me you'll come often? I can't bear not to see her after I've only gotten her back."

Reaching, he squeezed the hand of the woman he'd be proud to call family. "Of course we will. As often as we can."

Samantha sniffled, then turned to Blake with a cheeky glint in her eye.

"As much as I appreciate your promise, it doesn't change today's outcome. My ship's the fastest."

Laughing, Blake stood. "And just because you're to be my sister-in-law doesn't mean I'll let your ship win."

"I look forward to tasting your cooking later," she said, smiling.

"And I look forward to not paying my bill," he countered.

The sky was vivid blue. A gusting breeze blew in off the water, shoving at the gulls that scratched along the beach looking for whatever the outgoing tide had left behind.

Shading her eyes against the glaring reflection of the sun, Alicia grinned as the two ships drew alongside each other.

"They're like a bunch of children on Christmas morning," she said, grinning at her sister.

Sam nodded, pushed back her hair when the wind tossed it. "Luke was awake before the sun this morning. He and Aidan couldn't get out of the house fast enough."

"And Joe?"

Sam laughed. "He was fit to be tied when he woke and found out the other two had left without him. He charged out of the house without his breakfast and barely remembered to put his boots on."

Alicia's heart suddenly swelled and she grabbed Sam.

"What is it? What's wrong?"

"Nothing." Alicia wiped a teary eye. "I'm just so happy. We have a wonderful family. It's all such a miracle, isn't it?"

Sam hugged her close. "I'm thankful every day. I'll miss you when you go."

"We'll visit each other often. Oh, look," she said, squeezing Sam's hand. "They're about to start."

The ships were parallel, sails hung limply against the masts. A cannon blasted off the *Blue Rose*, smoke plumed in the air, and men scrambled about the decks. White sheets of canvas popped open and the ships took flight.

"He's leading, he's leading!" Alicia cheered, filled with pride at the sight of the *Blue Rose* out in front.

"It's not over yet."

They lost sight of the ships when they sailed around a small island. Alicia and Sam waited with bated breath until the billowing sails came back into view.

"It's ours!" Sam yelled, seeing the *Freedom* leading. She jumped up and down, yelling for Luke.

Blake wasn't far behind. Alicia's screams matched Sam's, drawing the attention of a few children who were out playing on the sand with the stray dog. They recognized Luke's ship pulling closer to shore and joined Sam's chorus of "Hurry, Luke!" The dog barked his approval.

In the end it was close, but the *Freedom* won by half its length. After the ships were anchored, Aidan ran off to boast to all his friends, and Joe, Nate, and Vincent became involved in boisterous recounts of the race. Sam ran to Luke and congratulated him with a kiss.

"It was close," Alicia said, wrapping her arms around Blake.

"It was fun," Blake exclaimed, stunning Alicia by the

excitement that radiated in his voice and shone in his eyes. Since she'd met Blake, she'd never seen him so carefree. Captain was right—Blake needed more fun in his life.

Luke stepped over, slapped Blake on the back.

"That's a fine ship you have. The wheel is yours, mate, my gift. But you're still cooking."

"Did I forget to mention I've a hold full of treasure?"

Luke laughed, pulled Sam close. "Not a bloody chance. I plan on sitting down and enjoying some rum while you look after roasting that pig."

"Speaking of the party," Sam said, "Alicia, we should get back, there's a lot left to do."

As they made their way to Sam's, she listed the chores yet to be accomplished.

"Sam, it's a small party. You don't need to fuss this much."

"Well, it wouldn't be so small if you'd let me invite more people," she reminded Alicia as they stepped onto the path that wound its way to the back of Sam's house.

"This is about family, about being together again. We don't need the entire village to celebrate that."

Sam stopped, turned. "I just want to tell the world you're here."

Alicia smiled, touched at her sister's words. "It's been a journey, hasn't it?"

"Yes, it has," Sam agreed, continuing on the path. The bold red and orange flowers that lined the walk scented the humid air. "But at least we can be thankful it's o—"

She stopped dead and Alicia bumped into her. "What is it?" Alicia asked, stepping beside Sam.

A cutlass protruded from the wooden door. Attached to its hilt was a rolled piece of parchment. Alicia looked around but saw nothing except palm fronds, ferns, and a splattering of color from the array of flowers Sam had planted. Still she had a cold feeling along her neck, like they were being watched.

"Should we wait for—"

"No, I'll deal with it," Sam answered.

Alicia watched as Sam removed the paper, her hands steady.

Over Sam's shoulder, Alicia read the words.

You've made quite a life for yourself, it's almost ordinary now. For someone as notable as you, it must have taken getting used to. Yet here you are, safely ensconced in St. Kitts with a family, a business, and a newly found sister. And nobody is the wiser. Well, almost nobody. Are you still feeling unidentifiable . . . Sam?

Sixteen

Sam crumpled the paper in her hand. She yanked the cutlass out, grabbed Alicia by the wrist, and wrenched open the door, banging it closed behind her. Once inside, she slammed both the letter and the cutlass onto the table and paced the floor, which had been scrubbed to a shine yesterday.

Squawk. "Don't slam the door. Don't slam the door."

"Who would do something like that?" Alicia asked, ignoring the parrot that bobbed on its perch.

"I don't know."

"What does it mean?"

"It can't be. It's not possible," Sam muttered, still pacing from the back door to the hallway that led to the parlor.

"What's not possible?"

Sam stopped, jammed her hands on her hips. Her steely gaze locked on to the door. "Dammit. Luke's not going to be happy about this."

"About what?" Alicia demanded. She placed herself in front of Sam so she couldn't resume her pacing. "What's going on? Luke's not going to happy about what?"

Sam blinked, as though remembering she wasn't alone. The hard look in her eyes softened.

"Luke's very peculiar about his things. He won't like that gouge in the door."

Alicia shook her head, set her jaw. Her sister was angry, and though she was trying to hide it, she was also afraid. But Sam wasn't the only stubborn woman in the Fine family.

"I'm not so simple, Sam, that I can't see this has upset you."

"Well, of course it's upset me. Someone's playing a mean trick."

Alicia grabbed Sam's arms. "We lost a lot, Sam. We lost our parents, our home, and for a time each other. Let's not waste the gift we've been given by lying to each other now."

Sam met her determined gaze, then bowed her head. "I was hoping you'd never have to find out."

Alicia's heart sank. Was Luke in trouble? It stood to reason. He was, or had been, a pirate. Surely the man had enemies. Despite the fact that she'd come to like him, Alicia suddenly felt a bite of resentment toward her brother-in-law as it appeared that his past life was putting Sam, and the people she loved, at risk.

"What did Luke do?" Alicia asked.

Squawk. "Luke's innocent. Luke's innocent."

Sam lifted her head, frowned. "Luke? He didn't do anything. Why would you . . . oh," she finished with a nod of understanding. "Because Luke was a famous pirate, you think this has to do with him."

It was Alicia's turn to be confused. "It doesn't? Then why would someone threaten you?"

"When you were in Port Royal," Sam began, her gaze watching Alicia closely, "did you ever hear of a pirate named Sam Steele?"

"No, I spent most of my time at the blacksmith shop, as did my fath—as did Jacob. He wasn't a man to gossip and neither was Anna. Why? Was Steele also responsible for what happened to our parents?"

Sam shook her head. "No, that's impossible. Steele wasn't in the Caribbean at that time. Not until four years later."

A heavy ball of dread fell into Alicia's stomach and she hoped to God she was wrong. "Did Steele hurt you as well?"

Sam's smile was sad. "Yes, but it was my own doing. Alicia, *I* was Sam Steele, and for four years, while I chased Dervish, I sailed under a pirate flag."

Alicia's mouth worked but nothing came out, so stunned was she by this unexpected turn of events. Granted she hadn't seen her sister in years, but neither the girl she remembered nor the woman she'd come to know in the last five days seemed capable of piracy.

"And that," Sam said, walking with her shoulders slumped in defeat to the table where she sat heavily, "is why I never wanted you to know."

Alicia finally managed to engage her brain and took the chair nearest her sister, grabbed her hand. "I'm sorry, I don't know what to say. I look at you, settled and married, and I think back to the girl who ignored me in favor of sailing, and it seems so unlikely that in the middle of those two things, you became a pirate. You're not that cold, Sam."

"No, I'm not. And neither was Steele. Steele was as fair and honest as I could manage. I abstained from hurting as much as I could, though it wasn't always avoidable. And while I amassed a fair amount of treasure, it was never about that. I needed to be Steele to find Dervish. The minute Dervish died, so did Steele."

Looking at her sister a little closer, Alicia saw the iron of her will, the strength of her convictions. Though the picture of Sam wielding a pistol and engaging in battles didn't come to mind, it was easy to accept that she'd crewed a ship. She'd have been good at that.

"But you've been pardoned, what's the problem?"

"No, Alicia," Sam said, shaking her head. "Luke was pardoned. My success as Steele was because nobody, other than the crew, knew Steele was a woman. A different member of my crew took the identity each time we made port."

"So," Alicia began, understanding now, "there was no need for you to get a pardon."

"No. In fact, Luke and I decided it was better to simply let Steele go, let people assume he'd died or left the Caribbean. It was never an issue until now."

"And you think whoever stuck that cutlass in the door figured it out?"

Sam shrugged. "It seems that way to me. I just don't understand. Why now?"

Alicia pondered that, but nothing made sense. "You're sure that's what this note means? He doesn't actually call you Steele."

"No, but he called me Sam. You, Aidan, Joe, and our father are the only ones to ever call me that."

Alicia bit her lip. "Do you think it could be a member of the crew that sailed with you?"

"Maybe. But what would they stand to gain? Besides, as I said, I was fair. They all made profits from sailing with me. If they admitted to me being Steele, to having sailed under me, they'd also be guilty of piracy."

Alicia was trying to absorb everything she'd learned.

God, the things that had happened to their lives since leaving England. And though it wasn't the least bit funny, Alicia chuckled.

"What's so funny?" Sam asked.

"To think, I was worried about what you'd think of me being a blacksmith."

The tension around Sam's mouth eased and the fear left her gaze.

"We aren't exactly the pillars of proper society, are we?"

"No," Alicia said. "Definitely not. But," she added, going over to Sam and taking her hand, "this doesn't change anything. Considering what you went through, who am I to pass judgment?"

Sam's eyes softened. "Thank you for not turning your back on me."

"Oh, Sam, how could I? You're my sister."

The sound of the men approaching sifted through the door. Sam wiped at her eyes and clutched Alicia's hand.

"Don't say a word. Not to anybody, even Blake."

"But—"

"Nobody!" Sam repeated, panic creeping into her voice. "We've worked diligently to keep my identity a secret. Should the truth ever come out, I could hang."

Sam was right, and as much as Alicia hated the idea of keeping any secret from Blake, she would. For Sam, she'd do anything.

"You have my word."

The door opened with a flourish of voices and the smell of the outdoors. The men had smiles on their faces and were all talking over each other. Regardless of the outcome of the race, it was clear to see that beneath the teasing and volleying of insults to one another's manhood was the affection of friendship. With a spring in his step, Blake came to Alicia and embraced her.

"That's as sorry an excuse as I've ever heard," Luke said. "Slipped on the deck. You couldn't come up with something better than that?"

"It was slippery," Vincent contested. "Tell him, Nate."

Nate held up his large palms. "I'm trying to accept defeat gracefully, Vincent."

"Ah, don't worry about it, lad," Joe said, thumping Vincent on the back, which sent the dwarf stumbling forward. "Luke hasn't managed that task well himself either."

"That's because I never bloody lose," Luke answered.

"What about the time—"

"Aidan," Luke warned with a narrowing of his eye.

Squawk. "Aidan bring food. Aidan bring food."

The boy grinned, danced on his toes. "Right. Never mind." He strolled to the cage, passed the bird something to nibble on.

"'Tis shameful the way you teach the lad to lie."

"It's called diplomacy, Joe, and if the boy ever hopes to get himself married one day, it's best he learn that skill early. Right, luv?" Luke lifted Sam in his arms, kissed her soundly, then set her onto her feet. His gaze slid over the table. "Is there a problem?" He gestured to the cutlass.

Sam looked to Alicia, then to Luke. "No, we found it on the ground. Can I talk to you upstairs a moment?" she asked, grabbing the sword and note.

Luke studied his wife, and Alicia saw by the tightness around his mouth that he didn't believe Sam's story. Nodding, he took her hand and they disappeared through the doorway.

"Sunshine?" Blake asked, but she felt the eyes of everyone else in the room on her. "Is everything all right?"

His hands were on her shoulders, his gaze tender. She forced a smile, prayed it looked better than it felt.

"Yes, everything is as it should be." The words weren't an outright lie but they nonetheless left a bitter taste in Alicia's mouth.

This had better work, Lewis thought later that afternoon as he leaned against one of the palm trees that skirted the market. While he'd been encouraged by how quickly Samantha had ripped the cutlass out of the door earlier that morning, it wasn't enough. He needed a more concrete confirmation that she was Steele. There couldn't be any doubt, not if he was to going to convince her to give him her fortune. And Lewis had no intention of failing.

He watched the boy he'd paid press a note into Samantha's hand before cutting through the crowd. There was no chance of her following; the boy was gone by the time she opened the paper to read the words. Lewis leaned forward, his hands curled into fists. He smiled at the distress that had her reaching for her husband.

Luke took the note, read the words. Though Lewis couldn't hear him, he was able to read the curse on the pirate's lips. Luke's gaze ripped over the crowd, but it didn't worry Lewis. Luke had no idea whom he was looking for, and Samantha was too busy trying to pull her husband out of the marketplace.

From a safe distance, Lewis followed as they raced back to their house. He slowed as they approached their home, and he melted back into the small group of people making their way to the beach. He chose a piece of waterfront that wasn't cluttered with noise and people and sank into the sand to think.

It had been a frustrating few days, watching them repair the ship. He'd caught Blake making his way back to the house on occasion, but each time he stopped to ask him about the treasure, he was told the repairs came first and that Lewis would just have to wait for his money.

He thumped a fist in the sand, wished it was Blake's face. He had a stake in that treasure and the fact that Blake was being deliberately slow about sharing it was infuriating! Especially since he kept someone from the crew watching over it at all times, which kept Lewis from fetching it himself. When he could, he'd ensure Blake paid for that, among other things, but he had to remember that as much as his former captain enraged him, he wasn't Lewis's main target.

Bending his knees and digging his heels into the sand while a few gulls flew low over the frothing surf, Lewis planned his next move. It was clear by the firm hand Luke had kept on Samantha, and the way he'd growled at everyone to get out of his way, that he'd been concerned for his wife. And only people who held secrets had reason to worry.

She was Steele, he knew it. Her reaction was too strong. He couldn't prove it, not with the changes she'd made to his father's ship, but she didn't need to know that. Besides, he'd had time to think it all through while he'd been on his damn hands and knees scrubbing Blake's ship and he'd worked through all the possibilities. They may be pirates, he thought, but they weren't the only ones who could be ruthless.

And once Blake had given him his share of the treasure, they'd find out just how ruthless Lewis Grant could be.

You look tired," Sam said. She handed Alicia a cup of tea and came to sit beside her on the couch.

"Thank you," Alicia said, accepting the cup. "I am. I don't know why but I suddenly feel exhausted." She'd already unlaced her shoes and now she tucked her stockinged feet underneath her as she sipped her tea.

"I'm sorry." Sam rubbed Alicia's arm. "The race and the party were enough excitement for one day. The letters certainly didn't help."

"No, but having the men hover throughout the party was almost as unnerving. I felt as though I couldn't breathe with Joe hanging over me."

Sam shook her head. "And then he spilled his rum all over you."

"I sneezed, for goodness' sake, and he jumped like a firing cannon. He acted as if I'd been attacked."

"And Luke was no better," Sam acknowledged, folding her legs beneath her. "I don't think he smiled all night." Sam sighed. "What was supposed to be a celebration turned into a nightmare. The way Luke scowled and refused to let me answer even the simplest of questions. I'd be surprised if anyone ever stepped foot near us again."

"Well, their attitude certainly kept the party from lasting too late."

Sam groaned. "Within two hours they managed to scare everyone off. Even with the amount Joe and Aidan can eat, we'll have food for a week. It'll spoil before we can get through it all."

Alicia finished her tea. "Blake's crew can take some. I'm sure they'd appreciate it."

"Is he still planning on leaving tomorrow?"

"I don't know," Alicia said. He'd figured out early in the evening that something was amiss and had asked her, on more than one occasion, what it was. Each time she'd had to lie or evade answering, it ate at her until she couldn't eat any supper because her stomach was in knots. "He's angry at the moment. He knows things aren't right and that I'm keeping the reason from him."

Sam found a loose thread on the sleeve of her gown and began wrapping and unwrapping it around her finger. "As much as I hate to say it, maybe it would be best if you did leave. Then I wouldn't worry about you."

"I'm not the one in danger, Sam."

"We don't know that. And I don't want to take the chance of you getting hurt because of something I did."

Alicia set her cup onto the side table, needing a few moments to gather her thoughts and emotions. Blake had spoken to her of leaving St. Kitts soon but they'd been too busy and too many people had been around for them to have a proper discussion about it. And the truth was, she wasn't ready to leave.

"Sam," Alicia began, her voice cracking. She waited a moment, started again. "I'm not ready to say good-bye." Her eyes stung as tears filled them. Inside her chest her heart was tearing in two.

Her sister drew her into her arms, held her firmly. "I know, the thought makes me queasy. But it won't be forever, Alicia. We'll just have to make a point of getting together as often as we can manage it."

"Luv," Luke said, stepping into the room and drawing their attention. He leaned against the doorframe and for the first time all night appeared at ease. "The doors are locked and Aidan fell asleep as soon as I doused the lamp."

"And Blake?" Alicia asked, coming to her feet.

Luke hesitated a moment. "Gone with Nate and Vincent back to his ship. He said to say good night."

Alicia swallowed the hurt. If Blake had something to

say, he would be the one to say it. It wasn't in his personality to speak through someone else.

"I appreciate the lie, Luke, but I know the truth. He's angry with me and I don't blame him. If I were in his shoes, I'd be furious as well."

"I'm sorry I had to put you in that position," Sam said.

"I don't blame you, Sam. We need to keep this secret to keep you safe."

"I know, but I didn't want my safety to come at the expense of your happiness."

Sam went to Luke, leaned into him, and Alicia felt both a twist of envy and a stab of fear. She had to make things right with Blake.

"It won't. Tomorrow, when I'm not so tired and he's had some time to calm down, we'll work it out."

"He's going to want to know what we're hiding," Luke warned.

"I'll think of something." Then, before she could control the sudden rise of despair, tears were cascading down her cheeks and she was once again crushed in Sam's embrace.

"Don't cry, Alicia," Sam begged, her own voice thick with sadness.

Alicia clung until her eyes burned. Then she sniffled and pulled back. She couldn't remember ever being so weary.

"I must be more tired than I realized. I'm not usually this emotional."

"Can I get you anything?" Sam asked, worry lurking in her eyes.

Alicia shook her head, wished them good night, and trudged up the stairs. In her bedroom she drew back the covers and slipped in fully dressed. Her thoughts were scattered; she couldn't seem to nail one down long enough to consider it. Then, with her head spinning, with every part of her body drained, she tumbled into sleep.

Consciousness crept slowly over Alicia. Judging from the brightness behind her closed eyes, it was daylight. She tried to move her legs but they felt tied. She gave a sound kick and untangled herself, only then realizing it was her skirt she was caught in. Flopping onto her side, she opened one eye. Through the curtain she'd been too tired to draw last night came a thick slab of sunlight and from outside came the sound of birds twittering from the treetops.

Neither the light nor the sound was welcome and Alicia tugged the covers over her head. Maybe if she pretended it was still night, she wouldn't have to face an angry Blake, wouldn't be forced to lie to him yet again. Wouldn't have to say good-bye to Sam.

When the air became hot and her lungs needed air, Alicia yanked the blankets down. The rising scent of food drifted from downstairs. Alicia inhaled deeply, wrinkled her nose at the smell of frying sausages, and immediately jumped from the bed when her stomach pitched.

Scrambling, Alicia reached for the bedpan with no time to spare. On her hands and knees, feeling much as she had on the first days on Blake's ship, Alicia retched until her face ran with sweat and her hands shook. When she was spent, she rolled onto her side and curled into a ball. She flitted back into sleep.

"Alicia," Sam called, knocking softly on the door and waking her. "Breakfast is ready."

When Alicia opened her mouth to answer, she had to slam it closed again before she got sick. She answered in the only way she could, with a moan. The door creaked open.

"Alicia!" Sam exclaimed. Her heels clicked as she ran across the room. Alicia felt the coolness of her sister's palm on her forehead. "Are you all right? Are you hurt?" She must have seen the bedpan then. "Oh, poor thing. Can I get you anything?"

"Do you have ginger tea?" Alicia croaked, her stomach clenching again. Sam rubbed her back while she was sick, then helped her to the bed. She tucked a light blanket around Alicia and took out the bedpan.

"I'll be right back," she said after bringing in a clean pan. "Just rest."

Alicia dozed again and was awakened by the coolness of a damp cloth being placed across her forehead. Her eyes fluttered open.

"Thanks."

Sam sat beside her, teacup and saucer in her hand. "You're not so worried about me that it's making you sick, are you?"

"No, I'm not sure why I'm sick. We all ate the same food. Is anyone else ill?"

"Not that I know of. Joe's keeping watch outside. Aidan and Luke went to check on our ships."

Alicia sat up, rearranged the pillows at her back, and leaned into their softness. "I was sick on Blake's ship but that was due to the motion. By drinking the tea and getting accustomed to the movement, I was fine." She frowned. "It feels the same but why would I have motion sickness on land? It doesn't make sense."

Sam was handing the tea to Alicia when she rattled the cup in its saucer. Alicia grabbed it before it spilled and scalded her lap.

"I don't mean to overstep, or insult you, but is it possible you could be with child?"

The cup rattled again and Alicia was vaguely aware of Sam taking it back and placing it on the bedside table.

"Alicia?" Sam placed a hand on her cheek. "Can it be?"

"I—" Alicia swallowed the panic and pressed a hand to her unsettled stomach. If she admitted this was a possibility, it would confirm she'd been with Blake outside of marriage. A burning flush crept over her face and into her ears.

Sam giggled. "You love Blake, Alicia. I won't judge you. Besides, I did the same thing. Well," she amended quickly, "not with Blake."

Alicia grinned. "I should hope not."

Sam grabbed her hand. "Then it is possible? You could be with child?"

"I don't know," Alicia said. "Anna died when I was a young girl and Jacob certainly never told me anything. Besides, we only just . . . um . . . well . . . it hasn't been that long since we . . ." Mortified, she closed her eyes.

"Having tried for a long time . . ." She paused until Alicia opened her eyes. "I've had time to gather every speck of information on the matter from friends who've had children. It's not uncommon to be sick, though mostly it seems to pass by midday, and some friends of mine have told me they knew within days of conceiving that they noticed some changes right away in their bodies such as their breasts getting tender. And," she added with a smile, "expecting women tend to be both unusually tired and emotional."

Alicia felt the blush drain, and knew all her color had gone along with it. "Oh, my God! It's true. What do I do now? I know nothing of babies."

"First," Sam said, and Alicia felt awful at the sadness that had crept into her eyes. "You tell Blake."

Alicia's stomach roiled again, but she fought the nausea. What would Blake say? He was already angry with her. They'd been together such a short time, they hadn't had a chance to discuss children. She didn't know how he felt about them.

"Don't be afraid," Sam soothed. "He loves you. He'll be pleased."

"And you?" Alicia asked, taking her hand.

"I'll be an aunt, how can I be unhappy about that? But," she added, wiping a tear from her eye, "I'd be lying if I said I wasn't green with envy. I've wanted this for so long, and it feels as though it'll never happen, that I'm the only one who can't conceive."

"I'm sorry, Sam."

She sniffled. "I know you are, but this isn't a time for sadness. Drink your tea, and I'll get you some dry bread. I've heard that eases a sensitive stomach. Then, when you're up to it, I'll walk you to the beach." She squealed. "A baby! How exciting."

Alicia waited until Sam had fled downstairs in search of bread before she allowed her own tears to come. It wasn't that she was sad, she was terrified. She knew how to hammer steel, how to mold iron, but she had no idea how to birth a baby or what to do with it afterward. Sam, on the other hand, was a natural. She was great with Aidan and had nurturing instincts that could be spotted for miles.

And Blake? Alicia pondered that while she finished her tea. She came to the conclusion that Sam was right, Blake would be pleased. The way he'd seen Eric's body home, the pain he'd felt when Jacob had disowned him, and the remorse he showed upon reading his father's letter all spoke of a man who, despite his mistakes, treasured family. No, she thought, setting aside her empty cup, Blake wouldn't be angry about a baby.

But before she told him about that, she wanted to clear the air between them. She hated knowing that he'd been so angry with her last night that he'd left without saying good night. Though she had no intention of telling Sam's secret, she could tell him there was one, but that it wasn't her place to divulge it. That way he'd know she wasn't maliciously hiding anything from him, that she loved him and treasured him too much to do that.

And knowing that, feeling it in the deepest part of her heart, she pressed a trembling hand to her belly. They were going to have a baby!

Seventeen

They were at the table when Luke swept in, radiating agitation the way the sun radiated heat.

"Are you all right?" he asked Sam, taking her arms and staring her down.

"Yes, why? What's happened? Is it Aidan? Joe?"

Alicia's heart began to pound.

"Not that I know of," he said. "I found this on the *Freedom*."

He smoothed out the paper that he'd carried in his fist. Alicia, sitting beside Sam, read the words as well.

> *You may have fooled everyone else by painting it, but I know this is Steele's ship, just as I know you, Samantha Bradley, were Sam Steele. I hope your life is valuable, because if you intend to keep it, here is what it will cost you. I want the* Freedom—*or should I call it the* Revenge?—*loaded and ready for sailing by the end*

*of tomorrow. You are to tie this bag onto the wheel and
fill it with doubloons and pieces of eight. If my terms are
not met, the Navy will be apprised of your location and
your identity. I have also made provisions that should
I not make it back to my home, my attorney is charged
with delivering the same message to the authorities.
You cannot hide any longer, Sam. Your time is up. You
have until sundown tomorrow.*

"Oh, my God," Sam moaned, her hands reaching for
Luke, "what do we do?"

Alicia was on her feet. "What do you mean? You give
him what he wants, Sam. It's the only way."

Luke's gaze cut to Alicia. The fury in it had her taking
a step back.

"No, it's not. I need to talk to Blake."

"You're going to tell him?" Alicia asked, feeling guilty
for the relief she felt. If Luke told Blake, then she wouldn't
have to lie to him any longer.

"I bloody have to. Whoever is doing this is someone
from his ship."

"What?" Alicia asked, grabbing a chair for support.
"That can't be."

"Then you explain to me," he growled, "how nobody
has bothered us until now. You and Blake come here and
suddenly Samantha's life is threatened. I don't believe in
chance."

Alicia's mind whirled with the possibility that Luke was
right.

"It's not their fault, Luke. You can't blame her, nor
Blake. They wouldn't hurt me like that."

Luke shifted his attention to Sam, but Alicia could still
feel his anger toward her. It hung in the air thick as fog.

"I'm not saying they did it deliberately, luv, but it doesn't change what's happened. If Blake brought this on us, he bloody well needs to know about it."

"But—"

"Stay here and lock the door behind me. I'll be back."

Squawk. "He'll be back. He'll be back."

And before Alicia could think of going along, which she realized too late she desperately wanted to do, Luke had shot from the room.

That's not enough," Lewis argued. "I deserve more than this!"

They were in Blake's cabin, along with Nate and Vincent. Blake leaned back in his chair, crossed his arms over his chest.

"We figured out the shares, and what you're holding"— he gestured to the small pouch that Lewis held—"is what you're entitled to."

"You're cheating me out of what I earned!" Lewis raged, spit flying from his mouth.

Blake bit down on his frustration. He'd thought of Alicia and the secret she was keeping all night, which had resulted in very little sleep. Behind his eye his head throbbed and all he wanted was to get Alicia and get back out to sea, where he belonged. Maybe then she'd trust him enough to tell him what was going on. Instead he was here with the lingering smell of the morning's breakfast and the constant whining of a man he never wanted to see again. They'd been over this already, four times by his counting. He'd shoot the blasted fool before there'd be a fifth.

"You can take it, or not. But either way, you'll not be

getting any more." Blake rose, deliberately using his height as intimidation, hoping it would put an end to the tedious discussion. "I'll warn you now, I'm not in the mood for bartering. You have ten seconds to take your money and get off my ship before I throw you off myself."

Lewis's gaze narrowed until his eyes resembled those of a snake. His nostrils flared. "You'll pay, all right," he vowed. "You just won't know how or when." He spun to leave.

Blake vaulted over the table, grabbed Lewis by the back of his shirt, and slammed him onto the floor. "Don't ever threaten me again, you little bastard," he growled. "Do you understand?"

Lewis's answer was a mewling noise and a jerky nod of his head. As easily as Blake had taken him to the floor, he wrenched him up again, then pulled him upstairs and onto the deck.

They nearly collided with Luke.

"I need to talk to you," Luke ordered.

"I'm busy," Blake answered, half dragging Lewis to the gunwale.

"My boat's over there," Lewis whimpered, pointing to the other side of the ship.

"Let him swim for it," Vincent said where he and Nate had taken position next to the main mast.

"Or we could keep it," Nate suggested. "For our troubles."

Blake scoffed, pulled Lewis to the port side. "There. Can't say I wasn't fair." Then, with a shove, he pushed Lewis off his ship.

The splash was soon followed by thrashing and cursing as Lewis pulled himself into his boat. The pressure behind Blake's eye eased and he sighed, leaned against one of the guns, and drew a deep breath, replacing the smell of breakfast with the tang of the sea. *Much better*, he thought. *One problem down, one more to—*

"Are you bloody ready now?" Luke grumbled.

Blake squinted. The glare of the sun off the chains around Luke's neck was enough to blind him.

"And we thought *you* were ill-tempered this morning," Vincent chuckled.

Luke didn't find the comment humorous and spun to Vincent and Nate. "This doesn't concern you," he said, glaring.

Blake cursed, rubbed the headache that was coming back with a vengeance, thanks to Luke.

"If you have something to say, then say it. I have work to do."

"In your cabin," Luke said, marching toward the hatch.

"Damn, we're going to miss it," Vincent complained.

Blake scowled at Vincent, then included Nate when the man rocked back on his heels, grinning. He stomped after Luke but didn't catch up in time. Luke disappeared below, leaving Blake no choice but to follow.

"Shut the hatch, this stays between us," Luke ordered.

Blake speared him a glare. "My bloody ship and everyone thinks they can give me orders," he grumbled as he slammed the hatch, the force of which rattled the breakfast dishes he'd left on the table.

Since Luke remained standing, so did Blake.

"What's so bloody important?" he demanded.

"Someone's threatening Samantha."

Blake couldn't have been more surprised. "Threatening her? How? Why?"

"Before I tell you why, can you account for your crew? Do you know where they are, where they've been, where they come from?"

Blake arched a brow. "Do I know where they are now? Besides Nate and Vincent, they're ashore. I've kept a few men here to guard the treasure, but the rest have been in town, spending their plunder. Why?"

"How long have you had them as part of your crew?"

Blake crossed his arms. "I'm not saying anything else until you tell me what this is about."

Luke bared his teeth, ran a hand across the back of his neck, and sighed. "Samantha used to be a pirate as well."

"Samantha used to be a pirate, too? Hell, I'm surrounded by pirates."

Luke scowled. "That's beside the bloody point, isn't it? Someone's found out and is threatening to turn her over to the authorities. Since she hasn't pirated in a year, and nobody knew until you showed up . . ."

"You think it's a member of my crew." Blake shook his head. "I can't account for the coincidence, Luke, but I can account for my crew. I've had the same one for a fair number of years and it's proven to be honest and trustworthy. Well, other than Lewis, who came onboard in Tortuga. But it can't be him. We didn't even know we were coming to St. Kitts until after we'd sailed from Tortuga and discovered Alicia had stowed away. There was no way anyone, including Lewis, could have planned to come threaten Samantha."

Luke shook his head, the anger replaced with worry. "You're sure?"

"I am. But I don't understand why this is an issue. You've been pardoned, why hasn't she?"

Luke inhaled deeply. "She was safer not asking for one. She's Sam Steele."

Blake whistled. "Sam's notorious."

Luke scowled. "So you know of Steele?"

"Everyone knows of Steele," Blake answered.

"Right, *her* you've heard of. Anyhow," he continued with a shake of his head, "someone has figured it out and is asking a huge ransom for his silence."

Suddenly last night's events made sense. "This is the secret Alicia was keeping, the reason you and Joe shadowed the women last night?"

"Yeah."

Blake mulled it over, decided he couldn't find fault with Luke's logic. In his place, he wouldn't have told a virtual stranger either. "But you're going to give in, I imagine?"

"Not yet." Luke set his jaw. "I'm trying to think of a way not to that can still ensure Samantha's safety."

"You could kill him."

"I could, but he's claiming to have provisions made that, in the event of his death, his attorneys have the information. We can kill him and Samantha can still hang."

Blake rubbed his eye. "This gets complicated."

"You've no idea," Luke sighed. "Can you spare some time? I'd like to go back to the house, discuss some possibilities."

"Sure."

On deck, Blake called Nate and Vincent over. "We need to do something before we leave. Follow us."

"Hold it," Luke ordered, stopping midstride. "They're not coming."

"I trust these men with my life, Luke, as well as Alicia's. You need help and there's nobody better than Nate and Vincent. They've been with me for years, and if they don't come, then I'm not going either."

Luke scowled but eventually relented, and the four of them rowed to shore. In the house, Blake took Alicia into the parlor. When they were alone, he pulled her into his arms. Relief melted over him when her arms came around his back and held him tightly.

"I missed you," he murmured into her hair. He smiled at the smell of oranges that teased his nose. She'd already become so familiar to him.

"Blake, I'm sorry." Alicia leaned back, cupped a soft hand to his cheek. "I didn't want to lie to you, but Sam had asked me to keep a secret and I couldn't betray her trust." Her eyes shone with tears that squeezed Blake's heart. "But by doing it, I felt as though I was betraying yours."

He looked down at her beautiful face, considered himself the luckiest man alive, then leaned in and kissed her. He savored her taste, the softness of her lips, which was that much sweeter after a long night of being without her. He moved his mouth and nipped at the delicate skin behind her ear. Her moan was for his ears only, but it went through him like fire.

"I'm sorry to interrupt," Vincent said, the humorous tone belying his words, "but we're ready."

Blake waited until Vincent had left. "I love you, and I think protecting your sister is an admirable trait. You've only found Samantha again and I know it must be hard to see her being threatened. I understand why you didn't tell me."

Alicia sagged against him. "I hated knowing you were angry with me. I—"

"Blake, man, are you finished?" Luke called.

"Come on." He grinned before kissing her again. "They're waiting."

They took their seats around the table, everyone except Luke, who couldn't stop pacing. Samantha stood at the head of the table, flanked by Joe and Aidan. She began to speak, but was instantly interrupted by Luke.

"Before she says anything," he growled, "I want to make

it clear that her words stop here. If any of you breathes a word outside these walls, I'll hunt you down and kill you."

Squawk. "Luke will kill you. Luke will kill you."

The insult scraped over Blake and had him scowling in return. If he could trust a pirate, then what was Luke's problem?

"Luke," Samantha said with a shake of her head. She turned to Nate and Vincent, smiled warmly. Blake shook his own head in disgust when Vincent blushed and sat a little taller. Nate, seeing this embarrassing display, rolled his eyes.

"Ignore Luke, he's out of sorts at the moment."

Then, with no more fuss, she began her tale. Blake grinned at the expected reactions of his friends. Vincent didn't blink, only stared at Samantha with a look of disbelief and awe while Nate nodded slightly, lips tugged as he fought a grin.

"I've heard of you," Vincent said, his voice thick with reverence, as though talking to the king. "I never dreamed Steele was a woman. Damn," he added, laughing now, "what a treat this is. I get to meet Sam Steele!"

Squawk. "Sam Steele. Sam Steele."

Samantha blushed. Luke stopped pacing, arched a brow.

"Excuse him," Nate said, shooting Vincent a look of incredulity. "He's easily excitable."

"But she was the best," Vincent argued.

"Excuse me," Luke growled. "She was tied with the best." He winked at his wife.

Squawk. "Luke was best. Luke was best."

Blake found the discussion quite humorous until Samantha mentioned the letters, *three* letters, and the fact that Alicia was mentioned in them.

"Why didn't you tell me?" he demanded, facing Alicia.

"I told you, it's Sam secret, not mine."

Fury had him standing. "It's no longer only about Samantha when your life is in danger." He spun to Luke. "You said Samantha was in danger, you never mentioned Alicia was as well. I could shoot you for that. How would you like for your wife to be threatened without you being the wiser? I can't protect Alicia if I'm not aware she needs it."

Luke nodded. "I'd be angry, too, mate, but know this, I was watching them and they were safe."

Blake gnashed his teeth. "You think a locked door would stop a grenade? You're a pirate. You should know better."

"From where I'm standing we're not so very different, mate, but if you have a problem with us having been pirates," he gestured to the door, "feel free to leave."

Blake rubbed his eye, sighed heavily. "I didn't mean it the way it sounded. I only meant that a locked door won't keep out someone who is determined to get inside."

"If he killed her, he wouldn't get his ransom, would he?" Luke reasoned.

"There are other ways. He could've taken Alicia. Did it never cross your mind that by taking her, he'd ensure Samantha's payment?"

Samantha paled. Blake turned to Alicia and saw she'd had the same reaction.

"I don't think whoever is doing this is that bold," Nate reasoned. "He left the cutlass in the door when nobody was home. He did the same with the note on the ship, and he used a young boy to deliver another."

"Well, that's not a chance I'm willing to take." Blake reached for Alicia's hand and pulled her to her feet. "We're leaving."

"Blake, we can't," Alicia said, yanking her hand back.

"The hell we can't," he argued and reached for her again. His hands closed over air when she stepped out of reach.

"You're right, Samantha isn't the only one in danger. But it seems to me that the way to ensure everyone's safety is to deal with this. I don't see running as solving anything," Nate said.

All eyes turned to Nate. He shrugged. "Blake, we can sail out of here, but what's to say we won't be followed? Do you really plan on having Alicia watched every minute of the day?" He leaned forward in his chair, looked to Alicia. "Would you want that?"

"No," Alicia answered. "I'd hate it."

Shit, Blake thought, Nate was right. They'd always be watching their backs if they didn't solve the problem now.

"Will you pay it, Sam?" Aidan asked.

" 'Course she will," Joe answered. "Won't ye?"

Samantha looked at Luke, her heart in her eyes. "He wants the ship."

Squawk. "Can't have the ship." Can't have the ship."

"Well, he can't have it," Luke said vehemently. Luke propped his foot onto a chair. "I agree with Nate and my parrot. I don't believe paying will make this stop. We'd always be wondering if and when he'll come back."

"Then what do you have in mind?" Vincent asked.

"Sam, if you don't pay him"—Alicia turned even paler—"you could hang."

"Why can't she apply for her pardon?" Vincent asked.

"Just because the Navy would forgive her, do you think every other pirate Steele has plundered would be as forgiving?" Luke asked. "Imagine them finding out they were bested by a woman."

Blake sighed. "I see your point."

"She'd 'ave every despot after 'er," Joe concluded.

The room fell silent as they contemplated what was best. Luke was back to pacing and Alicia was preparing tea. Blake figured they all needed something much stronger.

"The only way to make this go away," Nate said, leaning back into his chair and stretching his long legs under the table, "is to bring Steele back."

Luke stopped, looked at Nate as though he'd grown an extra head.

"You think the best way to save her life is to risk it all over again? Are you bloody mad?"

There was muttering from most around the table and they all agreed with Luke.

"I never said it had to be her," Nate explained.

Blake's mouth went dry. There was a reckless look on Nate's face he only saw when they were engaged in battle. He didn't like it, not one bit.

"What are ye proposin'?"

Nate looked to Blake. Blake shook his head. Don't do it, he thought. Don't do it.

"If Steele comes back, sailing and plundering while Samantha remains here in plain view, with her ship," he added with a wink for Samantha, "then your threat is gone. Nobody would believe him, and Samantha would be safe."

Vincent grabbed Nate's arm, looking as happy about this turn of events as Blake felt.

"You can't mean to do it?" Vincent asked.

Nate shrugged. "Why not?"

"What do you mean, why not? Then it'll be your neck on the line, won't it?"

"Not if they can't catch me. Besides, it might be fun."

Vincent cuffed Nate on the arm. "That's the dumbest thing that's ever come out of your mouth, and let me tell you, that's saying something."

"Boys," Luke interrupted, "you can squabble about it later." He turned to Samantha. "This could work. We have another sloop we can give him."

"Wouldn't it have to be the *Revenge*, uh, the *Freedom*?" Joe asked.

"Nobody would know even if it was, as we've changed her quite a bit. She doesn't look like the *Revenge* anymore. Besides, it's not unusual for pirates to take new ships. As long as we call her the *Revenge* and Nate claims to be Steele, then it'll work."

"There's a flaw in your plan," Blake said. "If this person knows of us, knows we're here, then wouldn't he know Nate isn't Steele?"

"Probably, but it's like I said. Once I'm out there plundering under Steele's name, using a ship he was known to have sailed, then it doesn't matter. The authorities won't believe his claim that Samantha, a woman, is Steele when there'll be proof Steele is somewhere else. And," Nate added, looking far too comfortable with this for Blake's peace of mind, "Luke and Samantha build ships for the Navy. They're not likely to do anything that would risk losing the two people that help them catch pirates by building the fastest ships. Not without rock-solid proof." Then he angled a look toward Luke. "The ship you're giving me will be the fastest, though, won't it?"

Luke nodded and turned to Samantha. "Luv, this will work."

Samantha looked stricken. She swallowed hard. "I can't ask you to do this for me, Nate."

"You're not asking. I volunteered."

Alicia set down her tea. Her eyes, Blake noticed, were shiny with tears. "What you're proposing is dangerous. I've witnessed two battles in my life and men died in both.

I don't want"—she choked back her sob—"I don't want anything to happen to you."

Nate rose and went to Alicia, tucked her into his embrace. Blake watched, knowing, as Alicia seemed to, that Nate's mind was already made up.

"I'll be careful. Besides, Luke and Samantha managed it. And Blake, Vincent, and I have survived many battles." He eased Alicia away, wiped her tears. "I know how to take care of myself."

"Then it's settled?" Luke asked.

" 'Tis mad is what it is," Joe argued.

"When you would leave?" Vincent asked, his voice unusually quiet.

Hearing the pain underneath the words and feeling the same squeezing in his own heart, Blake went to the cupboard where he knew Luke kept his rum. He took out a bottle, passed it to Alicia, who'd come to help. He grabbed enough glasses for everyone and passed them out. Alicia went behind him, pouring the rum.

"I'm sorry," he heard her say, "you're too young."

"Oh, give him a swallow," Luke said. "He's not that young."

Blake knew by her sharp inhale she didn't like doing it. Blake chuckled at the small bit of liquid he heard hit the bottom of Aidan's glass.

"To the new Steele," Luke said, raising his glass. "You have mighty big shoes to fill," he added, draping an arm around his wife. "See to it you do the name justice."

Nate grinned. "I'll do my best."

"What about a crew?" Vincent asked. He was standing on his chair. His rum was already gone.

"I know a few men that would be willing to help. I'll talk to them," Luke said.

"I'll go," Aidan volunteered.

"You most certainly will not," Samantha said with a glare.

Aidan set his mouth. "You promised."

"No, I did not. I said once you were older and you'd finished your schooling."

"I'm thirteen." He turned pleading eyes to Luke. "You taught me about ships, I lived on one for four years. I can do this."

Luke hissed in a breath. "Dammit, Aidan, don't put me in the middle of this. You and Samantha had an agreement. Until you're sixteen, you're staying with us to get your schooling."

Aidan shoved back from the table. "The day I turn sixteen," he vowed, "you won't be able to stop me." Then, grumbling, he stalked out of the room.

Nate was the first to cut through the strain that Aidan's departure had left. "I'll need those men right away."

"We'll have you ready by tonight. You can sail out in the darkness."

Nate nodded. "Good." Finally he seemed to remember Blake and his excitement dimmed when their eyes met.

"I need to get my things from the *Blue Rose*."

Vincent jumped off his chair. "I'll go with you."

Blake nodded, kissed Alicia, held her tightly. "I'll be back."

Then, with a heavy heart, Blake followed Nate and Vincent outside.

Eighteen

The walk to the *Blue Rose* was made in troubled silence. They strode side by side as they always did, and though the habit was the same, everything about it felt different to Blake. The easy banter was missing. Instead of badgering Nate about one thing or another, Vincent marched sullenly, his steps kicking up far more sand than necessary. Nate kept his eyes on the water, and as was usual with Nate, Blake was never fully certain of his thoughts.

The sun was bright in the sky, and as it approached midday, the beach was noisy with activity. If it wasn't children screaming and splashing, it was men shouting orders from the decks of their ships. It crossed Blake's mind that whoever was blackmailing Samantha could be amid all the ruckus without them knowing, but at the moment he couldn't summon up the energy to care. Not with Nate going back to the *Blue Rose* for the last time.

Vincent managed to hold his tongue until they were on the ship and Nate had gone below to gather his things. Then he let loose a string of curses, balled his hands into fists, and proceeded to pace from middeck to bow, stopping long enough to kick the gunwale every few steps. Blake held back, saying nothing, knowing Vincent's actions came as much from fear as from anger.

Finally he stopped, slapped his hands on a gun, and hung his head between his arms. "Has he lost his mind?" Vincent asked.

Blake leaned against the gunwale, sighed. As he'd watched his friend spew his frustration and worry, a thought had come to him. And it brought a jagged slice of pain. Nate and Vincent were as much his brothers as Eric had been. He hated like hell to lose them, but he loved them enough to do it. He was to blame for Eric's death, and there was nothing he could do about that. But there was something he could do for Nate and Vincent.

"I think you should go with him."

Vincent's head shot up and he whipped his gaze to Blake.

"What?"

"Tell me it hasn't crossed your mind."

Vincent pushed away from the gun, turned, and braced himself against it. "Of course it crossed my mind. Someone needs to keep an eye on the big lubber. Who knows what kind of trouble he'll get into otherwise?"

Blake couldn't remember any words being this hard to say. They wanted to stay caught in his throat, but he knew that was cowardly. He also knew Vincent wouldn't go otherwise. As much as Vincent loved Nate, he'd feel he'd be abandoning Blake and it wasn't in Vincent to leave a friend behind.

Blake cleared his throat, ignored the tightening in his chest.

"Go with him, Vincent. He needs a first mate."

"What about you?"

"I have a crew I've sailed with for years. I'm not saying any of them can replace either you or Nate, but at least I know them. Nate will be with a ship full of strangers."

Vincent grinned. "He'd likely get lonely."

Blake chuckled. "Yeah, Nate does that a lot. He hates being alone."

Vincent's face flushed at the lie. "I'll get my things."

"Get what things?" Nate asked. Somehow he'd come up without them seeing. He set his bulging bag at his feet.

"I'm going with you, you big oaf. Someone needs to make sure you toe the line."

Before Nate could do anything but gape at Vincent, the dwarf had fled down the stairs.

"He's coming?" Nate asked.

Blake shrugged. "You need a first mate."

"Don't you?"

"I'll pick one from the crew. Besides, I have Alicia."

Nate arched a brow. "I don't plan on kissing Vincent."

"You know what I mean. If you're captain, you need someone who can help you man the ship. Someone you trust. Who better than Vincent?"

From below came Vincent's off-key singing. It was bad enough to peel the paint from the hull.

"You're sending me with that?" Nate asked, pointing his thumb over his shoulder.

The weight eased off Blake's chest. "Can't think of any-one who deserves it more, my friend."

Nate shook his head, chuckled. "Thanks, I think." He took a deep breath. "I appreciate everything you've done."

"You're sure about this?" he asked, peering into Nate's green eyes. He saw the answer there before Nate confirmed it with words.

"I've never owned anything of my own, Blake. I can't pass this up."

It was more of Nate's past than Blake had ever known.

"He'll give you a fine ship."

"I know." His smile was wide. "I hope it's that green sloop he's got sitting there. I've had my eye on her."

"You found a woman already?" Vincent asked, setting his bag next to Nate's. "I've only been gone five minutes."

"You sure you don't want to keep him?"

Blake rocked back onto his heels. "Nope."

"Damn," Nate muttered and shoved Vincent. "If you give me too much grief, I'll feed you to the sharks."

He'd miss this, Blake knew. Their banter and arguing. They'd been a close group these last years, and Blake knew it would take a long time until he stopped missing them, if he ever did.

"Don't you have some rum we can drink before we go?"

"I do. It's in my cabin."

"Let's drink it down there, it's too bloody hot up here," Vincent said and began making his way to the hatch.

"That's because of all your hot air," Nate laughed, following the dwarf.

Blake held back a moment, watched them go. He placed a hand to his head and another over his heart.

He wasn't sure which one hurt more.

It had taken some doing, but Alicia managed to get herself out of the house without anyone noticing. She'd tiptoed past

Aidan's room, where she could hear Sam trying to reason with him. Judging by the lack of response on Aidan's part, he wasn't in a reasoning mood. In the parlor she found Joe slumped in a chair, hands resting on his belly. His snoring was loud enough to mask the sound of her slipping out the back door.

The sun was hot and hit her face with nearly as much heat as the forge in the blacksmith shop. She closed her eyes, pictured the shop and its assortment of tools, the smell of smoke and heated steel. Knowing she was going back to something she loved helped. She wasn't only leaving Sam; she was going home. With Blake.

Still, knowing she had Blake didn't make the thought of leaving Sam any less heart wrenching. Who knew when they'd be able to see each other next? It wasn't as though she'd simply be on the other side of the island.

The blasted tears snuck up on her again and she swiped at them impatiently. Forcing aside those kinds of thoughts because they weren't accomplishing anything but making her weepy, Alicia looked around at Sam's flowers, dropped to her knees, and began yanking out weeds. Moving along the row as she worked, Alicia tore weeds away, glad for something that kept her hands busy. Sitting around for so long was becoming tedious, and knowing she had more of it on the voyage back to Port Royal made her relish the simple task even more.

Working absently while her thoughts spun from Sam to Blake to the memorial she'd have for her parents once she returned, it surprised her when she looked up and realized she'd nearly completed one side of the path. Though her knees were getting sore and sweat was running down the back of her neck, Alicia felt useful for the first time in days.

She wasn't meant to sit all day. Proper or not, Alicia needed to work, needed to be productive in a way that entertaining and socializing could never be.

"Alicia?" she heard Sam call through the open windows of the house. She smiled when she heard a smack and an interrupted snore. "Joe! Where's Alicia? She's not upstairs."

"I'm outside, Sam," Alicia called. She came to her feet, wiping her hands on her skirt. She raised her head, was hit with a fierce wave of dizziness, and stumbled. Little white spots blurred her vision. Holding a hand in front of her, she groped for something to grab on to.

"Alicia!" Sam yelled and caught her just as she lost her balance. "Joe!" she screamed and heavy footsteps soon raced outside.

"I'm all right," Alicia said, her vision already clearing. "I simply got up too fast."

"Take her inside, Joe. I'll get her something to drink."

Before Alicia could argue that she could walk under her own command, Joe had her in his arms and she was being carried into the parlor. He set her down as if she were made of china, and when he stepped back, it was he who looked ready to swoon. His eyes were large in his face and his normally ruddy cheeks were stark.

"Joe, I'm fine. It was only the heat."

"And you should know better," Sam said, carrying in a tray with three tall glasses of sweet tea on them. She gave one to both Alicia and Joe and took the third for herself. Then she sat next to Alicia. "Drink," she commanded and didn't take any herself until Alicia did as she was told.

Sam had added a thick wedge of lemon to the tea. Alicia consumed half the glass at once. She sighed, closed her eyes, and felt her body cool.

"Alicia, you need to be more careful."

"I was only outside, Sam. I didn't venture so far away that I was in danger."

"That's not what I'm talking about, although you shouldn't have even done that without Joe going with you. I meant the baby, Alicia."

Joe choked on his tea. He coughed and sputtered, pounded a thick hand to his chest, while he wheezed in a handful of breaths. Sam grabbed his glass before he spilled it. He wiped his watery eyes and looked at Sam.

"What baby?"

Sam patted Joe's cheek. "Alicia's having a baby."

Alicia didn't think Joe could lose any more color but she was wrong. "Sweet mother of God," he muttered.

"Don't tell Blake, Joe. I haven't had a chance myself with all the excitement this morning."

Joe swallowed hard, dropped his gaze to his boots. When he lifted it again, Alicia was surprised to see he'd not only gotten his color back, he'd gained some. His face looked red as the flowers she'd had been weeding.

"Blake didn't . . . did he . . ." He rubbed his hands over his face.

Sam took pity on him. "No, Joe. Blake wouldn't do that."

Alicia realized what he'd been asking and reached over, taking Joe's hand in hers. "Blake didn't force me. And we are getting married."

His head reared. "As ye bloody should, too, or I'd have 'is 'ide."

"Have whose hide?" Aidan asked from the doorway.

"It's nothing," Sam said, dismissing it with a wave of her hand.

Because Sam was looking at Joe, she didn't see the anger that crossed Aidan's face, but Alicia did. And because she knew the boy was still stinging from being forbidden onto Nate's ship, Alicia couldn't bring herself to lie to him. He already felt as though he were being treated like a child— not that Alicia disagreed with Sam's decision not to let him aboard Nate's ship—and she didn't want to add to his hurt. She knew from Sam that he'd been whipped and beaten as a boy on the plantation they'd escaped from. He'd been Sam and Luke's family ever since and now he was hers, too. If Joe knew, she didn't see any reason not to include Aidan.

"Aidan," she called as he turned to leave.

He stopped, turned, crossed his arms over his chest.

Because she could remember doing the same thing when Anna didn't want her to go to the blacksmith shop, Alicia smiled.

"Aidan, you can't tell anyone, even Luke." Alicia turned to Sam. "Did you tell Luke?"

Sam flushed and Alicia sighed. Good Lord, everybody was going to know before Blake.

"All right," Alicia started again. "Don't tell Nate or Vincent or Blake, not until I have a chance to say something to him." She inhaled deeply. "Since you're now my brother, I guess it means you're going to be an uncle."

His forehead furrowed, then he dropped his arms. "You're having a baby?" he asked.

"I am, yes."

It surprised Alicia when Aidan's first reaction was to go to Sam. His expression lost all anger. If she wasn't mistaken, what she saw there was sympathy. He put an arm around Sam, who leaned her head on his shoulder. Alicia saw then that no matter what else was between Sam and Aidan, love was first.

"Come, me boy, let's go see if Luke's back to the harbor yet. Maybe he needs our help."

"Uh, congratulations," he said, then he sped off after Joe.

"You didn't have to tell him," Sam said.

"Sam, I know he's like a son to you, but he's growing into a man and all he wants is to be treated as one."

Sam sighed. "I know. And I know the time is coming to let him go, but I'm not ready. I love him so much."

"And he loves you. I didn't realize how much until just now. He was sad for you."

"He's a wonderful boy. I know I didn't raise him. I've only had him since he was eight, but I'm so proud of him." Her eyes misted. "As much as he calls me Sam, part of me wishes he'd call me mother."

Alicia's heart tugged, but she had no words for her sister. She couldn't promise it would happen one day; she could only hope and pray that it did. Sam went to get the pitcher of tea to refill their glasses. Judging by the length of time it took her to come back and the moisture that clung to her eyelashes, Alicia knew she'd needed a few moments to herself.

"Sam, you'll come back when it's time for the baby, won't you?"

Sam passed her the glass, sat slowly. "You'll go back to Port Royal for the birth?"

"That's where I live, Sam, where else would I be?"

"You've talked to Blake, then. He's changed his mind?"

Alicia's stomach knotted, and it had nothing to do with the baby.

"About what?"

Sam bit her lip, looked at the floor.

"Sam?"

"I went to the *Blue Rose* and talked to Blake before the race. I asked him if there was any chance you'd live here."

Alicia leaned forward.

"And?"

Sam took a heavy breath, raised her gaze. "And he said he couldn't be a privateer on land, that he'd come back when he could, but his life was at sea."

A ringing began in Alicia's ears. He couldn't mean to resume privateering. What about the blacksmith shop?

"He knows how much the shop means to me, I've told him. Besides, how can he think I'd live at sea knowing I not only almost died there once but the motion makes me ill?"

"Alicia, you need to tell him about the baby, about what you want and expect. You have to do that before you leave St. Kitts."

Her heart pounding, her hands still trembling too much to dare hold the glass, Alicia nodded. She agreed with Sam, the problem wasn't that. The problem was she was deathly afraid she already knew what it was that Blake wanted.

And it wasn't what she wanted.

In the end she simply didn't have a chance to tell him. Alicia and Sam made it to the beach—armed with small pistols underneath their gowns—just as the boat carrying Blake, Nate, and Vincent was coming ashore.

The men jumped into the calf-deep water. Blake passed the rope to Nate and trudged onto the sand.

"What are you doing here? Where's Joe or Luke?" he asked, his gaze hunting the length of the beach.

"Luke and Joe are getting Nate's ship ready. We're fine, Blake. Sam and I are armed."

Blake's eyes roamed her body, made her belly quiver. When his gaze met hers, she saw the spark of desire in his dark eyes and smiled. He stepped closer, brushed his thumb over her bottom lip.

"I'm curious to know where you've hidden your weapon."

"I'll show you later," she promised, earning her a low growl before he dipped his head and stole her breath with a kiss.

"Can I have one of those as well?" Nate asked.

"No," Blake answered.

Nate winked at Alicia. "He's scared if you kiss me, you'll realize what you're missing."

"Maybe he's more afraid of you passing along some disease," Vincent countered.

Blake threw his head back and laughed. Sam and Alicia giggled.

"I wasn't the one to have a disease. Wasn't that you?" Nate asked Vincent.

Vincent gaped. "That was Henry!" Vincent turned a flushed face to the women. "Henry was on our ship a few years ago. He had these sores—"

"Samantha," Nate interrupted, shaking his head at Vincent. "Has Luke picked a ship?"

"Yes." Using her hand to shade her eyes, she looked toward the harbor. "And it looks as though he's back. He must have found you a crew."

"Then I'd better get over there," Nate said.

Vincent turned to the women. "It wasn't me; it was Henry. I don't have any—"

"Go!" Blake ordered.

The dwarf looked torn between wanting to follow Nate, whose long strides had already taken him a fair distance down the white sand, and wanting to stay to defend his honor.

"I'll go with you," Sam volunteered, giving Alicia a pointed look. "I'm anxious to see who Luke's found to go with you."

Vincent nodded. Alicia grabbed Blake's hand before he could follow them.

"Blake."

He turned to her, gave her his full attention. He had the most beautiful eyes. She hoped their child had his dark eyes.

"What is it?"

She swallowed. "We need to talk."

"All right," he said slowly, watching her more closely now.

"When are you planning on leaving?" she asked.

"I thought we'd leave tomorrow night. That way it lets Nate leave tonight, and when we sail out tomorrow, it won't seem as strange as if both ships left at the same time. Besides, I want to stay until sundown tomorrow, just to make sure we settle this extortion issue. I don't want any other surprises following us."

"And where will we be going?" she asked. Before she said what she wanted, she needed to know what his plans were.

"Port Royal."

Alicia felt her anxiety dissolve. They were going home!

"I think a week there should be enough."

Her throat wanted to close. "Enough?"

He nodded, took her hand, and began walking. "Well, there's the service for your parents, and the markers you wanted to make. Then we need to sell the house and the shop."

If he noticed her step falter, he must have assumed she'd gotten caught up in the sand.

"The shop?"

"Don't worry. Even if we can't sell it right away, we can leave it to the attorneys to handle."

"And then?" she asked, though she knew the answer. It sat in the pit of her stomach like an anchor.

He brought her hand to his mouth, kissed it. The gesture, so intimate and loving, wrapped around her heart and squeezed. Her vision blurred as she walked blindly toward Luke's ships.

"And then we go back to sea." He inhaled deeply and his gaze turned to the ocean. "I can't wait; it already seems like an eternity since I've been on the water."

He turned back to her and this time looking into his eyes didn't warm her heart. It broke it.

"Is that what you wanted to know?" he asked.

"Yes," she answered dully. "That's everything I needed to know."

Nineteen

The rest of the day was a clutter of activity. While Luke introduced Nate and Vincent to their crew, Blake went around the new ship checking lines and canvas. It wasn't necessary, of course, as Luke and Samantha built quality ships, but it kept his mind busy. It kept him from dwelling on the fact that in a matter of hours he'd be saying good-bye to his two best friends.

Samantha and Alicia had been in charge of the food, and once the crew was introduced and the articles signed, the holds had been stocked with supplies, which included food, tools, and barrels of water. Luke had thrown in a few barrels of rum, claiming that no ship of his was going out dry.

Dusk was settling in, and from the porthole in Nate's cabin, Blake watched the sun ease into the sea. He wished he could yank it back out, toss it up high in the sky, and recover a few more hours. Judging from the lack of noise at the table behind him, he wasn't the only one who felt that way.

Blake turned from the bruised sky to the people who'd gathered in the cabin to say good-bye. Luke was sitting next to Samantha, his arm draped around her while her head rested on his shoulder. Joe and Aidan were to Samantha's left, and while Joe drank from his cup—Luke had brought a bottle of rum to share—Aidan's gaze roamed the cabin. Almost as if he were picturing it as his.

Alicia sat next to Vincent. As their backs were to Blake, he couldn't see their expressions, but both of them had their heads down, as though they found their laps of particular interest all of a sudden. Blake shifted his gaze. Nate, who was standing at the base of the stairs, met it. No words were spoken but Blake knew by the slight nod Nate gave him that he understood what Blake was thinking. And since Nate's green eyes were solemn, Blake figured a part of him felt the same.

"This is like a bloody wake," Luke grumbled and reached for his cup.

His comment earned him a poke in the ribs from his wife's elbow.

"What? They're taking one of the best ships the Caribbean's ever seen. They've enough food and a fair amount of rum," he added with a grin.

"Excuse my husband," Samantha said, getting to her feet. "But Luke's right. You deserve a better send-off than this." She raised her cup. "Nate, words can't tell you how much this means to me. You've only known me a week and you're willing to take Sam Steele and make him your own to save my life."

She wiped a tear that had leaked out and Blake watched, amazed, as that one small action had Nate shifting uncomfortably. He grinned. For all the strength a man possessed, it was nothing compared to the power in a woman's single tear.

"To Nate," she continued, "may God be with you, Vincent, and your crew, and may the wind blow you back this way once in a while so I know you're safe."

They all raised their cups and drank. Samantha rounded the table, leaned down, and hugged Vincent. He flushed scarlet. She went to Nate next, this time standing on her toes.

"Thank you," Blake heard her whisper before she embraced Nate and kissed him on the cheek.

A series of toasts and good wishes followed. Then, Samantha, Luke, Joe, and Aidan—who'd taken their own boat out—left.

"Be careful." Alicia hugged Nate, also adding a kiss.

"I'm sorry to leave you with the task of minding this one," he said, angling his head toward Blake.

Alicia smiled, though Blake knew her well enough by now to know it was forced. "I'll do what I can," she whispered. She embraced Vincent next and sniffled loudly when she drew away. "I'll give you some time alone," she said and went up on deck.

"You'd better take care of her," Nate warned, "or I'll come back and hunt you down."

"Just do me a favor and don't attack my ship if you see it."

"Scared you'd lose against a pirate?" Nate teased and his levity eased the pain that was creeping into Blake's chest.

"Pirate or not, the only way I'd lose is if Vincent was at the helm at the time," Blake countered.

"Good to know you haven't forgotten who's the brains in this pairing," Vincent said.

Blake finished his rum, taking the time to gather his thoughts and emotions. He wanted to give his friends the good-bye they'd earned.

"You'll be a great Steele, Nate." He put a hand on his

friend's shoulder. "Do what you did for me and you can't possibly fail."

"You don't have a problem with me being a pirate?" Nate asked.

"I'm learning that it's the kind of man behind the flag that really matters. And there's none finer than you."

Nate swallowed, nodded.

"And you," Blake said, turning to Vincent. "I trust you'll keep Nate from letting the idea of being one of the most notorious pirates go to his head?"

Vincent grinned. "Of that you can be certain."

"If anyone can do this, it's the two of you. I don't have any doubts about that."

Then, because it was killing him to do this, Blake stepped back. "If you ever need me, you can leave word with Captain at Doubloons. I stop in Tortuga often enough."

"Take care of Alicia," Nate said.

"I will."

Then, with nothing more that needed to be said, Blake headed on deck, Nate and Vincent following silently. Alicia hugged them again, while Blake simply looked at them and nodded. Turning away and climbing into his boat was one of the hardest things he'd ever done.

The boat rocked on the waves for a moment as Blake sat holding the oars and watched Nate and Vincent at the gunwale. Judging from Vincent's height, he must have found himself a crate already. The lanterns had been lit, allowing Blake a last look at his friends. With a heavy heart, he placed the oars in the water.

A lantern set in the middle of the table cast Blake's cabin with soft light and long shadows. Alicia remained at the

bottom of the ladder, watching him. He hadn't said a word
since leaving Nate and Vincent. When they'd arrived at
the *Blue Rose*, he'd stood on deck, bathed in moonlight,
and silently watched the *Revenge* sail away. He'd stayed
there, not moving, until the lanterns marking Nate's ship
had faded into the darkness. His silence was breaking her
heart.

And tomorrow she'd be adding to his hurt. She couldn't
go with him. Jacob had left her part of the shop. It had
always been his dream that his children take it over, and
if Blake didn't want it, she certainly did. She missed the
work, missed the certainty of knowing where she belonged.
There was nothing in England to go back to. Her father's
ship was at the bottom of the sea, and though Samantha
was in St. Kitts, Alicia's home was in the small house left
to her by the Davidsons. And the blacksmith shop, the only
place she felt she could be herself.

But she knew the sea was where Blake belonged. He'd
told her as much, and though she'd thought when he'd proposed that his intentions were to go to Port Royal, she'd
been foolish to assume he'd go home with her. When he
was on the *Blue Rose*, he was as at home as she was in the
shop.

She'd decided earlier that it would be best if Sam and
Luke took her home because dragging out her good-bye to
Blake over the days it would take to get back to Port Royal
would be agony.

But she wasn't going to think about good-bye now. She
had one night left with the man who'd come to mean everything to her, and she didn't intend on wasting a moment of
it. She shoved aside the sadness, willed away the despair
that lurked at the edges of her mind. Stepping behind
Blake, she wound her arms around his waist and pressed

her cheek to his back. The smell of the sea clung to him, as much a part of him as his dark brown hair and his slow smile. She inhaled deeply and closed her eyes.

"Trying to crush me?" he asked.

Realizing she was clutching, Alicia eased her grip.

"Sorry."

Blake turned in her arms, cupped her face, and lifted her gaze to his. "Don't be. It lets me know you love me."

"I do." She touched his face. The day's growth of beard scratched at her palms. "I'll never stop. Not ever."

He rubbed his thumbs over her lips. "I should hope not," he murmured. Then his hands fell away to her waist and his mouth slipped over hers.

The kiss was slow and sweet. It wrapped around Alicia until all she knew was the taste of Blake's lips and the feel of his hands moving up her back. She opened her mouth, invited more. He didn't take but rather nibbled and tantalized, giving little while promising everything. She felt the whisper of it in her soul.

While his mouth continued to tease, Alicia's hands reached for his shirt. She grabbed it and tugged it from his pants, sliding her hands over his heated flesh. Throwing her head back when his mouth moved to her neck, Alicia scraped her short nails over his stomach.

He shivered, then closed his mouth and bit her softly where her shoulder met her neck.

"Blake," she whispered. He pulled away long enough to help her slide his shirt over his head, then resumed where he'd left off. Alicia's head felt heavy, and her legs seemed soft as a jellyfish. She closed her eyes, and when Blake's tongue swept over her ear, Alicia's hands roamed his back. His muscles quivered where she touched, which was everywhere she could reach. His shoulders were broad and strong, his back smooth and warm. She lowered her hands over his backside.

She tugged him closer, purred when she felt the length of his need press against her belly. In a blur of movement, he grabbed her by the waist and set her onto the table. He backed away from her touch, a wicked gleam in his eye.

"You have far too much clothing on, sunshine."

Starting at her foot, he eased off one shoe, then the next. He took her right leg, placed her foot against the flatness of his belly, and caressed her ankle. His hands were strong yet gentle, and as they worked up her leg, Alicia had to fight to keep her eyes from closing in pleasure. With deft fingers, he massaged his way over her knee to her thigh and to the top of her stocking. His breath held for a moment when he encountered her skin, then he released it in a long exhale before slowly rolling her stocking down her leg. He tossed it over his shoulder, where it landed in the shadows with a soft plop.

Candlelight played over his naked chest, and desire rushed over her. His dark hair was falling around his shoulders, and his strong hands were on her body, though not where she'd like them. Her breasts ached for his touch and already her blood was humming everywhere. She pushed herself upright and tried to reclaim her leg. Blake held fast. From behind the fall of his hair she caught his ravenous look.

"You're not going anywhere," he whispered. "Not for a long . . ."

He'd been working at getting her other stocking off when his hands closed over something cold and hard. What the devil? But then he remembered her earlier words that she had a weapon on her person and her promise that she'd let him see where later. His hands followed the strap of leather that wrapped around her upper thigh where her skin was smooth as silk. All his blood moved below his waist. He wanted her. He wanted to rip off her gown, make her weak with wanting, and then plunge into her softness until he was spent.

But more than that, at the moment, he wanted something else.

He untied the strap enough to lower her stocking from underneath it, then tied it back in place. Though his loins screamed at him to hurry, he took his time rolling her stocking down her leg. It landed somewhere near the other one. Then, lowering her leg, he helped her to her feet.

"Blake, the pistol."

"I know, sunshine. It's fine where it is." With a grin he couldn't hide, he turned her so that her back was to him. And again, despite the hunger that threatened to eat him alive, he took his time undoing the buttons at her back. He kissed every inch of skin that was revealed and knew, by the low hum in her throat, that he'd chosen correctly in going slowly.

The dress slid down her body, followed by her undergarments. When she was naked but for the small pistol tied to her thigh, Blake turned her to him again.

His heart stopped, stuttered, then beat frantically against his chest. Lord, but she was a vision. Candlelight played in her hair and danced over her curves like a lover's hands.

"You're stunning," he said and knew he'd never spoken truer words in his life.

"I have a pistol tied to my leg, Blake."

He chuckled. "Yes, you do. And I hope it's comfortable, because you're not taking it off. Not for a long while."

Alicia arched a brow. "I thought you weren't a pirate, Mr. Privateer. Isn't this more something a pirate would do?"

Blake's grin was roguish.

"Tonight, sunshine, I am a pirate."

Then he swept her off her feet into the cradle of his arms and lowered her onto his bed, where he kept his word.

She didn't take the pistol off until morning.

Alicia had forgotten one very important fact when she'd made the decision to have one last night with Blake. It also meant she'd have one last morning. And she'd completely forgotten about her morning sickness, which rose quick and violent the moment she lifted her head from the pillow of Blake's chest.

Scrambling, Alicia tore off the covers and jumped out of bed, barely taking the bedpan from underneath the berth in time. If her stomach hadn't been cramping so badly, she'd have been mortified to have Blake witness her heaving, but as it was, she was glad for his support when she was finished and her body was devoid of strength.

He eased her back onto the bed and concern washed over his face, creating deep lines around his mouth.

"What can I do?" he asked.

"Ginger tea, maybe some dry bread."

He nodded and went to the galley while Alicia's mind worked to come up with an excuse for being sick. She wouldn't tell Blake about the baby. How could she? She was certain it would be a means of keeping him on land but at what price? He'd hate living in Port Royal and she didn't want to be an obligation to him. If he were to stay with her, she wanted it to be because that was what he desired, not what he felt compelled to do. She wouldn't hold him to something he didn't want the way Jacob had tried to do.

Blake was back quickly and set the tray next to the bed. He left again to deal with the pan, returning with both it and a bucket of water. He dipped a cloth and bathed Alicia's face. She closed her eyes for two reasons. One of which was it felt wonderful to have him take such care of her. The other was to hide the swell of tears that had risen as quickly as the sickness.

When he was done with her face, he placed pillows at her back, allowing her to sit up. He handed her the tea.

"Should we see a doctor?" he asked, watching her closely.

She was glad the tears were gone and any lingering wetness could be attributed to her being ill. "No. It must be the motion sickness is back."

He frowned. "We're hardly in rough seas."

"No, but I've been sleeping at Sam's all week. I suppose my body became accustomed to a motionless bed."

"I imagine that's possible," he acknowledged, though he looked less than convinced.

He hovered as she finished her tea and bread, helped her get dressed though by then her stomach was fine and she was feeling much better. Then, both anxious about the coming evening and the expected payment the blackmailer anticipated, they rowed to shore.

They'd just secured the boat when another rowed in down the beach from them. It was filled with men, all of them hollering at once. One, in his haste to get on land, leapt over the boat, caught his foot on the side, and plunged face-first into the water. The rest ignored him as they, too, jumped onto land.

Blake, curious to see what this was about, placed his arm around Alicia and walked with her toward the commotion. It didn't take long before a crowd had gathered. Blake stayed slightly back, but well within hearing distance.

"It's Steele!"

"He took our cargo, then blew the ship to pieces!"

"We were lucky to get out alive."

Blake's heart pounded. Nate did fast work.

"Steele's dead," a voice from the crowd called.

One of the men from the boat spun, his eyes wide. "He ain't dead! It was him and we was lucky to get the longboat off before his guns blasted us."

A murmuring passed over the crowd and Blake saw more than one concerned person looking toward the sea. He knew what they were thinking. If Steele was close, he could very well attack St. Kitts next. It was perfect. By the end of the day, everyone ashore would have heard that Steele was nearby and back on the hunt.

Blake eased Alicia back. He'd heard enough. The men were merchant sailors and had clearly been terrified. Whatever Nate had done, he'd done a convincing job of it.

"Let's go tell Luke and Samantha," he said. "Nate's done his part, now she needs to make herself seen."

It was nothing more than a feeling, but Blake stopped, wondering what had grabbed his attention. His gaze cut through the swelling crowd, and his eyes wandered from one man to the next before they connected with a pair he knew.

Lewis. He must have heard the commotion and come to see what all the fuss was about. But why hadn't he taken his money and left by now?

"Blake." Alicia nudged him. "Lewis is here."

Yes, and he didn't look any happier than he had the last time Blake had seen him, right before he'd pushed Lewis overboard.

"I know, sunshine. Let's go." He turned and walked toward Luke's, very aware that Lewis's gaze was locked on to his back. He could feel the bite of it gnawing at him as they made their way down the beach.

It was almost as though the man wasn't done with them yet.

They found Luke and Samantha at the breakfast table, lingering over coffee and biscuits. The yeasty smell filled Alicia's nose and brought her back to a time when she'd come from the shop with Jacob and they'd walk into a house that smelled of fresh-baked bread. Lord, but she missed Jacob and Anna, she thought with a tug of sadness.

"Good morning," Sam said, greeting Alicia with a hug that dispelled her melancholy. Sam squeezed Blake's forearm, walked by them, and took two plates and cups from the cupboards. She poured them coffee and placed biscuits onto plates.

"We have news," Alicia said.

"Oh?"

"Nate's been busy. A boatload of men came ashore claiming they'd been taken by Steele, that Sam Steele was back."

Squawk. "Sam Steele. Sam Steele."

Luke grinned. "That didn't take long."

"Nate's done his job." Blake's gaze turned to Luke. "Now it's your turn."

Lewis wasn't fooled. He knew exactly what Samantha and Luke were up to, strolling the beach together hand in hand as though they didn't have a care in the world. Somehow they'd gotten someone else to pose as Steele, and while word of Steele's return still rang up and down the harbor, Lewis knew it for what it was, a ploy. Something to get him to back down.

Well, he thought, using his hat to fan his face, which also helped shield him should Samantha look to her left and see him, they were in for a surprise.

Lewis Grant had no intention of backing down. Not until he'd gotten what he'd come for, not until he succeeded where his father had failed. And he knew just what he needed to do in order to accomplish it.

Alicia, stop pacing. Luke's with Samantha and it's midday. They're perfectly safe."

Alicia stopped at the back door, grabbed the latch, and clung to it. Sam and Luke had left the house nearly an hour ago, so she'd be seen by as many people as possible and thereby dispel any suspicion that she could be Steele. Alicia had spent most of that time walking around the table, to the door and back again, and a few times up to her borrowed room to fetch something she didn't need. And despite what Blake thought, her pacing had little to do with Sam and Luke's safety.

They'd both been pirates. Surely if anyone knew how to take care of themselves, it was Sam and Luke. But she'd let Blake believe that was the reason for her restlessness. Until now.

She pressed a hand to her quivering stomach and turned to the man she loved. He was sitting at the table, one ankle resting on the opposite knee. He'd tied his hair back, allowing her eyes to take in all his face from the strong angles to the shadow of his beard.

"There's something I need to tell you," she said. She stepped to a chair and grasped the back of it. His gaze followed her hands, then met hers.

"What is it?"

Alicia opened her mouth but, Lord help her, she didn't want to say the words. She bowed her head, hating the cowardice that kept the words from being said but she didn't know how to begin.

"Alicia?" She heard his foot drop to the floor, which propelled her into action. She once again looked into his eyes.

"Blake, I can't leave with you."

He paused a moment. "Do you need more time with Samantha? I could spare another day or so if I had to."

That he was willing to give her more time, despite his desire to get back to sea, brought tears to Alicia's eyes. Why, she wondered, did things have to be this way? She'd finally found a man who loved her, who treated her as she'd always hoped to be treated, and there was no future for them. She closed her eyes as a tear slipped out.

"Sunshine," Blake said and his chair scraped the floor as he stood.

Alicia jumped back, hurriedly wiped her tears. "Don't, Blake," she pleaded. "Don't come any closer." If he touched her now, she'd lose what little courage she had.

Squawk. "Don't come closer. Don't come closer."

His forehead creased into a frown, his eyes darkened. "Why? What's wrong?"

"I can't . . . I'm not that strong."

"What are you talking about? You're one of the strongest people I know." He took a step toward her.

"No!" Alicia held her palms up. "Don't. Stay over there."

Blake rubbed his forehead. "Why?"

"I just . . . I realized . . ." She took a deep breath and released it all at once. "My life is in Port Royal."

His frown deepened and he went still. "What are you saying?"

"I've told you how much I love the shop, that it's where

I belong. And now your father's given it to us. It was his dream for his children to take it over."

Blake inhaled sharply, ran his hands over his face. They fell heavily to his sides and smacked against his thighs.

"You know why I left Port Royal."

"I do, but he forgave you. He said so in the letter."

Blake shook his head. "That doesn't change anything. I can't walk into that house and that shop like nothing happened, Alicia. It's because of me that Eric isn't there. I feel the guilt of that every day. It would be tenfold if I were in Port Royal, surrounded by memories."

"Eric's death was an accident. And if anyone is to blame, it's Jacob. He's the one who sent Eric along."

"It doesn't change the facts. Eric's dead; they all are. Besides, I don't belong there. I've never made a secret of that."

"No," she agreed, feeling the despair creep inward like a thick blanket of fog. "You haven't."

His mouth thinned. "Why did you agree to marry me if you don't want to be with me?"

"I never thought you'd want to continue privateering with a wife on board. Look at the battle we had. You lost four men, Blake. Did you actually envision us living a life fraught with danger?"

"I can take care of you. I'd never let anything happen to you."

"Not intentionally. But some things are out of your control. The battle we had when my memory came back was awful. When it was over and silence had descended, I had no idea if you were dead or alive. In my head I saw the night I lost my family, but in my heart I pictured the same happening to you. I can't live with that fear. I already lost one family at sea, I will not lose another."

"You don't have a family in Port Royal either."

"I have Charles and I have the shop."

He flinched. "Are you saying you'd give up what we have for a blacksmith shop?"

"How is that so different from what you're doing? Do you love your ship more than you love me?" She sighed. "I thought when you proposed that we'd go back to Port Royal and run the shop together."

"Where the hell did you get that idea?" It was his turn to pace, swirling the air with his irritation. "I never once said that."

"I know. I just assumed."

"Hell," Blake muttered, stopping his pacing long enough to shoot her a confused look every few seconds.

Squawk. "Bloody hell. Bloody hell."

She waited for him to say more but all he did was grumble under his breath, rub his eye, and pace. Finally he stopped, and when his gaze met hers, it was stormy.

"I already had to make this choice once, goddammit."

"I know. That's why I'm not asking you to make it again. I know where your heart is, Blake, just as I know where mine lies. I'm not asking you to stay with me, nor will I use any machinations to force you into it."

His eyes narrowed and his ragged breathing filled the room.

"You're letting me go?" he repeated. "Well, how bloody generous of you."

Squawk. "Bloody generous. Bloody generous."

"Blake—"

"No." He stepped back, away from the hand she held out to him. "Don't."

He shoved a chair against the table. "You shared your body with me, professed your love, and agreed to be my wife. Yet you're walking away? At least my father was up front about his demands. He never promised me one thing while all along he was planning something else entirely."

Alicia jammed her fists onto her hips. "Do I want you to stay with me? Yes! But I won't have you hating me for it either. I watched Jacob stand on that beach every day, saw the hurt in his eyes, and felt his sorrow. I don't want that for either of us. I don't want to be the reason you're miserable and I don't want to be reminded every day that a part of you regrets the decision you made to stay." She pressed a hand over her heart. "I love you too much for that."

"You love me?" he spat. "You agreed to marry me and now you're telling me if I want that marriage, I have to give up a part of my soul. What kind of love is that?"

"That's not what I'm doing! I told you that you didn't have to choose."

"The hell I don't!" he argued. "If I want a life with you, it has to be in Port Royal. Isn't that right?"

Alicia stammered. She wasn't explaining this right. She was doing this for him, couldn't he see that? How could he not know how much it was killing her to let him go?

"You make this sound as if it were part of some elaborate lie to trick you. I'm no more at fault for assuming you'd stop privateering than you are for assuming I'd go along with you."

"That doesn't change where we are, does it?" he hissed. "I told you, time and again, that you were too young for me. I tried to stay away from you, but you kept at me until I gave in, until I believed we had a future together. If you'd left me alone, we wouldn't be in this fix!"

She struck her chin up. "I don't regret that, not for one moment. What we shared means everything to me."

He sneered. "Sure. It means so much that you can walk away."

"I wanted to be your wife, Blake. More than anything."

"And I believed you," he rasped, his eyes tortured. "That was my mistake."

Alicia gasped, her eyes stung with tears.

"Save them," he warned with a pointed finger. "They can't undo the damage that's been done here."

The door swung open suddenly and Sam strode in, followed by Luke.

"Oh," she said, stumbling to a stop. "We'll just wait outside."

She turned to grab Luke's arm but Blake moved faster.

"Don't bother," he said, his hard gaze slapping Alicia. "We're finished anyhow." He turned to Luke. "What time do you want me on the ship?"

Luke looked from Alicia to Blake. "I want to get there before he does. Come early."

Blake nodded. "I will."

"And come armed," Luke added.

Blake nodded. "I'd planned to."

And without another look or word to Alicia, he stepped out of the door and out of her life.

Twenty

Evening couldn't come fast enough for Blake. With Nate and Vincent gone, and his crew enjoying the last of their time onshore, the *Blue Rose* had been painfully quiet all day. Blake had been left with far too much time to think and too many memories to haunt him. He couldn't take a step anywhere on his ship without seeing Alicia standing there. He'd heard her voice in the breath of wind that swirled between the masts, and when he'd leaned over the gunwale, it wasn't the sea he smelled, it was oranges.

Every breath he took hurt, a pain he'd only ever felt once before. When he'd carried Eric's body home.

Now he'd lost yet another person he loved. He'd been so sure he'd finally found someone who understood him, understood his tie to the sea.

What he hadn't expected was to find a woman who made him feel complete, only to have her turn away. Turn away and rip his heart out in the same swoop.

"She knew who I was, dammit," he reasoned, slapping his hand against the side of his ship. The gull that was perched down the gunwale from where Blake stood ruffled its feathers and took flight. Blake watched the bird glide over the gently rippling bay as though it hadn't a care in the world.

Then, because he couldn't stand his own company any longer and it was close enough to the time to leave, Blake gathered his weapons, climbed into the boat, and rowed toward shore. Joe, Aidan, and Luke were waiting for him.

"I see you're prepared," Luke acknowledged, nodding his head toward the pistol and sword that Blake carried.

Blake couldn't help grinning at Luke's arsenal. Luke's sword hung from his side; he had two pistols tucked into his sash and a musket in each hand. Luke ran his tongue around his teeth, clearly enjoying himself.

"It's been a while, mate. I'm looking forward to this. In fact, you don't need to come at all."

Blake shook his head. "I want to be there. This isn't only about Samantha. He threatened Alicia as well."

"Fair enough. Joe and Aidan will row us there. That way there won't be any boats tied alongside to scare him off."

"And if he's watching us now?" Joe asked.

Luke shrugged. "I trust he'll be greedy enough to come anyway."

Blake helped push the longboat out, chuckling at the extra arsenal that lay in its bottom.

"How will we get back?"

"I'll light the lantern at the bow when we're finished. Joe can come get us then."

The row across was made quickly and soon the boat tapped the *Freedom*'s side. Luke went first, the chains around his neck jingling as he stepped out and climbed on his ship. Blake was right behind him. Joe and Aidan passed the extra weapons up to Luke before climbing onto the deck.

"Are ye sure ye don't need me to stay? Aidan can take the boat back."

Aidan glared at Joe.

"Thanks, Joe. But we're all right."

"Best watch yerselves, then. We don't know who this is, or how far he'll go to get what he wants."

"Let me tell you just how far I'll go," a voice said from the quarterdeck. The hatch slammed open and four huge black men, all carrying pistols, stepped onto the deck. Luke spun around at the same time as Blake, weapons raised and ready. Blake's eyes cut to the man who walked easily off the quarterdeck. His head spun at the reality.

"Lewis?"

"Miss me?" Lewis asked, looking smug as he stood beside his men, who, as far as Blake could tell, had no necks to speak of.

Luke didn't move his head, nor his weapon.

"Blake, who is this?"

Lewis spoke before Blake could answer. "Allow me. My name is Lewis Grant. I believe your lovely wife knew my father, Oliver Grant. In fact," he added with a laugh when Luke growled, "I believe they knew each other very well."

From there, it all happened in the blink of an eye.

Luke and Blake cocked their pistols. Joe lunged for the weapons at his feet. Aidan screamed a warning.

A shot pierced the air.

"Aidan!" Joe yelled.

Luke spun around. Blake's stomach fell to his knees. Luke dropped his weapon and raced to the boy, who lay deathly still and pale on deck. Blood stained his shoulder.

"Son," Luke said, placing a hand on his uninjured shoulder. "Aidan!" he yelled.

Aidan's eyes fluttered open. Luke's heavy sigh matched Joe's. His hands pressed against the boy's cheeks, lingered, then moved to his shoulder. He untied his sash from his waist and the pistols clunked to the deck.

"You'll be fine, son," Luke promised.

"Step away from him, Bradley," Lewis ordered.

"He's hurt," Luke answered, not moving from Aidan's side.

Blake saw Lewis nod to one of the men he'd come with. The man lifted his musket. Blake ran to Luke, yanked him upright.

"What the blazes? Let go of me, man!" Luke demanded as he shoved at Blake.

Blake held fast to Luke's arm, pulled him closer, and spoke low. "He threatened Samantha, Luke. If something happens to us, who's to stop them from going after her and Alicia?"

Luke's mouth tightened, but he nodded and stopped struggling. Blake let him go. Luke turned to Joe, pushed the sash closer with the toe of his boot.

"Keep pressure on it, Joe."

"Aye," Joe agreed.

"Tell me, Bradley. Did you show this much concern when my father lay dying at your feet?" Lewis asked. Unarmed, save for the group of men that had his back, Lewis strode casually toward Luke. He stopped when they were nose to nose. "Should I show you the same mercy you showed him?"

"He deserved everything that happened to him," Luke growled.

Blake's breath knotted in his chest. What the hell was Luke doing? They couldn't afford to be stupid, dammit.

But Lewis only laughed. "Luckily, Bradley, I agree with you. Still," he said, reaching down and taking Luke's weapons from the deck, "I suppose it should be a son's duty to avenge his father's death."

"I didn't kill him."

"Nor, I'm sure, did you mourn him."

Blake cringed. Don't say it, he begged silently. Please don't say it.

Luke's lip curled. "I danced over his body."

"As I thought," Lewis said, turning from Luke.

Blake released the breath he'd been holding. But it was premature. Using one of Luke's own pistols, Lewis spun around and brought the weapon down hard across Luke's face.

Luke's head shot back from the force. He staggered, one hand on his cheek and the other searching for support. Blake reached for Luke. He dropped his hand when Lewis's cold gaze met his. Luke fell to his knees.

Lewis looked from his men to Blake. Blake understood and made no further move. If he did, Lewis wouldn't hesitate to hurt him as well, or rather, one of his men would. Blake wouldn't risk it. He knew they were in trouble, and it was going to intensify once Lewis realized they hadn't brought any gold along.

They had hoped to come early, to catch the blackmailer unaware and instill enough fear, or pain, into him that he'd go back where he came from. With Nate posing as Steele, there was no real threat to Samantha's freedom any longer. Coming here tonight had really been more about taking a stand and letting whoever it was know that Luke and Samantha, and by association, Blake and Alicia, wouldn't lie down when they were threatened. They'd been prepared to do battle, but they hadn't anticipated that there was more in play than greed. They certainly hadn't planned on being caught unaware. From the moment they'd stepped on deck, they'd been at a disadvantage. And with Luke and Aidan hurt, the disadvantage was growing at an alarming rate.

"I'm tempted to shoot you now," Lewis said to Luke, "but it would ruin the rest of my plans." He knelt down, forced Luke's head up by pressing the pistol under his chin. "And I have such wonderful plans. Plans that involve your lovely wife."

Luke muttered oaths. Lewis grinned and stood. Then with a snarl, he pulled his foot back and kicked Luke solidly in the ribs.

Luke collapsed to the deck.

"Mother of God," Joe cursed.

Blake held his tongue, though his hand tightened around his pistol. He didn't dare use it, however, not when he had only one shot.

Lewis laughed and the sound slithered down Blake's spine. As though he sensed it, Lewis moved to stand in front of Blake. Arrogance poured from Lewis's gaze as he glared at his former captain.

"Underestimated me, didn't you? Thought I was nothing but a useless deckhand. Well, if I haven't proven you wrong yet, let me assure you that I will before the night is through." His teeth looked small in his mouth when he laughed, and it took all of Blake's will not to lunge for him. Only the thought of what lay ahead, what Lewis was capable of with those four men behind him, kept Blake silent and rooted to the deck.

"Nothing to say, Blake?" He tsked. "You disappoint me. Thought after all the bullying you did on your ship that you'd have some words for me. But you're not so confident now, are you?" He leaned forward, eyes narrowed. "You owe me. And I'm not going anywhere until I collect *everything* that's coming to me."

He stepped back, inhaled deeply. His hands came to rest on Luke's pistols, which he'd tucked into the waist of his trousers.

"Now," he said. "Where's my gold?"

Sam, stop pacing, it's making me dizzy."

Her sister stopped long enough to spare her a glance. "Well, if you'd try the food I prepared for you, then you'd be too busy eating to watch me pace."

Alicia sighed, looked down at the melon, oranges, and apples her sister had cut for her. It was all beautifully arranged and very colorful, yet Alicia had no appetite. She set the plate onto the side table.

"I'm not hungry."

"Alicia, you didn't eat supper. You need to feed the baby."

Because she knew Sam was right, she took a wedge of apple and sank her teeth into it. Sam nodded her approval, then went to the window and pulled back the curtain.

"It's too dark to see anything." She turned to Alicia. "How do you suppose it's going?"

"I wish I knew." Alicia finished her fruit and went to the window, taking the curtain from Sam and drawing it open farther. The darkness prevented her from seeing anything but her reflection and those of the candles that Sam had lit around the parlor.

"I thought Sam Steele was long gone, that it couldn't hurt me anymore," Sam said.

The distress in her sister's voice tugged at Alicia. Sam was always so strong, so sure of herself.

Alicia let the curtain float back into place and took

Sam's hand. "It'll be over soon. Then you needn't worry any longer. Luke and Blake will take care of everything. And with Nate being Steele, it's over."

Sam shook her head and something in her eyes made Alicia's belly clutch.

"I don't know, Alicia. I have a very bad feeling. Right here," she said, pressing a fist below her heart.

"They're fine," Alicia repeated, as much to reassure Sam as herself.

Lewis's nostrils expanded along with his chest. "What do you mean you didn't bring me any gold?"

Though Blake kept his gaze firmly on Lewis, he could see Luke out of the corner of his eye. Luke struggled to stand, and though he wavered and cursed, he managed to stay on his feet. Blake could only hope that they'd all be so lucky before this was through.

"It's not here," Blake said, trying for extra time. If they were going to get out of the mess they were in, then Blake needed time to think of a plan. "It's on my ship."

"Really?" Lewis asked in a syrupy voice that Blake didn't trust. "Shall I simply wait here while you fetch it?" Laughing, he turned to his men and gave a sharp nod. One of them strolled forward.

"Show this man what happens when I'm lied to."

Blake braced for it, but the fist that connected with his face felt like a cannon blast. His head rang with it, and a fiery pain ripped across his cheek. For a moment the deck of the ship rose and fell on a wave of dizziness.

"I'm through listening to your lies. You show me the gold I came for or not only will you regret it, but so will your precious Alicia."

Night had fallen fast, and though the lanterns hadn't been lit, the huge moon cast enough light for Blake to see the man wasn't lying. The problem was Blake was out of ideas. He looked to Joe. He still had a thick fist filled with sash pressed into Aidan's shoulder. The boy's eyes were closed and Blake wasn't sure if he was resting or unconscious.

"Restin'," Joe confirmed without being asked. But his face was drawn, and in it, Blake read the urgency. Aidan needed a doctor.

"I wouldn't bother keeping the wound from bleeding. None of you will be leaving this ship alive."

Blake's blood ran cold while sweat beaded on his upper lip. There had to be a way out. They couldn't let Lewis get to Alicia and Samantha. Despite their argument earlier, Blake loved Alicia and he'd give his last breath protecting her. He looked to Luke. The former pirate had a trail of blood running from his temple, his face was pinched, and he couldn't quite stand upright. He didn't look as though he could manage another fight.

"We'll get it, whatever you want," Blake said with his attention once again on Lewis.

Lewis grinned. "Oh, I'll get what I want, what I came for, and what I deserve. I'd always planned to. Your mistake, Blake, is thinking I need you alive to get it."

"We know where it is," Luke said.

Lewis turned to Luke. "So does your wife, I'm sure."

Luke snarled. "I'll kill you before I let you get near her."

"You won't have a choice," Lewis answered. He pretended to yawn. "This is getting tedious. You and you," he said, pointing to the two biggest men, "stay here. Feel free to hurt them, but leave them alive. I'd like to witness their final moments. I can't think of a better way to end a day. You two," he said to the remaining men, "come with me."

Blake didn't think. He went on instinct and he dove for Lewis. Blake landed on his enemy's back, Lewis grunted, and they both fell to the deck. Blake felt the back of his hands scrape against the wood. He pulled back his arm and ploughed his fist into Lewis's side. Hearing the man yelp drove Blake. Now they'd see how tough the little bastard really was. He fisted his hand again.

Before he could make contact, he was roughly jerked to his feet. A thick arm banded around his neck, choked his breathing until he was gasping. Luke, who must have followed Blake's attack, was also being held against a brick of a man.

Lewis wove to his feet, glared daggers at Blake.

"You'll pay for that, you son of a bitch."

Blake struggled. He knew what was coming, but he wasn't going to go down without fighting. He jammed his elbows back, wiggled, and shoved, but the pressure around his neck only increased. He saw little white stars and felt a fear the likes of which he'd never known. Alicia was in danger and there was nothing he could do about it.

With his lungs burning, Blake turned to Luke. The pirate was watching Blake, but Blake knew by the way Luke was clutching at his captor's arm that he was losing the same battle as Blake. Fog was creeping over Blake as he fought to remain conscious. He tried to shout when he saw Lewis and two men climb over the gunwale. But it wasn't until Blake felt himself slipping, saw Luke fold limply, that Blake knew true despair.

Alicia, he thought.

Then the world went black.

Twenty-one

"Why hasn't Joe come back yet? He and Aidan should have been back by now."

Alicia didn't bother answering, since she'd already done so three times. But as each minute passed, her concern also grew. Sam was right. Joe and Aidan should have returned some time ago. Sam had expressly asked Joe not to stay and watch so she wouldn't have to worry about them as well.

She angled her head toward the open window, prayed she'd hear their arrival. But the only sound that floated in with the damp air was that of palm fronds rubbing together. Even the night creatures were abnormally quiet.

"They have another few minutes, and if they're not back by then, I'm going down to the beach. I can't stand this waiting any longer."

Alicia stood up from the couch, where Sam kept insisting she stay. Her sister spun from the door she'd been watching, as though willing Luke to come walking through it.

"Don't think it, Alicia. You're staying here."

"I've a stake in this as well. And I will go. You're not the only one in our family that can take care of herself."

Their wills clashed in a long stare. A stare that was soon broken by the sound of boots on gravel.

"They're back!" Sam shouted. She raced for the door, Alicia right behind her. Sam threw open the door, gasped, and stumbled back a step.

Squawk. "Man in house. Man in house."

Alicia stepped around Sam and her heart sank. It was Lewis.

"You!" Sam said, grabbing Alicia's arm. Her grip was like iron.

Alicia shook her head. "You know Lewis?"

Sam's eyes were wide and her face was losing color by the second. "He's Oliver Grant's son."

"What?" Alicia sputtered.

"Allow me," Lewis said, coming into the room.

Sam scurried backward, pulling Alicia with her. Behind Lewis came two of the largest men Alicia had ever laid eyes on. The last one who entered closed the door behind him.

"Lock it," Lewis ordered.

The sound of the lock being slid into position had a ball of fear tumbling in Alicia's belly.

"In fact, Alicia, I have you to thank for leading me here. I had no intention of ever coming after Samantha until you came to the plantation."

Sam's gaze snapped to Alicia, and she released her arm. "You went to the plantation? When?"

"I—after I found Jacob's letter. He'd mentioned you may have been on the plantation. I didn't see Lewis there, Sam," Alicia said, trying to make sense of Lewis's presence. "I wouldn't do that to you."

"Ah, but you did. I heard you talking to that fat Fanny, heard you mentioning you were looking for your sister. At first I didn't care. You see, Samantha," he said, turning his attention to Sam, "I actually praised you for a while. You managed to elude my father. You were the one thing that bastard failed at. It proved I wasn't the only failure in our family."

His jaw tightened for a moment. "He kept journals on you, loads of journals about his desire to locate you, to make you pay for humiliating him. Had he known you were Steele, he would have succeeded. He'd have had the governor and the Navy and every other lawman and mercenary after you. But he didn't know. And neither did I until"—his gaze shifted to Alicia—"until you."

"But, but, I didn't even know until Sam told me."

"That was the key," Lewis said, holding up one finger. "Sam. Nobody had put it together that the time of her escape coincided very closely with the first sightings of Sam Steele. And I wouldn't have either, except you mentioned that you used to call her Sam. I started to put the pieces together. Same name, same sloop. From there it was really only a matter of following you."

"You're the one threatening me," Sam said.

Alicia's heart hammered. Lewis was the one who'd put the sword in the door, who'd scared Sam? Lewis had followed her, and all along she'd led him straight to her sister? She had brought this evil down on Sam, on all of them.

"You're wondering how. Well, let me tell you. But first, shall we move into the parlor, where we can be more comfortable?"

He led the way, confident he'd be obeyed. Alicia watched his arrogant stride and wanted to be sick.

"I didn't know, Sam. I swear."

Sam remained ashen, but she took her sister's hand and

Alicia drew comfort from the contact. They sat next to each other on the couch opposite Lewis. His men stayed in the entryway, blocking any exit.

"After I learned that you'd bartered passage to Tortuga, it was simply a matter of getting myself there and waiting for you. I followed you right to that little shack you spent the night at, the one with the giant." He grinned. "Luckily he keeps his window open. When he encouraged you to stow away on Blake's ship, I went there looking for employment. The dwarf was in charge at the time, and he hired me on. And now you know," he said. He leaned back, negligently crossed his legs.

"He'll kill you when he finds out," Alicia warned. Her voice held the conviction she believed. Blake wouldn't tolerate being used in such a manner.

"Oh, did I forget to mention that part?" He tsked. "I left Blake back on the ship. He's being, shall we say, well taken care of."

Alicia jumped to her feet. Fear clutched its long fingers around her throat. While they'd been sitting idle, had Blake and the rest of them been hurt? Or worse?

"What did you do with Blake?"

Lewis looked down at his fingernails, shrugged. "Teaching him a lesson he won't soon forget. But don't worry, I've ordered him not to be killed until I return."

"What about Luke?"

Lewis looked at Sam and chuckled. "He's in much the same position as Blake. Although I must say they're in much better shape than Aidan. He's probably bled to death by now."

With a keening wail, Sam went after Lewis like a cannon blast. She landed on his lap, where she began beating him with her fists.

"You bastard! I'll kill you!" she raged.

"Get off me!" Lewis shoved her just as his men came running forward. Sam sprawled to the ground but she immediately regained her feet. She faced Lewis, her hands curled into fists at her sides and her face red with fury.

Lewis also stood. He waved off his men before they grabbed Samantha. They stepped to the side. He then straightened his shirt, inhaled deeply.

"I see now why my father followed you across the Caribbean. Are you this boisterous in bed?"

The slap came fast and it echoed through the room. "You're as much a bastard as your father," Sam spat.

He grabbed her, yanked her against him. "Want to see just how alike we are?" he asked, thrusting his pelvis against hers.

"Let go of me!" Sam yelled while she strained against him.

Alicia ran to help but was cut short when one of the giants blocked her way. Without a hint of emotion in his ebony eyes, he stared her down. Alicia didn't stop to weigh the wisdom of her actions. She'd worked years in the shop and she'd become quite strong. She intended to use those muscles now.

She came at him, hand raised. As expected, he grabbed it easily before it made contact with his face. She tried with her other arm, putting more force behind it. He grabbed it as well, then yanked her hard against him. Alicia smiled sweetly.

Then she rammed her knee up between his legs with all her might. His eyes crossed. He doubled over and wretched all over the floor. Looking about madly, she caught sight of the other man coming at her. But she also saw a weapon. Dumping the fruit from the bowl, she swept the wooden vessel up and smashed it on the back of the fallen man's head.

"Alicia!" Sam yelled, but it was too late. The other man grabbed her. Taking her hair in his fist, he all but lifted her off the ground. Alicia gasped at the needles of pain that pricked along her head. Her vision blurred, forcing her to blink away the tears.

"Let her go!" Sam ordered.

Lewis laughed. "You're not the one giving orders, Samantha. Now, take me where you hide your gold. And don't think about lying to me or you'll see the same fate as your husband."

Alicia saw Sam's chin quiver a moment before she steeled it.

"If Luke didn't give you any, what makes you think I will?"

He cackled. "If you want your sister to remain alive, you'll do as you're told."

Alicia hadn't noticed it before, but the man holding her suddenly drew a pistol. He cocked it with his thumb and pressed the cold barrel to Alicia's temple. All Alicia could think of was her baby. The baby she might never get to see if Lewis ordered the man to pull the trigger.

"Sam, get the money," she said.

Sam locked gazes with Alicia and nodded. "I'll do it."

"That's better," Lewis said. He released Sam, who scrambled out of his reach. "But don't try anything stupid. If anything happens to me, you can kiss your sister good-bye."

"It's upstairs," Sam said.

Lewis pointed with his gun. "Lead the—"

"Alicia!" Blake yelled from the front door. It shook within its frame as he tried to force it open. "Alicia!"

Lewis's eyes went wide. "Don't let her go," he ordered to the man who held her. He grabbed Sam again. "Take me to the gold!" he barked. He pushed Sam toward the stairs.

Before they could cross the room, the front window exploded and Luke came crashing through the glass. He rolled to the floor. Lewis cursed and scrambled to get himself and Sam into a corner. Luke leapt to his feet, drawing his pistols at the same time. Both aimed at Lewis.

Her ears were still ringing as the front door smashed open and Blake barreled into the kitchen. His left eye was already swollen and his lip was split. He had a gash along his cheek and a trail of dried blood crept from there to his jaw. His hands, Alicia noticed as he aimed his pistols, were also scraped. Oh, God, what had happened to him?

"Luv," Luke said, drawing her attention back to Sam. "You remember the first time we took a merchant ship together? Remember what happened to the other captain?"

Sam nodded, and before Alicia could make sense of what they were talking about, Sam suddenly threw her weight to one side. It knocked both her and Lewis off balance. Lewis lowered his weapon as they staggered apart and he struggled to keep his balance.

"Luke, no!" Alicia yelled but her shout was lost as Luke pulled the trigger. The shot screamed through the parlor. Alicia's heart stopped until she realized Sam wasn't hurt.

Lewis fell and didn't move again. The man behind Alicia tensed. The pistol at her temple, however, didn't falter.

"Let her go," Blake ordered while Sam ran into Luke's waiting embrace. "You've no part in this."

"I was promised gold," the man said.

"Do you want to end up like your other friends?" Blake asked, pointing to the man who hadn't moved since Alicia had hit him with the bowl.

"I want my gold."

"There's two of us," Luke said, stepping near Blake. Since Luke had brought two pistols, they each had weapons aimed and cocked. "And you can't shoot both of us with only one shot."

The barrel pressed deeper into Alicia's temple. "I only need one to kill her."

"You kill her, mate, and you'll have two rounds in your skull before she hits the floor."

"It's a chance I'm willing to take."

Well, he may be, but Alicia wasn't. Following Sam's example, Alicia threw herself to the side. Only this man was much stronger than Lewis and he managed to keep them upright when they spun around. But then they tripped on a chair and tumbled over it. Alicia landed hard on her shoulder. When she caught her breath, she realized they'd landed near where Lewis lay. Or more importantly, within reach of his pistol.

The man was lifted off her, and Alicia saw it took both Luke and Blake to do it. Both were spent and the man knew it. Wrenching his arms free, he spun, knocking Luke down with a single blow.

Distantly, Alicia heard Sam yell for Luke but Alicia focused on Blake. She slid backward until her outstretched hand closed over the pistol.

"Stay back!" she yelled when Blake dodged a fist.

The man spun, and Blake leapt out of the way. Alicia had fired many pistols and her aim was true. Her single shot penetrated the man's heart and he fell to the floor.

"Luke," Sam whimpered. She knelt beside her husband, helped him to his knees, then wiped the blood from his mouth.

Tears formed in Alicia's eyes when Luke said nothing,

simply slid his arms around his wife and held her closely. He closed his eyes and pressed his lips to her hair.

"Are you all right?" Blake asked Alicia.

She blinked, pulled her gaze from Sam and Luke and the love that radiated from them. She looked up at Blake. His gaze was guarded; no sign of what he was feeling was visible. Though she ached to be taken into his arms and held tightly, she held back.

"Better than you, I'd wager."

He smiled, extended a hand. With a skip of her heart, she pressed her palm into his and allowed him to help her to her feet. Warmth spilled through her soul, brought home the fact that he was there and that they were both alive.

"Alicia," he said in a soft voice. He curved his other hand around her cheek. The slight tremble was unmistakable. "You're sure you're not hurt?"

She couldn't stop her chin from quivering. It took all her strength not to lean into him. God, she'd been so afraid. She swallowed the lump in her throat.

"I'm fine, truly."

He nodded, dropped his hands, and stepped back.

"Oh, my God, Luke!" Sam screamed, drawing everyone's attention. "Where's Aidan? Lewis said—"

"He's fine, luv. He was shot in the shoulder, but Joe's taken him to the doctor."

"Shot?" Sam said, her voice thick with tears. "I want to see him."

"I expect they'll be here before long."

"What happened on the ship?" Alicia asked.

"Lewis beat us there and he wasn't happy to learn we hadn't brought gold."

"Lewis did this to you?" Sam said, noting both Blake and Luke's wounds.

"Please, luv, don't insult me, I'm hurting enough. He had these two"—Luke pointed to the two men on the ground— "and two more." His gaze darkened. "Aidan should never have been hurt."

"It's not your fault," Sam said.

"No," Alicia said, wrapping her arms around herself, "it's mine."

"Don't," Sam said, coming to her feet. "You had no way of knowing Lewis had followed you, or what he was planning. You came looking for me and you found me, that's all that matters," Sam said, taking Alicia into her arms.

While Alicia wasn't looking, Blake snuck outside and leaned against the house. He needed the support. It had been dire on the ship, and all had looked lost when he'd woken on deck. He'd looked to Luke, thought for sure the man was unconscious, but then the former pirate had slowly opened an eye. Blake had known then that Luke was pretending to be hurt worse than he was and Blake had opted to do the same.

It had been agonizing moments before Luke had made eye contact with Joe. And somehow they had silently communicated the attack. Joe started it, screaming and cursing, saying they'd killed Aidan. Both captors had charged Joe, and that's when Blake and Luke had jumped and taken up the fight. It had taken all three of them. Joe, too, had his fair share of wounds, but they'd succeeded in killing Lewis's men before they could inflict further harm.

With Joe taking Aidan, Blake had been on Luke's heels running to the house. He'd envisioned all sorts of awful things as he'd run until his lungs burned, and all had entailed Alicia ending up in a pool of blood.

Now, with the scent of fear and blood still hanging over him, Blake took a shuddering breath. He drew deep gulps of air until he felt his heart beating normally again. Through the open door, he heard Alicia's voice and let it wrap around him. She was alive and safe.

"Where's Blake?" he heard Luke ask.

"I'm right here," he wanted to say. He wanted to walk into the room, take Alicia into his arms, and never let go. It killed him that he couldn't. But if he did, then what? It would only prolong the pain of losing her. They'd said their good-byes and nothing had changed. Alicia didn't want a life at sea and he did. The truth of that sliced through him every time he thought about it, but Alicia was right. Staying on the ship wouldn't be fair to her, and staying on land wouldn't make Blake happy. Best to walk away.

No matter how much it hurt.

"He's gone," Alicia answered, and in her voice Blake heard the same despair that was tearing him apart.

"What do we do with these men?" Samantha asked.

There was a moment of silence, then Luke's voice. "When Joe comes back, we'll take them out to sea. If Lewis left letters about Samantha, then the last thing we need is to have him die on the same island she lives on. Despite Nate taking over as Steele, it might raise too many questions and suspicions."

In the darkness beside the house, Blake nodded at Luke's logic. Then, knowing Alicia was in good hands, Blake cast a last look toward the house and walked away.

Twenty-two

Alicia stepped on deck and the full force of the sun and its reflection off the sea shot into her eyes. She squinted, dropped her gaze, and made her way to the bow. Though she heard Sam and Luke talking behind her and caught sight of Joe and Aidan sitting in the thin shadow of the lifeboat, deep into a game of chess, she ignored them all. She wanted only to lose her troubled thoughts in the undulations of the water.

But she should have known her sister better. The minute Alicia was settled against the base of the bowsprit with her mug of ginger tea, she heard the tapping of Sam's shoes moving toward her.

"Didn't take you very long," Alicia said and forced a smile.

Sam's lips twitched and she settled against the gunwale. "I've been waiting for days to talk to you, but since you stayed below, I assumed you needed some time alone."

Alicia nodded, took a long sip of her tea while she struggled to rein in her emotions. She'd wept enough since leaving St. Kitts three days ago, and though her mind knew that she needed to regain control of her life and stop moping, it was taking her heart much longer to catch up.

"I did." She took a deep breath of moist, salty air. After days below smelling nothing but wet wood, the freshness of the open sea had never been so welcome.

"And now?" her sister asked, her eyes filled with worry.

"I'm all right, Sam." She pressed a hand to her stomach. "I have to be, don't I?"

Her heart squeezed painfully, and Alicia turned to the water. Losing Blake was excruciating, but how would it be to look upon the face of his child and see its father there every day, knowing he was gone to her? She swallowed the sob that caught in her throat and hoped the moisture in her eyes could be attributed to the glare of the sun.

"It won't be easy."

"I'll be fine, Sam. *We'll* be fine. I have a home and a means of earning money. I'll hardly be destitute."

Sam frowned. "That's not what I meant, and you know it."

"I know, but it's too late for that, isn't it? I'm unmarried and with child. I don't hold any illusions as to the reception I will receive once it becomes apparent I'm pregnant."

And that was the truth. She'd thought of nothing else for days. But it wasn't herself she feared for, it was the child. The child who would be ridiculed, would be treated as less than he was because he didn't have a father.

"It's going to be awful. I really think you should have stayed with us. We could have lied and told everyone you were widowed. Nobody in St. Kitts would be any wiser."

"If I wanted to leave Port Royal, I'd have left with

Blake. I'm not ashamed of this child and I will protect it with everything that's in me."

Sam leaned forward, took Alicia's free hand. "I'm not saying you should be ashamed. The baby is a gift, a most precious one. I know it was conceived out of love, Alicia, and I want you to know I'll do what I can to help. Whatever you need, you've only to ask."

"Will you come back when it's time? I know there's nothing you can do to make it easier for me, but I don't think I can face bringing this child into the world without you there. At least for the first little bit, knowing I have someone to support me will give me strength."

Sam's eyes filled, which of course made Alicia's tear as well.

"Of course I will. We'll get you settled in Port Royal, then I'll come back for the birth. You don't need me for strength—you have enough of that all your own. But you won't be alone when it's born." She squeezed Alicia's hand. "I promise you that."

Alicia wiped a tear that was sliding its way down her cheek and clenched her teeth until she was sure she could talk. She set her cup down and held her sister's embrace.

"Thanks, Sam. That's all I needed to know."

There was something to be said for coming home, Alicia thought. It was a balm to the spirit and she felt its healing the minute she caught sight of the blacksmith shop. With joy pushing through the curtain of loss she'd felt shrouded in, Alicia ran the last stretch until she reached the door. There she stopped, placed a hand to it, and swore she felt it breathe. Home.

The hammering that had been muffled through the

thick door clanged around her ears when she threw it open. Familiar sounds and smells wrapped around Alicia until she felt the warmth of her tears on her cheeks. The coals of the forge glowed blood-red and the smoke from the fire curled up Alicia's nose. With his back to her as he pounded on a sword, Charles continued working, unaware she'd returned.

With a squeal of delight, she charged toward him. He stopped, his arm frozen above his head, and turned. Seeing her, he flung the hammer down, opened his arms wide, and crushed her to him when she raced within them.

He spun her around, her feet clear off the ground. Then he set her down, stepped away so he could look at her. "Blimey, it's good to see you," he said through his grin, then tugged her back for another hug.

Alicia closed her eyes and squeezed him back. He smelled of smoke and steel, and Alicia knew that by the end of tomorrow she'd smell the same. She grinned at the thought.

"Oh," Charles said, looking over Alicia's shoulder. He stepped back. "I didn't see you there."

Alicia turned. Sam, Luke, Joe, and Aidan were all standing inside the door watching. Well, the adults were observing Charles, clearly wondering if they could entrust Alicia to him once they left. Aidan's eyes were all about, jumping from the fire to the tools to the array of completed weapons that lay lined up on a table.

"Go have a look, Aidan. I'll explain anything you want to know later."

His smile was bright in the otherwise dim room and he made a direct line to the completed swords. He was healing quickly, and though his injured arm remained bound in a sling, the fingers of his other skimmed the intricate handles.

"Charles, this is my family."

His eyes flashed to hers, went round as moons. "You actually found them?"

"It pains me, Charles, that you have so little faith in me," she said, trying to look hurt but not able to wipe the grin off her face.

He scratched his head. "It seemed such a large undertaking and the chances of you actually finding them . . ."

"Would you like to meet them?"

His hand cupped her cheek, and his eyes danced with happiness. "I'd love to."

Then, feeling like a little girl preening in a new dress, Alicia introduced them.

Alicia pushed the bucket aside, groaned. Using the sleeve of her nightgown, she wiped the sweat off her forehead, then curled onto the floor. The wood was cool beneath her heated cheek and she took a deep breath, then another, as her stomach began to unfist. She had no idea how long these bouts of morning sickness were going to plague her, but she prayed it wouldn't be the whole nine months because it wasn't fair to Charles to run the shop every morning by himself. But as it was, she was too wrung out to move.

She was beginning to doze when she heard three sharp taps on her front door.

"Not now," Alicia muttered, throwing her arm over her eyes.

She'd recognized those knocks. Three crisp raps evenly spaced could only mean one person. Aunt Margaret. Moaning, Alicia sat up. Since they'd arrived in Port Royal toward the evening meal yesterday, she'd hoped her aunt wouldn't have yet had time to hear of her return. Another three raps. Damn.

Alicia came to her feet and pressed a hand to her stomach when it threatened to revolt. Taking deep breaths helped ease the nausea. Alicia took her robe from the foot of the bed and slipped it on, then padded barefoot to the door.

Her aunt did not look happy to see her.

She swept past Alicia and marched into the kitchen.

"I hope you have an explanation for what you've done. You left without word, without a chaperone. I had to hear it from that man that works at the blacksmith shop."

Alicia shut the door. "His name is Charles, and if he told you I'd left, then he also told you why."

Her aunt's mouth pinched. "Do not be obtuse, Alicia, it does not become you. You have a family here. You certainly did not need to go traipsing off by yourself to find perfect strangers. Do you know how that affected me? I had to make countless excuses for your absence."

Alicia frowned. "Why didn't you tell them the truth?"

"What truth?" her aunt sputtered. "That the love my sister had shown you all those years wasn't enough? That *I* wasn't enough for you, that you had to find better elsewhere?"

Sighing, Alicia sat at the table. She really wasn't up to this argument. The only good thing, though she hadn't thought so at the time, was that Sam had been adamant about sleeping on her ship. Better to wait until Aunt Margaret had some time to calm down before she introduced her to her sister.

"Aunt Margaret, this had nothing to do with either you or Jacob and Anna. You're right, they loved me as their own and I love them to this day, but it doesn't tell me about my past. This was about me wanting to know where I'd come from, what had happened, and if I did, in fact, have any family left."

Her aunt's cheeks turned fiery red. "You have me."

"And I appreciate you," Alicia said, trying for patience, "but I needed to know my past, and now I do. My memory returned."

"I see," she said, sitting primly with her hands smoothing her skirt.

"Aunt Margaret, I have a sister, and a brother-in-law, a longtime friend of my family, and a new brother. They live in St. Kitts and are actually here at the moment. Well, they're staying on their ship, but you can meet them later if you wish."

Her aunt rearranged her hat. "What does your brother-in-law do?"

"He builds ships. He and my sister both."

The older woman looked as though she was going to throw up. Apparently she'd harbored the hope that perhaps Alicia's sister could teach Alicia how to be a proper lady. If only her aunt knew that Sam had been a pirate, that she wore pants to work and cussed when angry. Alicia chuckled, then hid it behind a cough when her aunt's eyes narrowed at her.

"What are your plans, then? Are you going to remain in St. Kitts?"

Alicia wasn't sure if that was hope or dread in her aunt's voice.

"I'm staying. Nothing has changed, Aunt Margaret. Charles and I will run the shop and I'll continue to live here."

"And your sister?" she asked.

"Will be staying for a short time, then going back home. She'll be coming back—"

Damn, Alicia thought. She hadn't even told Charles about the baby yet but she figured since her aunt was here she may as well get it over with. Straightening her spine, she plunged ahead.

"Aunt Margaret, there's something else I need to tell you."

The older woman sighed. "I'm almost afraid to ask."

"I also found Blake, well, Daniel."

"Do not say that name in this house!" her aunt spewed, coming to her feet. "He broke Anna's heart when he left. I will not have his name spoken in her home!"

Alicia came to her feet as well. Despite how it had ended, she loved Blake and this was *her* house now. She'd speak his name if she wanted to.

"Anna loved Blake, Aunt Margaret, and what happened to Eric wasn't Blake's fault. It was an accident and he's sorry."

"It is too late for pathetic excuses! She went to her death bed sick over losing her sons and I will never forgive him for that!"

"He's your nephew."

Rage dripped from her aunt. "No, he is not, not any longer."

"Well, that's unfortunate as he's the father of the child I'm carrying."

Aunt Margaret swooned. Alicia grabbed her arm, guided her to a chair, and helped her sit. Since her aunt seemed incapable of speech, Alicia did the talking.

"I'm expecting Blake's child and I plan on raising the baby while I continue to work at the blacksmith shop, both before and after the birth."

Her aunt's mouth moved but it took more than one try before any words came out.

"Where is he?"

"Blake? I don't know. It doesn't matter, he's not coming back."

"Well then," she said, composing herself with incredible speed, "we'll act quickly. You'll come live with me, and when you start to show, we'll keep you inside and out of sight until the child is born. I'll tell everyone you've gone to spend time with your sister. Then, once the baby comes, we'll find someone to take it and nobody will be the wiser."

Alicia gasped. "I'm not going into hiding and I'm not giving away this child."

"It doesn't have a father and you don't have a husband."

"You're wrong. My baby has a father, a wonderful one. And I'll make sure he knows it when he gets older."

"This man you find so decent bedded you and left you, and you're going to parade that fact every day?" Her aunt looked pained. "I'm not surprised at Daniel's behavior as it is not the first time he has proven himself selfish. But you," she sputtered, looking down her long nose at Alicia, "have shamed this family and I am thoroughly disgusted."

"I can't help how you feel, but I am not ashamed. This child will be given Blake's name and it will be loved. If you cannot accept that, then you're welcome to leave."

Alicia had never seen her aunt look so ill. "Do you have any idea how difficult this will be for you, being unwed and with child? Everyone will think you're a—a—a whore," she sputtered.

The word wasn't unexpected, but it hurt. And because she knew it was the first of many times she was going to hear it, she decided to make her stand straightaway.

"Then so be it. But you're forgetting I've been through hard times before. This isn't the first trial I've had to survive and I'm certain it won't be the last. Just as I am equally certain that I can weather it. I've never been concerned with what people think of me."

"Yes," her aunt sneered. "I've been painfully aware of that."

"I loved Jacob and Anna and they gave me a wonderful life. I will forever be grateful to them, and their grandchild will know the wonderful people it comes from."

"Do not dare put yourself and Blake, or Daniel, or whatever he decides to call himself, in the same lot as Anna! She would be horrified to know you're unmarried and with child."

Seeing no reason to argue further, Alicia went to the door and opened it. The happy chirping of the birds outside was a sharp contrast to the storm of emotions that swirled inside.

"Please leave. And don't come back until you can find it in your heart to accept both me and this child."

Aunt Margaret huffed past Alicia, her head held at an unnaturally high angle. She stepped outside, then turned to Alicia.

"You have changed, and it is not for the better."

"No, I haven't. You've simply never been able to see me for who I am."

And with nothing left to say, Alicia closed the door.

Twenty-three

I thought I'd find you here," Sam said as she moved between the headstones. She sat on the grass next to Alicia, placed her bouquet of white flowers on the mound next to another bouquet, one of delicate blue blossoms.

Alicia looked from the carving that held the names of Jacob and Anna Davidson, to the intricate cross she'd made herself, to her sister.

"You didn't even know them."

"Doesn't mean I can't bring them flowers. Besides, they took such wonderful care of you, I feel it's a way of saying thank you."

"I keep thinking about what Aunt Margaret said, that they'd be disappointed in me. I can't bear that thought. I loved them, and knowing they weren't my real parents doesn't change that."

Sam rubbed Alicia's back. "Of course it doesn't," she said.

Tears of shame filled Alicia's eyes. The grass that had long since grown over the graves blurred into a carpet of green. "I keep seeing them in my head, Sam, and each time they're so upset that they can't even look at me."

"That's not you talking, that's your aunt, and she's wrong. I'm not saying they wouldn't have had a moment of disappointment, but they found you, a complete stranger, and took you into their hearts and home. They loved you as their own. That doesn't sound like the kind of people who would turn their backs on you at a time when you'd need them the most."

Sam was right, and the truth of her words eased a weight she'd felt around her heart since the day her aunt had said those hateful things to her. Jacob and Anna would have cherished their grandchild the same way they'd cherished her, unconditionally.

Alicia drew a deep breath, wiped her wet cheeks. "Thanks, Sam. I needed to remember that."

"That's what sisters are for," she said.

"Have I told you," Alicia asked, looking into her sister's eyes, "how grateful I am to have found you again?"

Sam smiled. "I think you've told me every day since you arrived in St. Kitts."

"It's all so extraordinary, isn't it? What happened to us, how we came to find each other?"

"It'll make an interesting bedtime story for your child."

"That it will."

Alicia lovingly touched the names on the carvings, then stood. Silently she and Sam meandered out of the graveyard. Though it wasn't a deliberate destination, Alicia wasn't surprised when they found themselves behind her house, on a small rise, looking down at a simple white cross.

"I always wondered who was buried here but all Jacob ever said was that it was a lost soul and that even lost souls deserved to be remembered. Somehow a part of me must have known, because I found myself here quite often." Alicia smiled. "I brought her flowers even before I knew who she was."

"She's not lost anymore, Alicia, and neither is Father. When I come back for the baby, I'll have their stones done and we'll give them a proper ceremony. She won't be a nameless cross any longer."

Alicia nodded. Sam would be able to make lovely head-stones from wood and planned to carve them with their parents' names as well as a likeness of the *Destiny*, their father's ship.

The blasted tears she'd come to loathe once again sprang to her eyes. Between the bouts of sickness, the tears that never seemed to dry, and the fact that Sam was leaving today, Alicia already felt exhausted and it was only midmorning.

"Are you sure you can't stay another few days?"

Sam bowed her head, then faced her sister.

"You know I'd love nothing better, but I'll be back for the baby."

Alicia's heart pinched. "That seems such a long time."

"It is, but I need to get back. I wish I could shelter you from what's coming, but I can't. Best I can do is to remind you to hold your head high. Words can't hurt you."

"They hurt Luke."

Sam's smile was troubled. "He told me he'd been by to talk to you."

"He gave me a lot to think about, about what my child will face as he grows up."

"It won't be easy, not for either of you."

Alicia sighed, reached down, and pulled out a few blades of grass. She toyed with them absently. "I know, and hearing it from Luke made it all worse. It's one thing to think I know what will happen, but it's another to hear it from someone who has lived it."

"There will be ugly names thrown at both of you, people are going to shun you, and your child will have just as difficult a road." Sam pressed her hand against Alicia's. "I hate knowing you'll be here alone, suffering through that, and there's nothing I can do to help you." She paused, gave Alicia a reassuring squeeze. "But Luke survived it and look at the man he is." Pride coated Sam's words, and made Alicia smile.

"He is a good man. I like him."

Sam's eyes sparkled. "As do I. And as I know he told you, the best you can do is love this child as the Davidsons loved you, completely and without reservation."

"That's easy, I already do."

"That's all you can do. Unfortunately we can't help what other people say or think. Luke's feelings toward his parentage didn't come from the townsfolk, they came from his stepfather."

"I don't have any intention of marrying anyone else."

"You're young, that'll change."

"If something happened to Luke, could you replace him?"

Sam smirked. "No, of course not."

"I wish Blake were here," Alicia said. Not simply because it would make her life easier, but because she wished she could share this experience with the man she loved.

"You'll have the shop and Charles, and a nursery to prepare. Besides, Aidan will keep you busy with his questions."

"I think he's still in shock that you agreed to let him stay."

"It wasn't my idea. But he asked, and Luke convinced me that letting Aidan stay here for a few months was going to be a good experience, that he'd learn a valuable skill." Sam sighed. "It doesn't seem that long ago that Aidan made me promise he could stay with me forever and already he's wanting to let go."

"That's only because he's secure enough in your love to know you'll be there when he gets back."

"Oh." Sam nodded as her eyes shone with tears. "I'll have to keep reminding myself of that for the next few months when I wish he was home. But," she said and smiled, "I feel better knowing you won't be alone. As he gets better, it will allow you to work less." She eyed Alicia questioningly. "You will work less?"

Alicia smiled sweetly and Sam sighed.

"That's what I thought."

The first few weeks after Sam's departure passed at a snail's pace. Knowing her aunt would not announce her condition, Alicia had decided not to tell Charles and had convinced Aidan not to either. If Charles knew she was with child, then he'd argue against her decision to work, and work helped keep Alicia's mind busy.

Her days were long, wanting to put in as much time at the shop as she could knowing her days of doing so were limited. Between her and Charles, Aidan was learning quickly and showed a natural skill for the work. He seemed to enjoy the shop as much as he enjoyed the evenings, which he usually spent with Charles's oldest son, Jack.

Alicia's favorite time was after Aidan had returned from visiting Jack and he spent the last hour before bed regaling Alicia with the many adventures of Sam Steele. Some made her laugh; a large number made her cringe. God, the things her sister had lived through!

As her life fell back into a routine, time began to slip away faster, and it wasn't long before her clothes weren't fitting properly and her belly was beginning to grow as much as her breasts had. She wouldn't be able to hide it much longer.

Alicia stroked her stomach and a warmth spread through her. In a handful of months there'd be a baby to hold. She wasn't sure how Charles would take her news but she was excited nonetheless.

She walked quickly, the morning breeze lifting the fine hairs at the nape of her neck. Unlike most mornings when she'd look out to sea and wonder where Blake was, today Alicia's focus was entirely on what Charles's reaction would be. She could only hope that after the disappointment wore off, he wouldn't treat her any differently than he had before. She couldn't bear the idea of losing his love.

She arrived at the door at the same time as Charles. His eyebrows angled into a frown.

"You're here mighty early, it's barely dawn," he pointed out as he held the door for her.

"I was anxious to get started." Alicia stepped into the shop and immediately went to the windows, throwing them open. The breeze whispered into the room, shifting the dust on the floor, and the pale dawn light was just bright enough to make lanterns unnecessary.

"Where's Aidan this morning?"

Alicia turned from the window, smiled. "Off to see your boy, said there was something he needed to tell Jack. Considering how fast he ate his breakfast, I'd say it was important."

Charles shook his head. "Those two took to each other like flies to horse manure."

Alicia laughed.

"All right," he said, leaning against the workbench and crossing his arms. "What is it?"

"What makes you think there's something?" she asked.

"Since you're first move wasn't to light the fire or pick up a hammer, I'd say you have news. Besides," he said, looking at her closely, "you're shiny as a gold piece this morning."

"You're right, I have something to tell you."

When she made no move to do so, he asked, "And you'll be sharing this news?"

She took a breath for courage. "I'm having a baby."

His jaw went slack. He stared at her, stunned, and before he could do more than sputter, Alicia told him the rest. How she'd met Blake, how they'd hoped to get married, how in the end their dreams kept them apart. How in four months' time she'd be a mother.

"Alicia," he said, scraping his hands down his face, then peering at her over his blackened fingertips. "Dear God, do you know how hard this is going to be for you?"

She set her jaw. "I do. But the alternative is unimaginable. My aunt wants to hide me, then give away the child as though it were nothing more than a used piece of clothing. I love this baby," she said and placed a protective hand over the slight swell. "And it's all I have left of Blake."

"Daniel," Charles said, shaking his head. "I can't believe you found him. And then to be having his child . . ."

"I'm not an idiot, Charles, I know the road ahead will be hard."

"It'll be beyond hard, Alicia." He pushed from the bench. "Business dropped off when your father died, not significantly but enough to notice. Now, you know I think you're a fine blacksmith but some people don't think a woman should be running this shop. It was fine when it was simply a father indulging his daughter, but a woman working a man's job is frowned upon, Alicia. And now." He huffed out a breath, waved his hand. "They'll never support this shop with a pregnant unwed woman at the helm."

"Then we pretend the shop is yours. We'll tell everyone I sold it to you."

"And you'll stay away from it? Because even if I *own* it, they won't bring their business to me if you're here. And what will you do after the baby? Who do think will want to look after a—"

"Don't say it! Don't you dare say this child will be a bastard!"

Charles ran his hands down his face again. "Ignoring the truth doesn't change it."

Alicia gasped. Charles grimaced.

"I'm sorry," he said. He walked to her, his eyes filled with regret. "You've blindsided me, Alicia. Of all the confessions you could have made this morning, this was the last thing I expected to come out of your mouth."

"I want this baby, Charles. I'll find a way to survive what is coming. If my life becomes too difficult, I can, in truth, sell the shop to you and move to St. Kitts. It's not what I'd want, but I'm not without options if I need them."

He took her hands. "You don't want to live in St. Kitts. If you did, you'd have packed up and left with your sister."

Tears pricked her eyes. "This is my home. My mother is buried here and so are the Davidsons. I love this shop." She sniffled, squeezed his hands. "And even if I can't own it, I want to be able to walk by, to see it, to be surrounded by the memories that are in my heart. I need to know you'll support me, Charles. Not with money, I can do that. I mean stand beside me. I need to know there's someone here I can talk to, who won't hate me."

He nodded, opened his arms. Alicia stepped into them, and felt the weight of her decisions ease. It wouldn't be easy. She knew that. As a woman proprietor, it had been difficult; she could only imagine the ugliness when her pregnancy became obvious. But at least with Charles behind her, she knew she could manage.

"Thank you," she sniffled.

"You've carved yourself a hell of a road, Alicia. But if you want to keep the shop going, then I'll do my damnedest to—"

His words were lost as cannon fire exploded over Port Royal.

Twenty-four

"Land ho!"

"Finally," Blake muttered and pulled out his looking glass. Through it he saw the unmistakable shape of Tortuga as well as the fact that it seemed particularly lively, if the number of ships bobbing in its only accessible harbor was any indication. Snapping the glass closed, Blake adjusted his course, taking the most direct line to shore.

They'd made port over the months since leaving St. Kitts, but only for the least amount of time Blake could get away with as he'd always been anxious to get back out. He'd worked his crew hard these last months and they had heavy pockets to show for it.

Unfortunately the sea didn't hold the appeal it used to. His ship, the very thing that had always brought him peace, had become an endless collection of memories that always chose the most inopportune moments to bob to the surface.

He'd almost been shot when an enemy's pistol had

reminded Blake of the one Alicia had strapped to her thigh and he'd paused almost too long when the vision of her wearing only that had exploded into his mind. He'd regained his senses in time to jump to the side and fire off a shot without getting himself killed, but it had been damn close.

There was also the time he'd gone ashore in Nassau. He'd spotted a woman walking in a way that reminded him of Alicia, even though logically he knew she was in Port Royal. In his excitement, he'd chased after the lady, only to have her whack him with her parasol when he grabbed her arm and spun her around.

That was weeks ago and he hadn't been ashore since. He'd worked until exhaustion had demanded he sleep, but that wasn't always enough. The bed reminded him of Alicia and there were times, in his dreams, when he smelled her.

And then there were Nate and Vincent, or the lack thereof. The ship was quiet. Who knew, Blake thought as he ordered the sails to be trimmed, that he'd miss Vincent's nagging and his and Nate's constant arguing? But he did. He often found himself turning to ask Nate a question, only to face nothing but air. There was no off-tune whistling, no friendly teasing. Nothing was as it used to be, and though Blake had known it was going to be that way when he'd said farewell to his friends, he hadn't realized just how much the changes would hurt.

"Drop the anchor!" he shouted.

"Captain? How long are we staying?" his new first mate asked from the main deck. The rest of the crew stopped their tasks to listen.

He decided if being at sea wasn't keeping his thoughts off Alicia, he'd give it a go on land. "Four days all right?"

It was the longest they'd stayed anywhere since leaving

St. Kitts and everyone cheered. They saw to the rest of their duties in record time and soon the longboat was cutting through the water to shore. Blake headed straight for Doubloons. If he was going to drink himself into oblivion, he may as well do it with a friend.

Doubloons was crowded and pulsed with activity. Singing, laughing, catcalls, and swearing all mixed together. Thick candles wavered on shaky tables, and the smell of rum and sweat hung in the air. Blake cast a glance around the room, saw whom he was looking for, and wove his way through bodies that already swayed from too much drink. A few women tried to waylay him, sliding an arm across his shoulders. Others were bolder and squeezed his backside. Blake didn't acknowledge any of them and continued to his destination, where he took a chair opposite his friend.

"Blake!" Captain roared. He grinned, caught a passing barmaid, and ordered two more drinks. The woman looked at Blake, her eyes dropped, and she leaned forward. It was a wonder her bosom didn't fall onto the table and snuff out the candles.

"Anything else I can get you?" she purred.

Blake shook his head and she pouted as she turned away. Captain's laughter shook the table.

"You really ought to teach me that trick," he said, his eyes dancing.

"I've told you, it's a curse."

"Well, then, it's a curse I'd surely love to 'ave!" He took a swig of his drink. "Haven't seen ya in a while. Been busy, have ya?" he asked with enough of a twinkle in his eye that Blake knew just what he was implying.

"You make a habit of telling people to stow away on my ship?"

"Only the pretty ones."

The barmaid came behind Blake, reached over, and set his mug on the table. Her breast brushed the side of his face. Blake shifted away, earning a disgruntled sigh from the wench and a disappointed shake of the head from Captain.

"Now ya see, Blake. That's why I did it. Ya need to have some fun. Ya could take her upstairs, forget yer troubles."

"I'm not interested," he mumbled into his cup.

"Ah, but were ya interested in Alicia?"

Blake took another gulp. Captain's belly jiggled with laughter. He should have known the man would want to talk about Alicia, and Blake couldn't help but wonder if perhaps that was the real reason he'd sought him out after all.

"I knew it!" He looked rather proud of himself. "And I was right about St. Kitts bein' where she'd find Samantha."

Blake frowned. "How could you possibly know that?"

Captain grinned. "They were here, Samantha and Luke, a few months back."

"With Alicia?"

"No. I figured Alicia was with ya."

Blake's mouth flattened. "No. She's back in Port Royal, running her blacksmith shop."

Captain guffawed. "If it's still standin'."

"Of course it is, why wouldn't it be?"

"Ya haven't heard?"

Fear slid low in Blake's belly and he leaned forward. "Heard what?"

"Port Royal was sacked about a month or so ago."

Blake's mouth went dry as dust. "How bad?"

Captain shrugged. "Ya know how it is. Some claim

there's hardly anythin' left, and others say the locals put up a hell of a fight."

He remembered the look on Alicia's face after she'd regained her memory, how pale and devastated she'd been. He remembered how close she'd come to being seriously hurt at Samantha's house. Now he pictured her in the shop, fighting off pirates while the town around her was being attacked. Had her shop survived? Had she been hurt? He shoved to his feet.

"Where ya goin'? Ya haven't finished yer drink."

But Blake didn't answer. He was too busy running out the door.

At first glance it looked every bit as awful as his mind had imagined on the interminable sail over. There were several skeletal remains of houses and businesses that hadn't survived the attack but they seemed contained to the streets closest to the water. As he ran farther in toward the blacksmith shop, the damage diminished considerably. There were fewer walls seared black, fewer windows boarded up.

When he rounded the corner and saw the shop, saw the same sign that had hung over the door as long as he could remember, he stumbled to a stop. It was there. It was still there.

The pressure eased around his heart and Blake leaned against a nearby business while he got his breath back. The shop was all right, which gave him every reason to believe that Alicia was as well. He could leave now, he thought.

Only it wasn't that simple. Now that he was here, he desperately wanted to see her. He didn't know what he'd say; he knew only that he had to see her.

He opened the door to the shop and was blasted with

memories. He saw his father stirring the embers, saw him turn at the sound of his sons coming in. He'd set aside whatever he was working on to give his boys his undivided attention. His hands had been gentle and his voice, as he reminded them to be home in time for dinner so that their mother wouldn't worry, was gentle. Blake closed his eyes. Why, before he'd run off to sea, hadn't he realized that everything his father had ever done for both him and Eric had been done out of love?

"Daniel?"

Blake blinked away the memories, the stab of guilt, and the sharp bite of regret. He focused on the man before him.

"Charles. It's good to see you." Blake stepped forward and shook the man's hand.

"Never thought I'd see you step foot in here again," he said, eyeing Blake cautiously.

"Never thought I would," Blake acknowledged. He looked around the room, saw it was exactly as he remembered, and for the first time in months, breathed a sigh of contentment. Coming home wasn't so bad.

"I heard about the pirate attack. Doesn't seem as though it touched the shop."

"We were fortunate. The town fought back, caught a few of the bastards before they could get too close, but I think they were new at the job. Bunch of young whelps thought they could get rich quick."

"Didn't work?"

"No, the Navy corralled them fairly quick. They're cooling their heels in prison while they await their hanging."

"Alicia wasn't hurt?"

Charles's gaze hardened. "Is that why you're here? You've come for her?"

Blake flinched. "I heard about the attack and wanted to make sure she's all right."

"She is. Does that mean you'll be leaving straight-away?"

Blake rubbed his eye. "I don't know."

"I see," Charles said. His mouth pinched. "Well, take it from me, she's fine. It's best if you simply left."

"I'd rather see for myself."

Charles grabbed a sword, swished it back and forth. Since he wasn't armed, Blake eyed it warily.

"You hurt her, Daniel." He stopped, grimaced. "Hell, I don't even know what to call you. She calls you Blake but I've only known you as Daniel."

"It's Blake now, and she wasn't the only one hurt by what happened between us."

Charles scoffed. "Perhaps not, but she's the one that'll keep paying for it, won't she?"

Charles's gaze widened and he clapped his mouth shut. Cursing under his breath, he turned and resumed working.

Blake's stomach dropped to his knees. "What aren't you telling me?"

Charles shuffled around the room, doing nothing more, Blake knew, than trying to look busy. Blake couldn't contemplate what the man's words hinted at. Unless Alicia told everyone they'd made love, which he couldn't see, there was no reason for Alicia to pay for what they'd done together. Unless . . .

"Where is she?" Blake asked. Silence followed, had Blake's nerves crawling along his skin. "Where?" he demanded.

Charles spun around, sword in hand, and before Blake could move, the tip of it was pressed against his throat.

"You break her heart again and I'll hunt you down myself. She's a good woman with a big heart and she doesn't deserve to be trifled with."

Blake didn't move but his eyes bore into Charles's.

"I'm not leaving until I find her, and since she's not here, she's likely at home. I'll simply look for her there."

Charles sighed heavily, lowered the weapon. Blake nodded and turned for the door.

"Do her a favor, Daniel," he called at his back, "and don't go to her unless you're going to stay."

Without bothering to answer, Blake let himself out.

Alicia traced her parents' names on the wooden headstones. Though there was only one mound, as her father's body was lost at sea, at least there were two markers. Her father's life wouldn't be forgotten.

"You did beautiful work on them, Sam." Alicia struggled to stand and gratefully accepted Sam's help. Though it had taken her a while to show, she'd made up for it and was now big with child.

"I enjoyed doing it. Just as I was glad to fashion the cradle."

Alicia grinned. "It's pretty."

Sam rubbed Alicia's belly. "How has it been?" she asked.

Alicia shrugged. "As expected. Charles's wife has been a godsend, though. She answers all my questions, and she's passed me clothing and blankets for the baby. She told me where to find that rocking chair I have in the nursery and she's also agreed to help look after the baby while I work with Charles."

"Aidan wasn't too much for you?"

"He's wonderful, Sam. We got a chance to really know each other. I'll miss him when he leaves with you."

"You could always come with us to St. Kitts."

"This is my home, Sam. I can't leave here any more than you'd want to leave St. Kitts."

"I know." She smiled sadly. "But I can't imagine not being around to see your child grow."

"It's lucky you make fast ships," Alicia said as she took Sam's hand. "You can get here quicker."

"And I plan on visiting often," Sam said.

Alicia leaned her head on her sister's shoulder. "I hope so."

Then, without warning, Alicia shivered. It was like the day of Jacob's funeral when she'd felt the intensity of a stranger's glare. Of course, that had turned out to be Blake. Alicia gasped, spun.

There he was. Her knees shook as her eyes drank in his presence. His dark hair was long and loose, framing a face that was carved in her memory. Except in her memory his eyes weren't like the banked fire in the blacksmith shop. In her mind they weren't blazing at her in anger. He'd never looked more like a pirate. Though she knew it was too late, she placed both hands over her belly.

Blake couldn't believe his eyes. He'd told himself, as he'd run to the house, that it couldn't be. Alicia couldn't be having his child. And when he'd first arrived, she'd had her back to him and had looked exactly as he remembered. But then she'd turned and he'd seen the roundness of her belly, knew she couldn't have much longer and felt as though someone had shot him in the chest. He strode toward her, cut a glance to Samantha when she tried to step in front of her sister. Alicia stopped her with her hand.

"You were going to keep this from me?" he asked when he found his voice.

"Yes."

The fact that there was no hesitation, no remorse in hiding his child, made Blake livid. He had a right to know, dammit! He took two steps closer and ground his teeth when she raised her chin and looked at him defiantly. He barely noticed when Samantha slipped away.

"Why?"

"You should know why, Blake. I can't live at sea and I wasn't going to make you give up your dream. I certainly didn't want to spend the rest of my life watching you gaze hungrily out to sea the way your father did."

His gaze kept dropping to her belly, which she kept guarded with her hands. "And so you took the decision away from me?"

"Yes. I had no doubt that if you knew I was carrying your child, you'd do the right thing and marry me. But I never wanted you with me out of obligation, Blake. That's why I didn't say anything in St. Kitts."

A sharp stab hit him in the forehead and he pressed his hand to the pain.

"Was our child ever going to know about me, or were you planning on keeping that a secret as well?"

She crossed her arms above the bulge of her stomach, a stomach Blake ached to touch.

"The child was going to have your name, Blake."

"And what about me? How can you think of giving my child my name, while at the same time denying me a chance to know him?"

Alicia's eyes gleamed with tears. "Do you think that was a decision I came to lightly?"

"How should I know?" Blake roared. "You never bothered to discuss it with me."

"Then let me tell you," she answered. "It was the hardest damn thing I ever did. I didn't set out to lie to you, but when was I supposed to tell you? When you were yelling at me for not wanting to be a privateer's wife? When you were accusing me of being manipulative? You tell me, Blake, when was I supposed to tell you I was pregnant?"

He rubbed his forehead, where an incessant throbbing was making it hard for him to think.

"I had a right to know."

She exhaled heavily. "Yes, you did. But I had a right to protect my heart. I'd rather know you're out at sea happy than miserable with me."

Blake scoffed. "Happy? I wouldn't go that far."

Alicia winced suddenly and pushed at the side of her belly. Blake was instantly at her side.

"What is it?"

"He's stretching and it hurts. Here, feel this. I think it's his foot."

She grabbed his hand and placed it over her belly, where a small bump was pushing outward. He circled it, amazed, then it disappeared. For a moment he lost his breath.

"Do you know if it's a boy?" His heart fluttered at the thought.

"There's no way to know but I prefer to call the baby a he rather than an it."

"How soon until we know?"

Alicia smiled and he'd never seen anything so beautiful in his life.

"A month or so."

Blake's head went light. "I think I need to sit down." Mindful of the fact that they were at a grave, Blake moved away from the mound and was relieved when Alicia followed him. He helped her down before he sat beside her.

"Why are you here, Blake?"

"I heard about the attack."

"Well, as you can see, I'm fine."

"And I made a decision about my half of the blacksmith shop."

She eyed him warily. "I don't have the money to pay you your share."

"I don't want money. I'm not selling my share. I'm keeping it."

"Why? You hate it."

He shook his head. "No, I don't. I realized that when I thought it was gone. When Captain said Port Royal had been attacked, I had to come. I had to see if you were all right. But what I hadn't realized until I arrived, until I opened that heavy door, was that a part of me had also been worried about the shop."

He shrugged his shoulders. "I thought if I was here that I'd dwell on the fact that Eric and my father are gone, but when I walked into the shop, it was as though they were there. There are so many good memories tied to the shop, Alicia, and while I can't bring either my father or Eric back, I can honor them by being there.

"You went looking for your past, Alicia. You needed to know where you came from and who you were. Perhaps I had to leave for the same reason, to learn who *I* was. I know the answer now. The shop isn't only my past, it's my legacy."

Alicia had to blink away the tears. If Jacob could see his son now.

"You love the sea, Blake."

His eyes latched onto hers. "I do, but it alone can't make

me happy. I learned that these last months. You were gone, Nate and Vincent were gone. I love the water, Alicia, but I realize that I love the shop as well. And more than anything in this world, I love you."

Her heart jumped, and Alicia had to fight to keep from doing the same. She'd never doubted Blake's love and she'd seen his eyes when he'd felt the baby. But it would take more than that to make a life together.

"Living here won't make you happy, Blake."

"Yes, it will."

"What about your ship?"

"There's always a need for merchants to run supplies. If you'll agree, I hope to do that now and again, no more than once a month, and we'll run the shop together the rest of the time. What do you think?"

"I think . . ." She stumbled on a sob. "I think it sounds fantastic."

Blake smiled and wrapped her gently in his arms. He found Alicia's mouth waiting for him and he kissed her deeply and thoroughly. There'd be time later for gentleness; for now he simply couldn't get enough. He plundered her mouth, drawing soft moans from her throat. Her hands tangled in his hair and he nipped at her lips with his teeth. He stroked her tongue with his, knowing he'd never again let her go. When he was breathless, he took her hands. Pride be damned, this was what he wanted and he'd beg her forgiveness if need be.

"You already have my heart, Alicia. Take my name as well and be my wife."

Tears streamed down her face, and from nearby he heard a sniffle—apparently Samantha hadn't gone as far away as he thought she had.

Alicia's heart had never felt so full, and as though the

baby knew, it began to move in earnest, letting his desires known. Luckily, they were the same as hers.

"You're sure? This isn't out of some sense of responsibility?"

He frowned. "I've been damn miserable since you left. Granted it's taken me a while to figure it all out, but I knew before I even saw you again that it was going to take more than a ship and the sea to make me happy. For a time it had, but not once I met you. I need *you*, Alicia."

His eyes melted as he looked at her stomach. If she hadn't already loved him, she would have tumbled then.

"I need both of you."

Alicia placed both hands onto Blake's stubbled cheeks. His brown eyes were wet with emotion as he looked into hers. She saw no reason to make him wonder any longer.

"If it's a boy, I think we should call him Daniel Edward Jacob."

He bowed his head, and when he lifted it again, she had to wipe the tear from his cheek.

"And if it's a girl?"

"Helen Anna Samantha. That all right with you, Sam?" she asked, knowing full well her sister had heard every word.

Sam nodded, wiped her eyes, and this time she disappeared into the house.

"Is that all right with you?" she asked her soon-to-be husband.

Blake drew her into his arms, pressed a kiss to her head, and held on for life. Never again would he let her go.

"Whatever you want, sunshine," he answered. "But there's something you should know, though, before we get married."

"What's that?"

He grinned. "I think there is a little pirate in me after all."

She tossed her head, laughed. "I wouldn't have it any other way."